Again

Diana Murdock

To Toria, my cousin, the driving force behind this story, the one who made me cry a little and laugh a lot. The one who pushed me to be the best writer I could be.

To Kathleen, my dear friend, my sounding board, and voice of reason. The one who took pages and pages of words and made them look pretty.

To Jesse and Jett. For all the times I shut you out while I escaped into my world. I hope to make it up to you one day.

Chapter 1

Eryn scrubbed intently at the residue baked on the casserole pan, as if doing so would uncover some sort of hint. Her head ached from the tight knit of her brow, and still she was no closer to an explanation.

For the fourth time that week, the date on her computer was off. Way off. Hell, by like 500 years. January 1501 to be exact. It didn't matter that she kept changing the computer clock to the right date and virus scans kept coming up empty. January 1501 would be there every time she would turn on the computer.

It was too big a coincidence that the glitch had started the day before the dream. Unlike her other easily forgotten dreams, this one was different. This dream wouldn't let her forget. It invaded at will, regardless of what she would be doing. It would press against the back door of her mind, pushing until the door gave way.

The mundane task of washing dishes was certainly no match for the dream now. It merely nudged everything out of its way and played center stage again, as if it had a life of its own.

She and Bryce were sitting at a table somewhere. His words were a simple request. "Look at his eyes," Bryce said. "They look like stars." Eryn studied the calm face of her husband. Normally so jealous and possessive, it was totally unlike him to ask her to look at another man - and even stranger for him to make such a poetic statement - so she could hardly resist. Eryn turned to face the stranger sitting next to her. But he was no stranger. Well, she didn't know him in the conventional sense, but he was familiar

5

somehow. She knew him from…where? She couldn't
be sure. A slight shift in the air around them
whispered his name…Jonathan. She let the name
brush across her lips as her gaze slid over his clothes.
His shirt, she thought, was the kind that a pirate would
wear. It hung loosely over his broad shoulders and
tucked into black pants, and the shirt's billowing
sleeves flowed down his arms and closed snugly
around his wrists. The sun-darkened skin of his face,
chest, and hands contrasted sharply against the
whiteness of the shirt. Thin laces across his chest were
lazily tied, granting her a glimpse of the strong muscles
underneath. Her nails bit deep into her palms as she
fought the urge to trail her fingertips down his chest.
Somehow she knew exactly what it would feel like.
Smooth and powerful. Her gaze slid upwards. She
loved the way his dark brown hair fell freely, a little
past his shoulders, brushed back from the smooth skin
of his face. His hair had a bit of a wave to it, adding to
the thickness of his locks. The curve of his lips was
kind, and at the same time, so sensual. His amber eyes,
fringed with thick, long lashes, were warm and gentle.
And they sparkled. Yes, she thought, definitely like
stars. He sat there quietly while she looked into his
eyes. He didn't have to say anything. She could feel
he loved her - and she loved him back. She just
wanted to stay there forever, looking into those depths.
There in those eyes she felt at home, safe and accepted.
Those eyes held so much, almost as if they were
keeping memories for her, things he wanted her to
remember. But he would be patient, she knew, until
she was ready.

And one of those memories managed to find a
way into her mind. Just one. Like a seed dropped into

fertile soil, it grew quickly. A dawning of sorts gave way to realization. She drew in a quick breath as it became clear. He was the one she had given her soul to so many centuries ago and it was in that moment she realized that he still had her heart. His smile grew wide as he saw that she understood. She suddenly felt embarrassed to stare so long. She dropped her gaze for a moment and when she looked up again, he was gone.

Tom Petty's music rattled her cell phone to life behind her and Eryn's attention jerked back to the bright-lit kitchen. She stood at the sink, her limp hand now barely hanging onto the soapy dishrag. Outside the bay window, the sun was breaking over the rooftops across the street, throwing long shadows across the grass, the rich blue skies deepening in color with each passing moment.

Shaking her head to clear her thoughts, Eryn dropped the dishrag and dried her hands on the back of her shorts. She yanked on the knot holding her hair from her face and let the long, soft strands cascade down her back in a downpour of bronze before picking up the cell phone. Her brows pressed together into a frown. With her mind still saturated with the dream, it was hard to focus on the incoming phone number. She gave up and flipped the phone open.

"This is Eryn."

She held her hand out to touch Bryce's when he walked into the kitchen. A hint of a smile managed to find its way to the corners of his lips, but only after she mouthed *good morning* to him.

Silence on the other end of the phone, begging for some kind of response, drew Eryn's attention back. She had no idea what had been said.

7

"Can you just fax that to me and I'll look it over?" Eryn asked.

Their fingertips brushed lightly as Bryce walked past her. She sighed. Their marriage seemed solid enough, but there were definitely things about it that lacked. It was too hard to explain, even to herself. It was nothing tangible, just some underlying current she couldn't quite grasp.

Eryn absent-mindedly adjusted the strap of her tank top. "I'm sorry, what was that?" She pressed the phone hard against her ear. "Yeah, that's fine. Hey, when do you have the decorating crew coming out?"

Her attention wandered again as she watched her husband pour his coffee. Where Eryn's beauty complemented any space she stood, Bryce's body completely possessed the room. Strong, yes. Silent, yes. Commanding, definitely. And he looked good. Today he wore his jet-black hair slicked back, the ends loose. His black button-down shirt hugged his impossibly strong shoulders and rode the line down his slim waist and disappeared into gray pants. The role of the successful, most sought-after young architect suited him well. He handled everything in his personal life like he did his work - deliberately and calculated. Even the task of pouring his coffee. Always in control.

A big breath escaped her again. Too much control, she thought. "I'm sorry. I was distracted. What was that again?"

Bryce turned his head slightly as he locked onto her conversation.

She grabbed a pencil and paper and turned to the counter before Bryce could see her face. "Ten o'clock. Friday. Great. Okay. Thanks. Bye." She scribbled a few more notes while things were still fresh in her mind, trying in vain to focus on something other than Bryce. During the entire time they've been together, she always felt like he harbored some kind of resentment, maybe some anger towards her, but for what, she hadn't the slightest idea. She did whatever she could to make him happy, but it never seemed enough.

Two deep breaths later, she turned to face him. She knew he would be standing exactly as he was now, leaning against the counter, one hand in his pocket, the other holding his cup to his lips. He looked at her as if she was a jigsaw puzzle and he was trying figure out where to place the next piece. She hated it when he did that. It made her feel uncomfortable, like maybe she did have a piece missing.

Intent on distracting him, she gestured across the kitchen. "Your breakfast is warming in the oven."

He made no attempt to move or even look away. "Going to have to pass today. Meeting with some builders this morning." A perfect mix of blue and gray, his eyes refocused.

An exasperated breath rushed over her lips. "You passed on breakfast yesterday." She walked back to the sink and resumed scrubbing the casserole pan with a vengeance. "And the day before and the day before," she mumbled under her breath. She didn't mean for him to see how annoyed she was, but she couldn't help it. He never asked for breakfast. She just wanted to make it for him. But this was the third time in a row he refused it. Still, as annoyed as she was with herself, she knew she'd probably do it again.

"I did, didn't I?" He took a few swallows of his coffee before pushing away from the counter. "I'm sorry." He reached around her and placed his cup in the sink.

Her mood sagged a notch to resignation in one heavy breath. "You don't need to apologize." She dropped the dishrag into the sink and turned to face him. Her pale blue eyes held no challenge to his gray ones. "Really, you don't. It's my fault."

His hands slid down the length of her arms until he held her hands in his. Stooping a little to level his face with hers, he said, "Don't think I don't appreciate what you did." He took her silence as understanding. "I don't always have time to sit around and eat."

"You could take some time off," she suggested, but she knew it was pointless to have said it. He seemed perfectly content to immerse himself in his work. "Sorry. Stupid thing to say," she mumbled, and turned away.

He cupped her chin in his hand, turning her back, giving her no choice but to look at him.

She hated it when he gave her no choice.

Intense focus darkened his eyes. "I'm doing this for you. For us." He held her face until she nodded in acknowledgement. "Good." Releasing her, he grabbed his keys and wallet from the counter and headed towards the garage. "Don't forget about Montgomery this morning," he said over his shoulder. The door slammed behind him, sharply cutting off his reality from hers.

It never ceased to amaze her how quickly the atmosphere around him could change so fast. Predictably unpredictable.

With her lips pressed together in a tight line, she tried to reel in her thoughts. *Don't do it to yourself. Don't do it.* Eryn closed her eyes tight against the tears that burned. I'll never get used to this, she thought.

She never knew exactly where she stood with him. A long time ago she convinced herself she was willing to wait, but now she finally had to admit defeat. Defeat in a battle that would continue as long as their marriage did. *What went wrong?* She pressed her fingers to her temples. *Were we not meant to be together? Where did the love go?* She straightened up and turned to the kitchen window. The brightness of the morning was starting to fade. The fog was rolling in like a smoke screen, eating up everything in its path, turning everything of which she was so certain of into gray shades of nothingness.

She now dared to think of the one thought she had been denying for so long. *Maybe the love had never been there in the first place. Maybe this was all a big mistake.*

For the second time that morning, Tom Petty yanked her thoughts back to the kitchen. Snatching up the phone and flipping it open, she answered. "This is Eryn."

"Hello, this is Sonja from Mr. Montgomery's office calling to confirm today's photo sitting for Mr. Montgomery."

Eryn tried to picture the type of person Sonja was. Perfectly composed face, impeccable makeup, long nails that were painted red. Probably a silk blouse smoothed over a nylon-mix fabric skirt. Older, trying to look younger. Eryn rolled her eyes at the image she conjured up in her head.

Corporate. Ugh.

"Yes," Eryn dug her planner out of her purse and flipped the pages. "Let's see. Tuesday. Right. I have him down for 1:00 this afternoon at my studio."

Sonja reconfirmed the address before expressing a perfectly polished goodbye.

Biting her lip and drumming her fingers on the counter, Eryn stared hard at her planner, trying to concentrate on her schedule. She finally gave up and turned to face the thick gray that was drifting past the bay window. She shivered just thinking about being in the fog. The way it muffled and distorted everything, always gave her the sense of dreariness and gloom. Despite that, though, she loved living at the beach. Something about it just kept her there.

She glanced at her watch. Good, she thought. She'd have time to get in a run. The dishes can wait. She needed to get outside.

Her bare feet felt cool on the tile that stretched from the kitchen into the living room. The house, designed by Bryce, reflected his preference for open space and windows. Lots of windows. To Eryn, it lacked intimacy and had a certain coldness about it. The cream-colored furniture that dominated the house was broken up with blotches of bold color in the paintings, lamps, and sculptures scattered throughout the rooms. Bryce spared no expense. She felt guilty for not appreciating how much work he put into the construction and the elaborate furnishings, but sometimes she thought it was just too much. If she had her choice, she would be happy with a little cottage on the beach, something plain and simple.

Running her hand along the smooth mahogany rail as she slowly climbed the stairs, she remembered how often Bryce said he wanted her to have the best in life. The best of the tangible things, she thought, dryly. What about the things you can't touch? Like unconditional love. Romantic love. The kind of love that makes your insides rage like an inferno only to be quelled by the waves of passion. The kind where you can't wait to see each other again. When every touch and every glance means something. *The same kind of love in my dream.* She smiled as it drifted in and swirled around her mind again. She sighed. *I could get used to a love like that.*

She took the rest of the stairs two at a time to get her blood pumping. Only slightly winded, she breezed to her room and sat in the middle of the floor, stretching her long, toned legs in front of her, reaching well beyond her neatly manicured toenails.

Forming a mental checklist, she planned out her day. After her run she would take the portrait of Montgomery, grab some salmon from the store on the way home, edit the pictures and get them out in time for corporate approval so they could hang it up on the board members' wall. He would be just one of a handful of board members she would be photographing this week. They were the heavy hitters at World Commerce Bank and her pictures would document their status for the world to see. Well, maybe not the entire world, but their world anyway. New pictures for a new building. The very building that Bryce designed. He worked hard to prove himself, but whether he wrapped himself around his work *for* her or *because* of her, she wasn't completely sure.

She got up and stripped off her clothes. Brushing past the line of designer clothes she rarely wore, she headed for the back of the closet where her chest of drawers stood in the corner. This was where she placed her stash of favorite clothes - soft, worn, comfortable clothes. She pulled out a pair of black sweat pants, a sports bra, and a bleached-out sweatshirt.

"Now that's what I'm talkin' about," she said out loud. After she quickly threw on her running clothes, pulled on a baseball cap, and slipped into her old running shoes, she ran down the stairs.

A glitter of light caught her attention as she dashed past the kitchen, compelling her to slow her pace and stop. She knew what it was. She had seen it a hundred times. But since her dream, it had become another reminder. She looked over her shoulder at the crystal hanging in the kitchen window. It had taken hold of a few shards of determined sunlight and threw out flashes of white across the room. Like bursting stars. Like his eyes. Eryn let the delicious warmth of her dream run over her for only a moment before she stopped herself.

Run, she thought. *Get out and run.* But she knew that miles of running would never let her escape the memory of Jonathan's eyes.

Chapter 2

The Year of Our Lord 1501

Emelie stopped short, catching her breath.

Lady Catherine turned and stared down at her maid. "What is it?" she demanded. The afternoon sun was too warm, putting Catherine in a slightly foul mood.

Not put off by her mistress' tone, Emelie stood with fists clenched to her stomach, her whisper strained with excitement. "It is him, milady. The merchant Elizabeth and I spoke of."

Catherine rolled her eyes at Emelie's melodramatic air.

At fourteen, Emelie was perched on the edge of womanhood, and she took notice of any and all males. Compared to Catherine, one would consider Emelie plain. Where Catherine's thick auburn tresses fell heavily over her shoulders down to her waist, Emelie's fine, pale blond hair was braided and wound tightly about her head. Emerald green eyes adorned Catherine's beautifully delicate face, while her maid looked at life through eyes of muted brown. Emelie's still developing shape was flat in places where Catherine, at 17, had developed curved hips, rounded breasts, and long, shapely legs.

To humor the girl, Catherine turned her attention to the groups of village folk milling busily around the port where merchants regularly came and went to sell their wares, restock goods, or to wait out foul weather. Catherine often came here for the diversion it held as well as the variety of goods the many merchants brought with them from lands Catherine had never dreamed existed outside her world. It was here that her hunger for the finer things in life was often sated.

Lady Catherine and Emelie now stood on the fringes of a circle of village women crowded around one merchant in particular. Catherine followed her maid's gaze to the man who stood alone before the titillated throng. Without effort, he lifted bulky rolls of fabric and displayed them for the women who stood shoulder to shoulder, two or three deep, constantly shifting themselves for a better view.

He reminded Catherine of the traveling performers who visited the castle from time to time - animated, carefree, playing to the crowd. The air about him was charged with energy. Standing a full head above everyone, but without a hint of superiority about him, his mere presence commanded attention.

Twittering laughter assaulted her ears. Catherine's lip curled in annoyance as she looked upon the women before her. None of them seemed the least bit interested in this merchant's goods. Young or old, it made no difference. All of them openly ogled this man and giggled like nervous girls. Some clung to each other as they swooned. Others blatantly adjusted their dresses in hopes of enticing him. It all seems incredibly *carnal,* Catherine thought contemptuously.

The merchant's deep laugh drew Catherine's eyes back to him as he leaned closer to one of the women, a large-breasted blonde. The woman looked at him from under lowered lashes, twirling a strand of hair around her finger. As he leaned closer to her, his dark, rich brown hair flowed easily across his broad shoulders while his unlaced white shirt with its

16

billowing sleeves, revealed a well-muscled, smooth chest, with skin darkened by the sun. Catherine strained to hear his words, but they were smothered by the chatter.

One voice suddenly rang out above the others, "What of payment with a kiss?" Shouts of approval welled up from the crowd.

His smile broadened as he raised his voice to be heard, "A fine payment, indeed." His eyes now focused on the one who stood on her toes in order to be seen. "But as tempting as that is, my good woman, these lips are for another." A mix of laughter and groans of disappointment rippled through the air.

Catherine's eyebrows arched. A merchant with scruples? She might not be well versed in what happened between men and women in the bedchamber, but she was not so naïve as to be unaware of what occurred when the merchants came into port. She had heard stories of late night gatherings and most questionable behavior. Could this man be different than the rest? Could he possibly be loyal to only one woman?

Mirroring her thoughts, the villager beside Catherine leaned toward her and said, "Whoever his mistress is, she must be awfully good for a toss in the hay!"

Catherine turned sharply to face her, her eyes narrowed. "You dare speak to me in that manner?"

The crowd fell silent as Catherine's words cut through the gaiety.

The woman's face drained of all color and her eyes widened, her hand flying up to stifle her quick inward breath. Stumbling backwards, she dropped into a deep curtsey.

"Forgive me, milady!" Her voice quivered. "I meant no disrespect!"

Like a ripple through water, the other women curtsied and quickly stepped back, distancing themselves from Catherine, some managing to slip away. Catherine's scathing look raked those who remained. No one dared look at her - save one. And now Catherine met his gaze, her chin set, challenging him.

His eyes held hers briefly before his gaze traveled down the length of her, clearly enchanted by what he beheld.

"Milady," he said, bowing deeply. "You grace me with your beauty." When he looked at her again, his eyes sparkled with a light that shone like the brightest stars in the night. Their depths were as intense as their color rich, amber with flecks of gold adorning the borders. They beckoned her to come closer.

A chill ran the length of Catherine's spine, causing her to stiffen. Blinking several times, she could not stop the way the noise of the village or brightness of the sun dimmed when her eyes locked with his. This stranger reached out and enveloped Catherine without so much as touching her. Her pulse quickened and her skin tingled as if his fingertips traced the very curves of her body. She caught her breath as her body responded in a way she didn't understand, tightening in some places, weakening in others.

The sound of Emelie clearing her throat finally broke Catherine's gaze. She looked around at the village women who stood unmoving, staring, waiting in anticipation.

Catherine squared her shoulders and stepped closer, ignoring the whispers that followed in her wake. Uncertain if her knees would continue to hold her were she to look at him again, Catherine instead tried to focus on the jewelry, brushes, trinkets, and fabrics that lay before her.

Be not a fool, Catherine! Remember who you are! She was legendary for the number of her potential suitors who called on her, all of whom she rebuffed. This was partially due to their boorishness and partially because Galen, her companion since childhood, intimidated them. His size and possessiveness was enough to send them scampering away.

Not one man has ever done so much as to give Catherine pause, let alone enrapture her in the way she was experiencing right now. Why was this man so different?

She gave into her curiosity and let her gaze wander upward. Her eyes touched upon his trim waist and moved their way up to his broad chest barely concealed by the shirt that clung to his wide shoulders. She nervously licked her lips as she imagined sliding her arms around his bronzed neck, kissing the strong line of his jaw. She closed her eyes abruptly and clenched her jaw hard.

Fabric, she chided. *Look at the fabric. Not him.*

Eyes still held tight, she said, "I could not help but notice your magnificent fabric." Her words were strained, struggling against the tightening of her throat.

She opened her eyes to the fabrics that lay before her and gasped in astonishment. For the moment all else was forgotten. The fabric was truly something to behold. There were layers of brilliant, vibrant colors glowing in the sunlight, with textures so soft and shimmering, like nothing she had ever felt before. The rich-colored fabrics of blood red, deep green, royal blue, and pale lavender glistened under her touch. She could almost feel what it would be like to be wrapped in a dress made from such exquisite material.

"Magnificent," she whispered.

"Milady recognizes fine quality."

She looked up and met his eyes that were studying her so intently. Control slipped and her pulse quickened. She fought to focus once again on the fabric spread out before her. She then looked to the sky. *By the saints, how can one shiver when it is so impossibly hot in the sun?*

"Might I suggest the jade? It matches your eyes." His voice was soft. Though the other women still lingered around them, he spoke to her as if she was the only one in his world that mattered.

She chided herself for being weak. It was so unlike her to allow her feelings to have free rein. This situation in which she found herself truly chafed her to the core. Taking a deep breath, she tried to look at him again, this time with cool assessing eyes, free of emotion.

He stood with his hands on his hips with an impossibly contagious smile curving his lips.

Her resolve faltered as an unfamiliar feeling of surrender muddied her thoughts. Like a caged bird, her heart fluttered desperately in her chest, rising to her throat. She struggled to maintain an impassive expression as a battle raged within her. How could this merchant, with one look, take away her control? Ire gripped at her now as she realized this man who stood before her was not even *trying* to win her favor, that just his presence alone caused her body to betray her mind.

"Milady?" His voice was questioning.

Oh, how this one made her feel so vulnerable. Her soul felt naked under his gaze. Somehow he managed to erase the line between their social classes. They were man and woman, not lady and merchant.

Fighting the urge to settle herself in his eyes again, her gaze flickered here and there, focusing on nothing in particular. She wanted to press her hands to her ears to shut out the pounding of her heart.

"Yes, yes. Of course. I would like the jade. All that you have." She felt the words rushing out. "Have it delivered to Elderidge castle." Catherine fumbled in her purse and held out a stack of coins, horrified to see her hand shake ever so slightly. She still refused to look at him.

The merchant glanced at Catherine's maid questioningly.

Emelie, who had been staring at him unabashedly, giggled. "May I present the Lady Catherine, sir. Daughter of Lord Roberts."

Once again his eyes took in Catherine's entire form, but unlike the lust she saw too often in other men's eyes, this man held open appreciation, sincerity, and genuine interest in something other than her wealth.

"The fair Lady Catherine. I am pleased to make your acquaintance." He bowed low. "I am Jonathan."

His eyes spoke words not heard, but felt, as they penetrated to her soul. She sensed that not only did he understand the way she was feeling, but that he was drawn to her as she was to him.

She released a breath of impatience as she continued to hold out the coins, her control sorely tested.

He lifted his hand to take what she offered. Though she steeled herself against further assault of unbidden feelings, she was unprepared for the sensation of his touch as he took the coins from her hand. A shock like a lightening bolt sent a flame through her body, and she recoiled in surprise, swallowing hard. How could she be such a fool? She was not some commoner who crumbled at the feet of a man! So why was it that with a simple look, an innocent touch, this man had the power to take all that away?

Jonathan smiled.

And she shivered. Again. *Oh, that smile will surely be my undoing.*

He turned around and called to a man not far off.

For the first time Catherine took notice of the men working behind Jonathan who were organizing, sorting, and tending to his ship. In sharp contrast to Jonathan's refined and confident presence, the crew was haggard and weather-worn. A certain camaraderie flowed in and out of their conversations, but it was clear Jonathan was the master.

"Will there be anything else, milady?" Once again, he turned to address her. His brows arched with encouragement and perhaps a bit of hope. "You have only but to ask."

"No." She shook her head, suddenly wishing she was anywhere but where she stood. "Nothing." It unnerved her that she couldn't trust herself, yet she made no attempt to stop him when he reached down and placed her hand in his. Ivory white against bronzed skin met with a sizzling burn. Time meant nothing to her as she watched him bring her hand upwards, his lips branding her knuckles with a mere whisper of a kiss.

"Perhaps then, we shall meet again?" His easy smile triggered a fluttering in her stomach.

Catherine withdrew her hand quickly and stepped back, bumping into Emelie. "I doubt that. Good day, sir."

Walking quickly through the marketplace, Catherine hardly noticed the other merchants and villagers. She walked past those calling her, waving perfumes, gems, and cloths. She rubbed the place on her hand where Jonathan's lips kissed her. The softness with which he held her hand, the tenderness of his kiss upon her skin, the warmth that spread through her body as he looked at her, fogged her thinking. *This is madness. 'Tis a blessing Galen is not here to see me falter this way.*

She sighed. Galen had been her champion since they were children, swearing an oath of loyalty to her when they were but eight years old. How could she be so shallow as to already forget the devotion he had shown her this morning? He had been so pleased when he presented to her a small sapphire brooch with diamonds circling the gem.

Catherine trailed her fingers along the contour of the brooch that was now pinned to her dress. Solid like the gem, Galen had been her rock, her pillar of strength, and as close to her as if he were her own brother, but for months now she knew his affections for her were growing far deeper than that. Everyone expected them to wed, being as close as they were, and they should have by now, but it was Catherine who begged to wait. She was still waiting for that spark, the telltale sign that love was true. She wanted the same kind of love that permeated the castle when her mother was alive, a soul-searing love that bound together her mother and father. Theirs was a love that knew no bounds. And yes, they had shared lust, too. Catherine's mother never hid her shivers of desire when Lord Roberts brushed his lips against her cheek or atop her hand. Much like the desire Catherine, herself, felt today with…

A ripple of uneasiness swept through Catherine as she realized her mind refused to dismiss this merchant. She shook her head. At this moment she was no different from the women in the village. The same heated desire ran through her blood as did theirs, only she needed to escape those eyes and the touch that would have her stay.

"Enough!" Catherine said, shaking her head.

"Milady?" asked Emelie, running along at her side, trying to keep up with Catherine.

"Nothing, Emelie." She released a ragged sigh. "I have had enough for today. Let us fetch our horses."

"There you are, Catherine!"

Catherine turned to the sound of Galen's voice. Relief washed through her. Galen's presence would make it easier for her to control her wandering thoughts, so she did not object when he put his hands around her waist and drew her to him. Catherine felt Galen's strong arms through his tunic as he held her close. She tensed with agitation, finding herself wondering if the merchant's arms were as strong. She simply could not help but compare the two men - Galen so fair with his blond hair framing high, strong cheek bones, a slender nose and strong chin, serious eyes, and lips that promised passion; the merchant, with dark locks that flowed freely, softer, yet oh-so-masculine features, and laughing eyes that showed no trace of regret, sadness, or pain.

Galen held her at arm's length and searched her face. "Catherine! Is anything amiss?"

He knew her only too well. She forced the thoughts of Jonathan back and mustered a smile.

"No, of course not, Galen." She rested her forehead on his chest, hiding her face. "I merely wish to go home."

He lifted her chin. His eyes narrowed with suspicion. "You are certain you are well? Has anyone upset you?"

The memory of Jonathan's eyes hung in her mind as she looked back at Galen.

"Really, Galen, I am well," she said, pushing herself from his arms. "I believe I have spent far more time in the sun than I should have." Hooking her arm through Galen's, she tugged him in the direction of the horses. "I have arranged for my purchase to be delivered to the castle, so we need not dally here any longer."

"But I am here now. I will fetch your goods myself."

"No!" she said quickly.

Galen's raised eyebrows invited an explanation from her.

She thought quickly. Had he any knowledge that another man filled her senses the way Jonathan had, he would put an end to it. It would take but one word from her and Galen would see to it that the merchant maintained a fair distance from her, but no such hint passed her lips.

"Emelie will fetch it." She turned to her maid and gestured in the direction of the ships. "Quickly, Emelie," she hissed.

"Wait but a moment, Emelie." Galen turned to Catherine. His words were deliberate and measured. "I shall accompany Emelie to make certain that your purchase is handled properly. These merchants cannot always be trusted."

Catherine's mouth went dry as she squirmed under his gaze. She knew that her eyes, nay, her entire body, was betraying her. The heat in the air was palpable as a bead of sweat trickled agonizingly down her spine. It helped her not that Emelie's own face had gone pale, her lips pressed into a thin line.

"Aye, that would be best," Catherine whispered.

"I pray you wait for us here, then," Galen said.

He looked at her a moment longer before turning and motioning for Emelie to lead the way.

Catherine could not still the frantic beating of her heart as she made her way to her horse. She would not wait. She could not face Galen until she could once again gather her wits. Feeling like a coward, Catherine mounted her horse and spurred the mare homeward, anxious to once again be safe within the castle walls.

Chapter 3

God, what a long week, Eryn thought, as she stretched her arms to link her fingers behind her back. Almost like some supreme being shoved a few extra days in just for laughs. She had spent the better part of the week taking pictures of the board members of World Commerce Bank, editing and re-editing until she was satisfied with the results. All of them were far wealthier than anyone she knew. Also more pompous than anyone she knew. Their air of superiority filled her studio, making Eryn grimace at the stench.

She could never understand how people thought money could make one person superior to others. In her opinion, money had become a wall that separates one human from another, drawing the line between the Haves and Have-Nots, never giving the Have-Nots the chance to prove themselves as worthy or lovable a human being as the Haves. It gave everyone the excuse to ignore each other and not get involved.

Though jobs like this corporate photo shoot paid her well, she preferred the simplicity of the average person, the innocent child, the spontaneous event, and capturing life in action. Given the choice, that would be her world, but it wasn't. She lived in Bryce's world, filled to the top with corporate royalty.

He led. She followed.

He fit in. She didn't.

Tonight she would have no reprieve. In less than twelve hours, their house would be filled with the banking elite, puffing on their expensive cigars, boasting of their latest acquisitions, bemoaning the plight of the world between bites of caviar.

She sighed. Maybe she would invite Brandi when she saw her later this morning. If anyone could shake up a party, it was Brandi. Outspoken, brash, playing it just like it is. Brandi definitely had her own way of doing things.

But now, this moment was for Eryn. The beach was her temple. Her runs were her meditation.

Reaching high above her head, she stretched her arms, shoulders, and back, releasing the tension that seemed to have found a permanent place in her life.

She set herself in motion, feeling the firm sand at the water's edge give way easily to her strides.

It had been dark when she slipped out of bed that morning, too early for Bryce to be up. She liked to be on the sand at the precise second when night struggled for control one final time before shrinking silently behind the growing strength of the day.

Now as she began her run, the sun was peeking over the horizon, reaching its rays towards the few people who walked the beach and the surfers who dotted the early morning waves. Eryn liked the solitude at this time of day, the unobstructed view down the beach, and the soft lull of the ocean.

Her puffs of breath kept pace with her steps, carrying her further down the beach, away from the life that waited for her just a few streets away. She closed her eyes as she ran. She'd learned to trust her instincts, to sense rather than see. She felt a rush of anticipation as she dared herself to take a few more steps in her darkness. Feeling her feet hit softer sand, she opened her eyes to see that she had strayed from her straight line. She looked behind her to see her footsteps in the wet sand, her trail zigzagging, and then heading up past the water line. "Geez, I'm glad nobody was watching me," she laughed, checking around to make sure.

Her run slowed to a walk and her smile dimmed as she looked down the stretch of beach that lay before her. Something about it stopped her, even though the wet sand ahead was empty, save for sandpipers pecking for crabs and a few seagulls swooping in disorganized formation. The hair on the back of her neck prickled at the eerily familiar sensation and her brows pulled together hard.

She could see, though a ghost of an image, a big wooden rowboat with tall sides approaching the shore. She squeezed her hands into fists, trying to bring the image closer...

She stood on the beach, close to the cliffs that she had carefully descended with her horse moments before. The strong waves made it easier for the boat to lift onto the wet sand. Three men jumped out to drag the boat higher on the beach. Before they had it pulled completely ashore, one of the men let go and came running toward her. Her heart pounded in her chest, beating faster the closer he got. Just a breath away now, he stopped in front of her. Unable to contain her joy, she threw her arms around his neck. A rush of relief consumed her as his strong arms tightened around her waist, his lips finding hers...

Eryn quickly drew in her breath and the specter was gone, just like that. She stood there, eyes searching, body frozen, unable to release her breath. The pounding of her heart swelled to a roar in her ears and she pressed her lips together to stop their tingling. As streams of sunlight, no longer soft, devoured the magic of the morning, replacing it with harsh reality, she fought to keep the vision alive, playing it over and over in her head. The boatman who ran up the beach had worn black pants and his white shirt hung loosely over his strong chest and arms. His brown shoulder-length hair flung against his face, shadowing his eyes from the sun. She focused on his beautiful face, his sensual lips. His eyes were so full of emotion! And the kiss – ah, that kiss! – had stopped all too soon.

"What the hell?" she said out loud, finally breathing. She squinted against the sun, turning in place to scan the beach once again. Only the squawking of the circling seagulls answered her. Her heart beat unreasonably fast.

One thing was undeniable. The man who sat next to her in her dream and the man who ran up the beach in the ghostly vision were definitely the same man. This time it was *so real,* though. She could still feel his firm lips on hers; could still feel the excitement of seeing him again. Again? That same sense of familiarity surrounded him, as if she *knew* him.

She took a deep breath while turning around and walked back to her car, willing her still-racing heart to slow down its pounding.

"It's got to be stress," she said to a seagull that landed near her. She wanted desperately to believe it. A reaction to stress would make it easier to explain the incident away. But something told her it wasn't just that. She didn't have enough stress to trigger hallucinations or even a minor breakdown. Besides, she highly doubted a breakdown would come in the form of an extremely sexy pirate with eyes in which she could lose herself.

She couldn't help but glance back over her shoulder. She actually hoped to catch another glimpse of him! *Ok, maybe a little counseling wouldn't hurt.*

She picked up her pace and ran as hard and fast as she could.

~ ~ ~

Brandi wrinkled her nose as Eryn plopped in the chair across from her. "Did you by any chance go for a run this morning?"

Young, energetic waiters and waitresses flitted around cloth-covered tables like bees, sweeping up empty plates, laying down fresh linen and silverware, and jotting down orders, all while instinctively dodging busboys and hostesses. Perky staff, perky greetings, perky smiles. Sometimes the place was too perky for Eryn, but the coffee was good.

"How'd you guess?" Eryn countered sarcastically. She quickly guzzled the water the waiter had placed in front of her, then reached for her coffee.

"For one thing, the sweat stains, and for another thing, the smell of sweat."

"Yeah, well, exercise does have some drawbacks," Eryn said, shrugging.

Brandi shuddered. "A lot of drawbacks, I'd say. My way is a whole lot easier."

"Popping diet pills may be easier, but not smart." Eryn studied her friend. Only a few months younger than Eryn, Brandi's face reflected the effects of her lifestyle. Too much booze had turned her skin so sallow and pale that she had to cover it with a thick layer of concealer dusted over with bronzer. Her blond hair, with carefully touched-up roots, was pulled into a loose ponytail, accentuating her slightly sunken cheeks.

"If you would just go running with me…."

Brandi waved her hand in dismissal. "Not a chance. Besides, serious competition in the acting world calls for drastic measures."

Eryn knew there would be no conceding on Brandi's part. They'd had this conversation too many times before and it always ended up the same. It was easier just to change the subject.

"So what's up with you? Got anything brewing?" asked Eryn over the top of her coffee cup.

"Oh, you know, a little bit of this, a little bit of that." Brandi's hands gestured animatedly. "I'm up for a part in a new sitcom and I'm waiting to see about a print job for a catalog."

Eryn's eyebrows raised ever so slightly. "Really? That's great! What kind of catalog?"

"Oh, it's a new one. Fashion...you know." With a wave of her hand, she dismissed the subject. "Hey, guess who I saw last night." Brandi didn't wait for a response. "Cole Hamilton. Boy, is he a hottie! I sure would like to get together with him!"

"Isn't that the guy in that new vampire movie?"

Brandi nodded enthusiastically.

"A little young for you, don't you think?" Eryn teased.

"Hey, I'll take whatever. I haven't had a serious relationship for a long time." Brandi shrugged, pulling a cigarette out of her purse and putting it between her lips. "I'm desperate. What can I say?"

"You know you can't smoke in here."

"Oh yeah. Damn rules." Brandi shoved the cigarette back in the pack. "Speaking of hotties, how's Bryce?"

Eryn's stared at her coffee. "Oh, he's fine. Business as usual."

Eryn looked up in time to see Brandi raise one brow high. It curved in a much-too-perfect arch. Eryn wondered if she practiced that look.

"What wrong?" Brandi leaned closer, her chin resting on a fisted hand. "I mean…really."

Drawing a big breath, Eryn let it out slowly. She pressed her lips together in indecision. She knew her friend's interest in her marriage was fueled more by the possibility of gossip rather than by concern, but sometimes that didn't matter. It helped Eryn to air it all out.

"I don't know. Things have changed. Maybe they were never really right to begin with." She took a sip of her coffee, trying to keep her voice light. "Who knows? Maybe it's just me." Maybe it *was* her. As hard as she tried, she couldn't seem to get through to Bryce. When they first met, they just clicked, but even then there always seemed to be something wedged between them. There was never any warmth or emotion in his eyes, certainly nothing at all like…

"I had a dream the other night that started me thinking," Eryn said hesitantly.

Brandi picked up a yellow packet of sweetener and shook it, waiting for an explanation.

Eryn shook her head, unwilling to go into detail. "Probably just a symbol of something lacking in my life." She shrugged. "I was thinking I should have my dreams analyzed."

Eryn leaned back as the waiter topped off her coffee. "Thanks." She poured some more cream, watching how it to sank beneath the dark surface and reemerge at the top. She stirred until the contrasting colors blended seamlessly into one. *Why can't people blend that well? Why are people and their relationships so damn complicated?*

"Sometimes I wonder what attracted us in the first place," Eryn said.

Not that she had much perspective on the matter. She has never been serious about anyone but Bryce.

"You could have done a lot worse." Brandi pointed out. "Remember Derek from our Science class? He was always after you to have his babies."

Eryn shuddered at the thought. "Eww. How could I forget?" She paused, biting her lip. "Bryce is a good guy. I'm probably just going through a midlife crisis."

That was it, wasn't it? Most marriages hit a stale spot once in awhile, right? If it's as simple as that, Eryn thought, I can make it work. Yeah. Just a little bump in the road. Feeling a little better, she changed her focus. "Anyway, are you free tonight? Bryce is inviting some heavy hitters over. Who knows, maybe we can land you a quality husband, huh?"

Brandi's eyes brightened. "You know I'm always up for a party. What time?"

Eryn pulled some money out of her wallet and put it on the table. "Show up around 6:00." She took one more swig of her coffee before standing up. "Gotta go get cleaned up." She rounded the table and gave her friend a quick hug. "See you tonight."

~ ~ ~

Eryn stopped short just inside the kitchen. She had thought Bryce would be gone by now. Bryce looked up from the newspaper so briefly Eryn would have missed it had she not been staring right at him.

He glanced at his watch. "Long run?" he asked, his attention returning to the paper.

She skirted the marble island and opened the refrigerator to grab a bottle of water. His question lacked real interest, so she answered in the same way.

"Not really. I had coffee with Brandi," she said. She certainly wasn't even going try to explain what she saw, or thought she saw, on the beach. How could she, when she couldn't even explain it herself?

He folded up the paper and placed it on the counter. Drinking the last of his coffee, he joined Eryn at the counter, keeping a thin distance between them.

"Everything set for tonight?"

"Of course." Her face darkened. Why was it so hard for him to show some intimacy? She drew a deep breath and let it out. "The cleaning service will be here this morning."

"Good. I have to go. I'll be back early."

As he turned to leave, she grabbed his arm. She couldn't deny the physical attraction she felt for him, still as strong as the day they met. Refusing to conform to the corporate image, he kept his hair long enough to pull back at the nape of his neck, giving him an untamed, roguish air. Eryn traced the line of his strong jaw, brushed his high cheeks and his perfectly shaped nose.

His eyes often hid his feelings, but now impatience filtered through the steely blue eyes.

"Do I get a kiss before you go?" she asked.

He hesitated a moment before dipping his head to meet her upturned face. He kissed her quickly, but Eryn pulled him closer, keeping his lips to hers. When he didn't respond, she pulled back, her arms dropping to her sides.

"Sorry," she laughed self-consciously. "Don't know what got into me."

He kissed her on the forehead and headed toward the door.

She watched as it closed behind him, cutting off any further contact between them. Her nails dug deep into her palms. *What got into me?* she chided herself. She just wanted some reaction from him. She wanted to feel a toe-curling, lip-puckering, sweaty-palm feeling. Did that kind of feeling really actually exist? She loosened her now aching hands and leaned hard against the counter. Yeah, it does, she thought. But maybe just in dreams.

Chapter 4

Catherine sat in a chair in front of the fire, Emelie's rhythmic brushing of her hair relaxing both her mind and body. Here in her chambers, the village seemed so far away, fading with the setting sun. Now Catherine could think more clearly. Her mood had lifted since this afternoon when her horse had brought her thundering through the castle gate. A warm bath, food, and wine did wonders to bring her emotions back under control. Undoubtedly, she told herself, her muddled thoughts and shaking limbs had much more to do with the effects of the hot sun than with the handsome, bold-eyed, young merchant.

The door was thrown open, shattering the serenity of the evening. Catherine sighed. There was only one person who opened doors with such vigor and without a considerate knock. There would be no further peace for Catherine tonight.

Sara, her young sister, bolted across the room to stand before her. The girl's eyes were wide with anticipation, her face flushed with expectation. Sara had been away for some weeks, accompanying her father to Dirkstowe, another holding of his. Within hours of her arrival this afternoon, the gossip about the merchant had made its way to her.

"So what is he really like, Catherine? Is he as handsome as Emelie says?" She leaned forward in insistence. At 14 summers, she stood almost as tall as Catherine, yet was considerably thinner, and her dark tresses spilled down her back, reaching down to hang at her thin waist. Sara's almost too-round eyes feigned innocence, but there was a depth to them that often spoke otherwise.

Sara was four years old when their mother died. Since that time her father had indulged her without boundaries. Much to Catherine's dismay, Sara has grown to be impetuous and demanding, flirtatious and teasing. Despite Catherine's promise to her mother to watch over Sara, the older girl has found it increasingly difficult to control her sister's behavior.

Sara demanded again. "You simply must tell me everything!"

Catherine closed her eyes, drawing a deep breath. "Pray tell, Sara. What gossip is keeping the maids from their duties?"

Sara's gaze flickered to Emelie for a moment before darting back to her sister. "Emelie told me he is most handsome. Tall and strong. And his eyes alone were enough to make her knees weak."

When Catherine did not respond, Sara went on. "It seems all the women in the village nigh lost their senses in his presence."

Catherine fought to keep her expression passive. If Emelie had mentioned Catherine's own behavior that morning, Sara's face did not betray such.

Sara persisted. "What of you, Catherine? Emelie said you spoke to him. Did you think he was so wonderful?"

Catherine sighed. There would be no satisfying her sister, whatever her answer would be. "What does it matter what I think of the man, Sara? You can see him for yourself and make up your own mind."

Sara's face brightened. "Truly that is an excellent idea! Then we shall seek this merchant at first light on the morrow!" Sara was on her feet and rushing out of the room before Catherine could object.

There was no point to fighting her, Catherine knew. Sara would find a way to see the merchant whether Catherine forbade it or not. She frowned. Had it not been for Emelie and Elizabeth's need to gossip, Sara's curiosity would not have been so piqued.

"Emelie, what exactly did you say to her?" she asked.

Emelie came around and knelt before Catherine, looking at the floor. "My apologies, milady. I meant no harm. You know that Lady Sara can be very persistent. She would not let me rest until I told her what she wanted to hear."

The silence stretched as Catherine contemplated Emelie. Yes, Catherine knew only too well how her young sister could be. Sara allowed nothing to stand in her way when the end result was to her benefit. Catherine could not fathom how her own mother, so kind and beautiful, could have spawned such a devious and manipulative child as Sara.

"I shall have my privacy now, Emelie."

"Yes, milady." She stood before her mistress, hands held tightly together, showing no inclination to go.

"What is it?" Catherine's voice was impatient. She wanted to be alone.

There was a slight quiver in Emelie's voice. "I…I said nothing to Lady Sara about milady's…behavior today."

Catherine stood, her back stiffening at the implication. "Of course you did not! There was nothing *to* say."

"Yes, milady. Naturally not," Emelie agreed.

Catherine gestured toward the door and now the maid curtsied and hurried out. Catherine bolted the door behind her. She slowly turned and leaned against the door, sighing deeply. Nothing to say, indeed, she thought. But what Catherine had *felt*, well, that was something altogether different.

~ ~ ~

Sitting resolutely upon her mare, Catherine silently cursed her sister. If Sara would only behave in a manner befitting of a young lady, she would not have been compelled to accompany her sister this morning to ensure that the girl stayed within the boundaries of propriety. If not for Sara, Catherine would not have spent the morning trying to convince herself that she had no desire to see the merchant again. She inclined her face to meet the morning sun, mixed with the warmth of the air, and breathed deeply. It would be easier to convince herself that the sun would one day forget to rise.

"Oh! Catherine! That must be him!" Sara reigned in her horse and waited for Catherine to join her.

Indeed, it could only be him. His too-virile body, naked from the waist up, assaulted her senses once again. Catherine's heart quickened at the sight of his bare shoulders and muscled back glistening with sweat. His corded muscles moved easily with the weight of the boxes he carried. Sara's sharp intake of breath broke Catherine's stare.

Averting her eyes from the merchant, she turned to face Sara. "Do close your mouth, sister, lest he sees you gaping like a fool." Catherine cringed. *And you would do well to tame the beating of your own heart.*

40

Catherine dismounted, allowing her horse to graze on the grass beneath their feet. "Come, Sara. Let this be done with." Her slippered feet were quick and firm upon the ground as she approached where he stood.

Jonathan looked up to see the women approaching. His eyes flickered a moment to Sara, then firmly settled on Catherine, his smile radiating only for her.

"Fine morning, ladies!" Jonathan called out. "Tis early for you to be up and about, is it not?"

As he turned around to reach for his tunic, Catherine couldn't help but to look at his broad back that he unwittingly put on display before her. Many years of hard labor have chiseled the strong muscles that rippled when he moved. Her gaze followed the edge of his tunic as it slipped over his bronzed skin, then snapped back up to his face when she dared to look no further.

Turning once again, Jonathan took Catherine's hand in his and raised it to his lips, his eyes never leaving hers.

There was no denying it this time. 'Twas not the heat that caused her knees to weaken as his lips lingered upon her skin, but an undeniable attraction.

"'Tis a pleasure to see you again, Lady Catherine." His voice, low and husky, slid over her like a lover's caress.

Sara made a sound of impatience, stomping her foot on the ground.

Dragging his gaze from Catherine, he turned to Sara. "My apologies for my rudeness. Whom do I have the pleasure of meeting?"

"I am Lady Sara." She thrust her shoulders back to display her still-developing bosom. "Would you take me aboard your ship?" she added with a pouting lip and a batting of her eyelashes.

Catherine groaned and closed her eyes.

Sara's response was quick. "What of it, Catherine? I am not afraid. Unlike you, mayhap?"

Catherine's mouth opened to reply, but shut it promptly for words would not come. Sara's insolence knew no bounds.

Jonathan watched the exchange between the two, clearly amused. Laughing, he turned to Sara. "You are a bold one, Sara. I daresay your father would have my head if I succumbed to your desires. I am sure there are other younger squires that challenge one another for your affections?"

Sara sighed. "Yes. Of course there are many." She waved her hand to dismiss the notion. "But they are merely boys."

Jonathan laughed. "Come, ladies. I have something for you."

Casting a warning glance over her shoulder to Sara, of which Sara returned with a shrug, Catherine allowed Jonathan to lead them to several boxes set aside from the rest.

"Ah, here it is." He picked up a doll, exquisitely dressed in velvet, its face painted with a solemn smile. "For you, Lady Sara. 'Tis what all the young noble ladies have."

Wide-eyed and disbelieving, Sara gasped, "'Tis beautiful!" Her fingers ran gently over its painted face. "Thank you!" She threw her arms around Jonathan so enthusiastically he stumbled backwards.

His laughter filled the air as he carefully pulled Sara's arms from around his neck, holding her away from his body.

Catherine was relieved to see the youth once again return to Sara's face. This was the sister that Catherine longed to see, not the impetuous, stubborn, young woman she was becoming.

Sara moved away and sat upon a crate with the doll cradled in her lap. She looked every bit a little girl, enraptured with her unexpected gift.

"As for you, milady," Jonathan said, "I thought of you when I unpacked this today." He retrieved a red velvet pouch from another crate and, untying the gold cord, he drew out a hair circlet, a string of pearls interspersed with rubies, sapphires, and emeralds.

Jonathan gently took her hand and turned her palm upward, draping the circlet across it. Though heavily laden with jewels, its weight was feather-light. The sunlight pooled in the depths of the stones, swirling and flowing, begging for her attention, but Catherine saw only her hand in his and felt only the intense heat that inflamed her skin where they touched.

"My gift to you," he said quietly.

She knew she should lift her hand. Her mind screamed for her to do so, but the circlet seemed to weigh heavily upon it.

"Nay, I cannot accept it." Her voice was a whisper. She was walking on dangerous ground now. She knew she should turn away before she lost herself completely.

"It would be honor if you would, milady," said Jonathan. His smile faded. "I can think of no other woman who could wear it as elegantly as you."

Catherine blushed, her resolve broken. "I cannot possibly…"

Jonathan gently placed his finger to her lips, silencing her. "Yes, you can. Allow me this."

That simple gesture, and the warmth of his touch, left her without the desire to refuse. The heat lingered even after he pulled away.

So many men have tried to seduce her for their own gains and for her wealth. Their words were woven with flattery, promises, and shallow complements. She searched Jonathan's face for such falseness, but she saw none. She found nothing more than kindness and affection in the endless depths of his eyes.

"Then how can I not accept?" she said. The words were scarcely audible to her ears, but he heard.

His face broke into a smile and the air that surrounded him sparked to life, crackling in the morning light. Such enthusiasm was contagious and Catherine laughed, unleashing the tension in her body.

"Master Jonathan!" The shout came from the ship. A young man stood on the deck and beckoned him to follow.

Jonathan looked back at the ship and then to her, reluctant to leave her side, but then conceded. "I shall be but a moment."

With another bright smile, and a light touch to her arm, he turned and ran towards the ship.

Catherine watched his retreating back before turning to where her sister sat, smoothing the doll's dress.

"Master Jonathan is a kind man," Catherine said thoughtfully.

Sara set aside the doll and took the circlet from Catherine, turning it over in her hands.

"Yes, he is." She paused, looking up at Catherine, her eyebrows raised ever so slightly, the youthfulness now gone from her face. "I wonder what Galen will say of the merchant's generosity."

Catherine stiffened at the mention of Galen. "'Tis merely a gift, Sara," she said in defense. "I have received gifts before. Galen takes no notice."

"You speak the truth, yes," Sara said, "but I daresay Galen would not approve of this gift, coming from him." She inclined her head in the direction of the ship.

"Galen has naught to worry about." Catherine was quick to respond. "A gift is but a gift." She placed her hand out to reclaim the circlet and to place it safely back in its pouch. Sara gave it back, her face sullen.

The number of villagers walking about grew as the sun rose higher.

Looking around at the gathering crowds, Sara sighed. "He truly is utterly handsome. I fear, though, that I am but a child to him." Sara reached for the doll and ran her fingers across the smooth face. "Once again, Catherine, you have won."

"What do you mean?" Catherine felt her ire rising once again. "What have I won?"

"'Tis nothing." Sara dismissed Catherine's question with a wave of her hand. "Just once I would capture the affections of a man and not a boy! Master Jonathan would be that man had I been alone."

"Sara, you *are* but a child and he *is* a grown man."

Sara raised her hand to silence her. "Say nothing, Catherine, but one day I shall rival even you."

She stood and faced Catherine. "I am ready to leave. I shall await you at the horses."

Catherine watched as her sister walked away. Defeat seemed to weigh heavily on Sara's thin shoulders. What is this that she speaks of? Catherine wondered. Her sister harbors jealousy?

"You must leave now as well?"

Catherine did not notice that Jonathan had appeared at her side. She chanced a glance at the merchant whose mere presence addled her wits. A head taller than Catherine, he stood with his hands on his hips, looking at her expectantly. Aye, but he made it difficult for her to even think! His manner tore down all of her defenses, leaving her to feel vulnerable. She was drawn to this man in a way she could not explain. What a fool she was for believing she could withstand the sweet torment to her senses while she stood beside him. His closeness sent a heady rush through her body, a longing that confused her. She needed to leave, to put distance between them sooner than later.

She straightened in resolve. "Aye, I have much to do. Guests of my father will be arriving before too long."

"Might I escort you back to the castle?"

She shook her head. "That will not be necessary." As much as she would like to accept, she could never allow it. He did not seem to understand what havoc his offer would create if she accepted, however innocent it would be.

She paused, placing her hand atop the velvet pouch as if to ensure her gift was still there. "I thank you for your generosity, to both my sister and me."

Jonathan put his hand over his heart and inclined his head in acknowledgment.

Though the need to be away from him was strong, her feet seemed rooted to the ground, and her eyes locked with his. A boldness she did not know that she possessed raged through her. "When do you set sail?"

His eyes, still glittering, shadowed ever so slightly. "In two days' time."

Catherine nodded her head and managed a smile. It is for the best, she knew, for there was no place in her life for him, though her body seemed to feel otherwise. His nearness and his smile made her feel so alive. With her lips pressed tightly together, she lowered her gaze. She had to turn away. This man was making her feel everything she had searched for, but being who he was, a man of the sea and not of noble blood, made it impossible for her to succumb to her desires.

It took every ounce of strength for her to walk away.

Chapter 5

Leaning closer to the mirror, Eryn blotted her lips, using her little finger to smooth around the edges. One last run-through with the hairbrush and she was done. She padded to the bedroom in her stocking feet and scrutinized herself in the mirror. For the party tonight she had chosen a simple black cocktail dress, with a lace-edged bodice, that lay smooth over her flat stomach and slender hips, and instead of pinning her hair up in a twisted knot as she usually did, Eryn decided to leave it loose to fall across her shoulders and spill down her back. She put on her black strappy heels and, turning sideways one way and then the other, decided the effect was just right.

"Good to go, Eryn? It's almost..." Bryce had thrown open the door and then stopped, his words fading away.

She caught a softening of his usually serious eyes as he slowly crossed the room to stand behind her, his eyes taking in the way her dress molded to the curves of her body. For a moment she couldn't remember why she was annoyed with him. She had his attention now and his guard was down. It was seductive the way he wrapped a bit of her hair around his fingers and held it to his nose, closing his eyes while inhaling its fragrance. A shiver rippled through her body when he traced his fingertips down her arms.

"You're beautiful, you know," he said.

Their eyes held as they looked at each other in the mirror. Their image reflected a perfect couple. Bryce was much taller than Eryn and his wide shoulders and chest formed a strong wall that Eryn longed to lean on. Those few seconds seemed to hover around them, unsure where to go, but then Bryce quickly dismissed them. Her heart dropped when she saw the desire fade from his eyes. Once again control took over.

"Better be careful. Old man Michaelson will be here. He likes pretty women."

She couldn't figure out if that was meant to be a warning or a compliment.

"Come on," he said. "We should get downstairs." He led the way, not looking to see if she was following or not.

~ ~ ~

Eryn leaned against the bar, half-listening to Carl Michaelson as he went on about his newly-acquired 80-foot yacht and all of its can't-do-without amenities. Her cheeks hurt from smiling so much, but that was part of being married to Bryce. His was a world where pretenses and ass-kissing was not only a way of life, but expected. She stoically made nice and hated every minute of it.

Scanning the room over her wine glass as discreetly as she could, she watched the usual groupings of guests. The men, clad in Italian-cut suits, wrists heavy with Rolex watches, were in deep discussions about financial matters, while their wives were scattered about the room in clusters, either looking bored or trying to one-up the other women in the room, using whatever means they possessed – attitude, pricey dresses, or diamonds. Some of the wives were younger, with perfectly bouncy breasts, nipples in a perpetually frozen state jutting through thin fabric. The older women, with attitudes closely resembling that of a Doberman, fiercely guarded the lifestyle they felt were due them, often ignoring their husband's infidelities.

Eryn looked at the clock on the wall. It was still fairly early. She hoped everyone would eventually loosen up and draw each other to the dance floor the DJ had set up by the pool.

Sweet and spicy aromas drifted up from the buffet table spread out in the dining room and the three different bar stations were constantly busy. The decorators had transformed the house into an island paradise, complete with Polynesian statues, Birds of Paradise, and gardenias with burlap covering most of the walls and palm trees dotting the edges of the pool.

After nodding her head with a "Really?" thrown in for good measure, Eryn chanced a glance over Carl's shoulder where she spotted Brandi by the fireplace, absolutely sparkling. Eryn was glad her friend was enjoying herself, but then, parties always were always Brandi's favorite pastime. In college, Brandi had made it a point to know where all the fraternity parties were and then somehow got herself invited to each one. She may have failed every college class, but she scored high on mastering the party circuit.

Brandi glowed, animatedly talking to Dylan, a newly divorced banker. By the way he had Brandi cornered, he seemed to have bounced back quite nicely from the collapse of his marriage.

"Speak of the devil! Here he is right now!" Carl bellowed.

Heat flooded Eryn's cheeks. She had been so engrossed in her thoughts she didn't notice the man who had appeared at Carl's side.

Impeccably dressed, the newcomer stood with his hands in his pockets, looking like he just stepped out of a men's fashion magazine.

"Eryn, this is my nephew, Troy," Carl's voice carried across the entire room. "Troy, this is Eryn, the gorgeous hostess of this party."

God! Eryn cringed. *Does the man ever speak quietly?*

Barely over the first blush, she felt a second wave come on; not at Carl's compliment, but at the way Troy was looking at her.

His sandy blond hair fell carelessly over his eyes, but didn't hide the intensity of them. His gaze raked her body ruthlessly and with obvious appreciation. He leaned slightly back on one leg, biting his lower lip, his shocking blue eyes giving her a definite come-hither look.

"Why don't you two get acquainted? I need to find my wife before she thinks I'm flirting with you." He winked at Eryn and slapped Troy on the shoulder before walking away.

Eryn watched Carl as he made his way through the room, until he reached his wife.

"I apologize for my uncle." Troy grinned. "He gets so excited about his boats, he forgets not everyone is interested."

Eryn wrinkled her nose. "Was it that obvious?"

"Don't worry about it," he said. "I can guarantee you he was totally oblivious." He turned to the bartender and ordered a beer. "Let's go outside."

Without waiting for her response, he took his drink and gently guided her towards the door leading to the patio outside, his hand placed firmly on the small of her back.

She looked around the room to find Bryce deeply engrossed in conversation with one of his clients. She wondered how long it would take for him to notice that she was gone.

The air outside, though warm, was still cooler than it was inside. She breathed it in, trying to clear her head.

"So what is it that you do? You seem to be new to the circuit." Eryn waved her hand to indicate all the partygoers.

"My mother convinced Uncle Carl to take me under his wing," he said, gesturing with his bottle toward the house. Through the patio doors they could see Carl engrossed in a conversation, his wife at his side. "She's afraid I'm going to waste my life, so she feels the need to save me from myself." He looked over his bottle at her, gracing her with a smile meant to put her at total ease. His charm was hard to ignore.

"Oh yeah? What would you rather be doing?"

"Rock climbing," he said.

That seemed to fit him, Eryn thought. She could tell he was in good shape by the way his suit fit snugly over his shoulders and tapered sharply to a trim waist.

"So what about you?" he asked. "Are you a career hostess?"

"Oh, God, no," Eryn quickly responded. "I'm a professional photographer." She definitely wanted to make that distinction. Though she did what she needed to help out Bryce, she had her own life. "So, where do you climb?"

"There are some nice spots in Colorado and Idaho. I go to Yosemite a lot and when I can't get away, I like to practice over by the cove, just past the tide pools." He tilted his head to one side, contemplating her. "You could get some great shots there. In fact, I should take you with me some time," he said, his smile just this side of suggestive.

"Take her where?" Bryce seemed to have materialized out of nowhere. In an instant he had his arm possessively around Eryn's waist, pulling her close. "How's it going, Troy?"

The two men shook hands. Bryce held his grip a moment or two longer than necessary, his eyes locking with the younger man.

Eryn looked down, pressing her lips tight. The green monster of jealousy was raising its ugly head right under their feet. Although Bryce had thrown the preverbal gauntlet, Troy was not in the least intimidated.

"I was just telling Eryn that rock climbing would give her an incredible photo experience," Troy said coolly, yet searing Eryn with a blazing look.

She looked up at the mention of her name, stunned by Troy's hot intensity. She smiled, though, enjoying the fact that Bryce tightened his grip around her waist. *My ego will never be the same.*

"I'm sure you're right." Bryce's tone was controlled. "She always gets great shots."

Bryce ignored her sharp glance in his direction. If he had ever noticed the quality of her photos, this was the first time she had heard about it.

Bryce pressed his lips to her hair and pulled her closer. "There's someone I'd like Eryn to meet. So, if you'll excuse us…" He led her away without waiting for an answer.

Eryn felt Troy's eyes following her as they left.

"Just like his uncle," Bryce sneered.

She could hear the tension in his voice. She didn't have to look to know Bryce's face was grim, his lips pulled into a thin line. Eryn knew only too well what lay beneath that look. He was battling for control. He had always been jealous throughout high school and college, making sure no boy, especially the extremely attractive ones, got near her.

She looked back at Troy. He grinned and raised his bottle in a salute.

She didn't mind so much when Bryce not so gently pushed her ahead of him inside the house.

Chapter 6

The last of the sun's rays reached across the waters, skimmed the top of the castle walls, and forced their way through the open window where Catherine sat atop silk pillows, tucked within the window seat.

She leaned against the wooden shutters with the circlet on her lap, and watched the jewels spark to life in the sun. The gems, their colors deep and brilliant, and the sun's rays, still warm and strong, sought one another and touched in an intimate and seductive way To Catherine, the duet between the gems and sun was an allegory for love, of belonging to one another. She flushed as thoughts of Jonathan crowded into her mind unbidden.

Turning her face to the setting sun, she tried to imagine what he would be doing at that moment. Would one of the ever-present women around him find her way into this arms this night? A sigh feathered away a tendril of hair that had loosened itself and fallen across her eyes. Oh, what difference would it make, she thought. Whatever it was that she felt, whatever it was that she saw in his eyes, mattered not. Their worlds are far apart – he, a merchant on the seas, and she, the Lady of Elderidge. Their stations alone placed an insurmountable barrier between them. He would set sail two days hence and her life would continue as if their paths had never crossed. She would go on with her life, go on with Galen, and she would more likely than not forget about Jonathan altogether, as surely as he would forget about her.

She picked up the circlet and hesitated a moment before rising to put it away. Catherine yearned to wear it tonight, but was not prepared to answer the questions it would evoke, so she put the circlet carefully in its pouch and tucked it away on the bottom of her trunk. Taking out the black velvet bag that Galen had given her, Catherine emptied its contents into her hand. The brooch weighed heavy against her palm. The sapphire's deep vibrant blue stared back at her, solid and brooding. It was worlds apart from the lightweight and colorful circlet from Jonathan. Catherine smiled wryly at the difference. How befitting that the two gifts should be such a contrast, for each man was as different as the gifts they gave. Night and day. Black and white. Galen was the moon. Jonathan carried the sun.

Deep inside her, something stirred, reaching for the light.

No! Her fisted hand pressed against her mouth. *It would not be wise to encourage such feelings!* She pushed that emerging self back into the shadows, and resolutely turned her mind from it. Slowly unclenching her hands, she saw the brooch had bitten into her palm, leaving a crescent line of scarlet, a stark reminder of to whom she belonged.

Resolutely she fastened the brooch on her bodice, smoothed her dress and took a deep breath. With one last look over her shoulder at the fading sunlight, she prepared herself for the evening ahead.

~ ~ ~

Catherine stood at the entrance to the great hall and took in all that had been done. Large tapestries hung from the walls and fresh rushes had been strewn across the floor in preparation for the feast tonight. Two dozen places had been set on long tables that would soon be laden with beef, fish, wine, and ale. An intimate party, to be sure, reserved for Lord Oakley and his entourage.

Catherine grimaced at the thought of Lord Oakley, the neighboring landowner that reminded her of a leering rodent. Why her father chose to keep his company, she did not know. Perhaps their love of hawking was the thread that bound them. Catherine shuddered. She despised the man and his relentless advances, but as he was a guest in her home, she would be expected to endure his company tonight without complaint.

The guests had arrived sometime earlier, first being shown to their chambers to rest after their journey. To her relief, Lord Oakley had not yet come down. She relaxed a little as she watched the servants light the candles on the tables and stoke the fire, bringing it to its full force within the hearth.

"As always, you look radiant."

A chill ran along the length of her body as the fetid breath of Lord Oakley blanketed her neck. She stepped sideways and turned to face her father's guest, keeping a fair distance between them. His attempt to be charming made her skin crawl.

Close-cropped hair revealed the ugly scars of battle, scars he wore as trophies of his survival and power. His lopsided smile could not hide the coldness of his eyes, like a hunter surveying his prey.

Catherine made no effort to hide her distain. "Lord Oakley, you humble us with your visit. To what do we owe this honor?" Her lips curled with the words.

Stepping closer, Oakley reached out to stroke her cheek. His calloused fingers chafed her as he brushed them across her skin. Though the touch was meant to be gentle, she could feel a controlled violence vibrating underneath the surface. Catherine stiffened under his touch and backed a small step away.

He let his hand drop to his side. "Such beauty you possess, Catherine." His small, dark eyes raked lewdly down her body as his tongue licked his thin, shiny lips. "In answer to your question, I am here at the invitation of your father." Looking at the tables in the hall, he said, "As always, your hospitality is most welcome." He stepped closer and took hold of her hand. "I wish to discuss a matter with you, Catherine, if we might have a moment alone this evening."

"Catherine, I believe your presence is needed in the kitchen." Galen's broad shoulders, twice the size of Lord Oakley's, filled the doorway. He drew himself up to his full height, his feet firmly planted, with arms folded, drawing his tunic tight across the muscles of his chest.

Lord Oakley's slight build straightened at the dangerous tone of Galen's voice.

Catherine wasted no time pushing past Lord Oakley, and with a grateful glance at Galen, left the hall.

"Again, your timing is impeccable, Sir Galen." Lord Oakley turned slowly to meet his foe. Not nearly as tall as Galen, he stood with an arrogance that almost made up for his size.

"Your business here is with Lord Roberts, not Lady Catherine," gritted Galen.

Surveying his competition, Oakley chose his words carefully. "Catherine is a woman of free will. Unless she has pledged her heart to you...?" Taking pleasure in the tightening of Galen's jaw, he continued. "So, Catherine has yet to make her choice, has she?"

His words dripped malevolence. "Do you not realize, Sir Galen, that you cannot hold onto that which is not yours?"

Lord Oakley's words had found their mark.

With dangerous calmness and his steel-colored eyes growing dark, Galen answered, the threat implicit. "You will tend to your business here and stay away from Lady Catherine."

Sensing the danger, Oakley shrugged. "If you will excuse me then, I shall see to my hawks before we dine." He studied Galen, unmoving before him, and smiled, his face contorting with a twisted grin. "Should the fair lady be seeking me…"

At Galen's sudden advancement, Oakley's hands flew up in defense as he darted just beyond the other man's reach and out of the hall.

Slowly, Galen let his breath out, unclenched his fists, and released the tightness of his muscles. Lord The man was despicable. Oakley preyed upon his victims' weaknesses, and like a viper, he had struck at Galen's very heart with his words.

Galen ran his fingers through his hair in frustration. It was all too true. Catherine has not yet pledged her love to him. He felt he knew her reasons, and thought that she just needed time. Time he was willing to give. For him, there was no other woman. Even as a young boy, he knew she would someday be his wife. He has spent his life protecting her, being her strength and her companion. Yes, he would wait…a lifetime if he had to.

Chapter 7

The hot rays of the sun soaked into Eryn's skin, melting away the effects of last night's party...and what had happened afterwards. Bryce had made love to her last night and though he had been passionate, it had been far from fulfilling for her. His lovemaking had been over-laid with possessiveness, as if he was reclaiming his territory. And Eryn knew why. Troy had dared to challenge Bryce and she had been caught in the swirling vortex of testosterone. She knew, though, that it had more to do with Bryce's damn pride than with her actions. He could never stand the thought of another man even *thinking* he had a chance with her, let alone show open interest, like Troy did. All six feet four inches of Bryce's muscular frame was usually enough to put them off. But there was Troy, shorter by three or four inches, daring to taunt him.

"I didn't get much sleep last night." Brandi, who was lying in the lounge chair next to her, broke into her thoughts. "That Dylan is an animal!"

Eryn winced. Brandi was much too accommodating for her own good. "Busy taking care of his wounded heart, eh?"

"I wouldn't talk, girlfriend. I saw you cozying up to that good-looking guy."

Was everyone watching them last night? "Oh, pu-leeze," Eryn grumbled. "I wasn't getting cozy. We were just talking."

"Uh-huh." Brandi wasn't buying it.

"Really," Eryn said. "It was totally innocent."

Brandi groaned. "It's always been so easy for you. Men just flock to you and you dismiss them like its nothing. I, on the other hand, usually get the leftovers."

"What are you talking about?" Eryn asked. "Dylan is a real catch." She started counting on her fingers. "He's good looking, single, and if you didn't know, very wealthy."

"Yeah, well, the jury is still out on him being a catch. Hey, who was that guy you were with, anyway?"

Before Eryn could answer, a shadow moved over her and instantly cooled her baking body. "Hey, who's in my sun?" Shielding her eyes, she squinted up at Bryce.

He stood above her, his cool gaze sliding down the length of her body. If he had any lingering passionate thoughts from last night, his expression certainly didn't show it.

"I'm going to play golf with a client. Need anything while I'm in town?"

She was disappointed, but what was she expecting? Roses the morning after? "No thanks." She settled back on the chair. "I've got to head down that way later anyway. Got a call for a photo shoot today."

"Really." He challenged. "With who?"

Eryn frowned, peering at him through her lashes. It sounded like he didn't believe her. "Troy. You know, Carl's nephew," she said matter-of-factly. "He wants some shots for his portfolio."

The tension shooting off Bryce was palpable.

"Wow," said Brandi. "Innocent, huh?"

Eryn shot her a look that had Brandi back-peddling. "Sorry."

"You think that's what he really wants?" Bryce gritted.

"Careful, Bryce, I might think you're actually jealous," Eryn dared to peek at him, hoping he was smiling, but his jaw only tightened. "Oh, come on! Is it so hard to believe that the man actually might want a good photographer? Isn't that what these parties are all about? Networking?"

"She's got a point there." Brandi piped in.

Bryce ignored her as he continued to stare at Eryn. "At least tell me where you'll be."

She shielded her eyes and looked at him again. His eyes challenged her, serious and penetrating. His face was like a fortress. She couldn't tell what was going on behind it, but the way he stood over her was protective and possessive. It was sexy and yet at the same time extremely annoying. Maybe he did care after all, she thought, but he had a hell of a way of showing it.

Eryn finally answered him. "I'm meeting him over by the tide pools at four o'clock." She could almost hear the mental math playing out in his head, calculating how far along in his game he would be by the time four o'clock rolled around.

"Just be careful." He stopped himself just as he was turning. "Oh yeah." He tossed a small manila envelope onto her chair. "This came for you."

"What is it?" Eryn picked up the envelope and shielded her eyes as she read the handwriting on the front.

Not bothering to answer, Bryce turned and walked away.

Eryn forgot the envelope for a moment as she watched him walk back to the house. She wanted to crawl into his head and poke around in there. What was it that kept him so far away from her? Last night his hands roamed her body as if making sure she was still all there, that his property was still intact, and when he drove himself into her, his eyes were closed, lost in his thoughts, a place she could never follow.

"That is one good looking man," Brandi said under her breath.

Eryn shot her a sidelong stare.

"What?" Brandi shot back. "Well, it's true! God, I remember in high school how every girl just flocked to him." She closed her eyes and lay back. "They all had crushes on him, but you were the only one he would look at. Now here you are, married to him, with a house, career. Like a damn fairy tale."

It was true. Almost. "Not quite like a fairy tale," Eryn muttered.

"More trouble in paradise?"

Eryn thought about it for a moment. "I don't know. It always seem like he's blaming me for something. He kind of keeps his distance, but never completely pushes me away." She sat up straighter in her chair and stared at the sun bouncing on the surface of the pool.

"Well, it can't be that bad. I mean, look at all the shit he buys you. You gotta love that," said Brandi.

"Maybe that's part of the problem. He confuses all that stuff with affection."

"Well, I'll be more than happy to take some of it off your hands if you don't appreciate it," Brandi said, putting out her hand.

Eryn laughed and slapped her friend's outstretched palm. "I might just do that." She picked up the envelope again and recognized her brother's rushed handwriting. She flipped it over, looking for a return address. "Typical," she muttered.

"What's typical?" Brandi tipped her face higher into the glaring sun.

Eryn carefully ripped open the top of the envelope, not sure what to expect. "Oh, James is never in one place long enough to bother telling me where he is." She peered inside. "He usually sends legal papers for me to take care of for him." She sighed. "I wish he would stop traveling long enough to visit once in awhile."

She pulled out a wad of paper that apparently was supposed to pass for wrapping paper. Pulling back the edges, she uncovered a scribbled note on top of a stone pendant engraved with three spirals, hung on a thin, black cord. She studied the round, nickel-sized ornament, wondering what possessed her brother to send it to her. Even more surprising was that he had taken the time to write a note. *"Eryn - Was in England this past month. Cornwall in particular. Found this. Thought you might like it. - James."*

"Now that's a first." He never acknowledged her birthday, let alone sends her gifts. "I wonder why he did that?"

"What?" Brandi asked.

"He actually sent me a souvenir." She flipped over a small card attached to the string and read the description. "It says the symbol is a *triskele*, a triple spiral. It represents the sun, the afterlife, and reincarnation. The one continuous line represents continuous movement of the universe within eternity." Eryn dangled the stone in front of her, her brow creased in thought. "I've seen this symbol before. I just can't remember where."

Eryn put the smooth stone in her palm and traced the lines of the interlocking spirals with her finger. "Hmm. From Cornwall of all places." She liked the sound of that. Cornwall, England. When she was young she wanted to be a princess and live in a castle, a big white fortress with looming towers that brandished flags bearing her family's colors. She imagined walking in the gardens, dreaming of her knight in shining armor, who would sweep her onto his horse and protect her with his shining sword. The memory made her smile. What little girl didn't dream of her knight? She carefully wound the cord around the pendant and put it back in its envelope.

Placing the package beside her, she swung her legs over the side of the lounge chair. The water looked too good to pass up. Looking at Brandi out of the corner of her eye, she got up quickly and jumped into the pool, hooting as she folded her legs into a perfect cannonball, splashing Brandi thoroughly. It felt good to cut loose, something she didn't do too often.

The cool water slid past her skin, slowing her drift to the bottom, dropping her down into the hushed silence. The sun's rays penetrated through the ceiling of the watery space, illuminating the floor of the pool with dancing lights. Crouching low, she pushed off the bottom to the surface.

Brandi was sitting up now, drying herself off, a scowl on her face.

Eryn laughed. "Aw, live a little. You're like Bryce. Too serious." She swam to the edge of the pool and climbed out, then grabbed a towel and patted her skin dry. "I've got to get my stuff together for the shoot."

Brandi looked over at Eryn, scowl still set. "God, you're so skinny." She looked at her own waist. "I'm still working on these love handles here." She pinched some skin between her fingers.

"You're kidding, right?" Eryn asked incredulous. "If you lose anymore weight, you'll be a poster child for anorexia."

Brandi dismissed Eryn's reaction. "It's the way of the world, girlfriend. Gotta do what it takes to get ahead."

It was hard for Eryn not to worry about Brandi. She was like a sister to her. Over the years she had watched Brandi nearly break in her efforts to bend to the demands of the fickle Hollywood scene. She jumped from man to man, molding herself to be what they wanted, and when they tired of her, Eryn was there to pick up the pieces.

"What are you looking at?" Brandi had lowered her glasses to peer at Eryn.

Eryn hadn't realized she was staring. "Nothing. I was just thinking. Sorry about that." She finished drying off, gathered her towel, lotion, and envelope and headed for the house. "I'll be here for a bit. I'll let you know when I leave."

"I want a full update on...what's his name...Troy? See if he's got a girlfriend, will ya?"

"You got it," Eryn called over her shoulder. She smiled. She should set them up. Who knows? They might just be good for each other.

Chapter 8

Catherine woke before the sunrise, feeling hollow-eyed and tired. The events of last night wore on her even as she slept. She slipped out of the bed, drawing the bedcovers close to her body to ward off the chill lingering in the air. The stones beneath her feet were as cool as the morning air wafting through the window, bathing her face with its crispness. Outside, the grounds were still swaddled in that moment between night and day, when time weighted in the balance, almost undecided as to what to do next. Catherine held her breath and counted the seconds. Reluctantly the night released its grip as the morning light began to unfold, luxuriously stretching its light across the pale hills, reaching towards the sea. She relaxed, letting her breath out slowly in concert with the rising sun.

The evening past had drawn on endlessly as Lord Oakley's leering stares and inappropriate remarks escalated with each tankard of ale he emptied. Beside her, Galen had endured her father's guest in strained silenced. Though Catherine sat between the two men, she had proved to be a poor buffer, for Lord Oakley took thorough pleasure in baiting Galen. She could see by the tightening of Galen's strong jaw, the flexing of his hands, that if Lord Oakley had not been under the roof of her father, Galen would have gladly taken the nobleman apart limb by limb.

On more than one occasion she heard the word *marriage* pass across Lord Oakley's thin, twisted lips, but much to her relief, her father dismissed the idea. Though his lands bordered their own, and such a union would strengthen their holdings, she knew her father loved her enough not to force her into a marriage with someone as vile as Lord Oakley.

Catherine rubbed her arms vigorously, but could not suppress the cold feeling when she thought about him. So long as he was within the castle walls, she felt the need to escape. In a short time her father and Lord Oakley would be headed towards the open hills, but until then, she would ride to the ocean and stay there until the stench of the man's presence was gone.

She turned on her heel and crossed her bedchamber, dropping the bedcovers to the floor as she pulled on a red velvet robe. Quietly, she opened her door and stole down the hall to the room where the maidservants slept. Slipping in and closing the door behind her, she crossed over to where Emelie lay sleeping.

Catherine spoke with hushed urgency, gently shaking her shoulder. "Make haste, Emelie. You must rise!"

"Milady! Is something wrong?" She sat up, rubbing her eyes.

"Shh!" Catherine put her finger to her lips. "Ready yourself and then come to my chambers. I wish to ride this morning before the others arise!" Turning to Elizabeth, who was now awake, Catherine said, "Tell Jarrid to ready our horses, and be quick about it. Speak to no one of my plans."

Elizabeth wasted no time in scrambling to her feet.

Back in her chambers, Catherine felt the urgency grow as the light outside began to spread. Impatiently, she pulled on a burgundy velvet gown with gold-beaded trim above the elbows and waist and gold silk that peeked out from the slashed sleeves and skirt.

Emelie hurried in, lending a hand to tie the laces at the back of the dress and then to tuck Catherine's hair into a tight braid.

Signaling for her maid to keep quiet, Catherine headed for the stairs leading to the kitchen, preferring to avoid the great hall where many of the guests would lie, having fallen asleep in their drunken stupor.

The cook, a jolly, plump woman, was the only one about, busy preparing breads and meats for Lord Roberts and his guests that morning. Startled by the sudden presence of her mistress, she dropped into a deep curtsy. Catherine waived it away as she hurried out the door to the courtyard.

Catherine focused on the two figures ahead of her, Elizabeth and Jarrid, who obediently stood holding the horses. She could hear Emelie's panting breath behind her as Catherine's long strides brought her fast to the stables. Without a word, Catherine took Jarrid's hand as he assisted her onto her saddle and looked around impatiently, waiting for Emelie to mount her horse. Confident that no one was watching them depart, Catherine urged her horse toward the gates. It was not until their horses were a good distance from the castle walls that Catherine began to relax.

Turning her head, she hid a smile. What, Catherine wondered, must Emelie be thinking? One moment she was awoken from sleep, the next moment the poor girl is atop a horse, all before the birds had stirred. Still, Catherine had not offered her any explanation, for her reasons to leave the castle this morning were her own. Lord Oakley would be staying with them for a few days and Catherine had no desire to feel the lecherous eyes of Lord Oakley dirty her any more than she was required to. She turned her horse for the port, determined to put as much distance between them as possible.

~ ~ ~

Galen had awoken early that morning, still sorely agitated from Lord Oakley's goading. He felt helpless at not being able to strike back at Lord Oakley for his words, his lewd expressions toward Catherine, and the smug looks that Lord Oakley directed his way. Under the table Galen had found Catherine's hands, clenched in tight fists, and held them in his, trying to protect her as well as he could. Loathsome or not, Lord Oakley was Lord Roberts' guest, and by Lord Roberts' law, all guests were to be treated with respect.

He put his hands behind his head, staring at the ceiling. Today would be a hard day of training, Galen thought, sharpening his skills as well as the squires'. He would fashion a post and hay in the likeness of Lord Oakley, and shred it to ribbons. Though it would bring immense satisfaction to him, it would do little to ease Catherine's mind. She spoke little last night, but he knew only too well the contempt she held for Lord Oakley.

It was no secret that Lord Oakley had an interest in Catherine. It was apparent that Lord Roberts had no intention of entertaining Lord Oakley's repeated requests for Catherine's hand in marriage, but that did little to put Galen at ease. Lord Oakley was a constant thorn in his side.

Catherine is mine, Galen thought fiercely, and always will be.

Unable to lie still any longer, he got up and crossed his chamber to the chair where his clothes lay As he passed the window, movement at the gate caught his eye. His brow furrowed as he watched Catherine's and Emelie's horses race away from the castle.

Chapter 9

"Ok, Eryn. I guess we can stop now." Troy began unhooking the gear he had strapped to his waist. "I'm sure you have plenty of shots I can use."

Eryn rolled her neck to loosen up the muscles. The past three hours had been a new and welcome experience for her, having never before explored the sports side of photography. She was actually excited about the pictures she'd gotten. The strain of gripping the rock, his arms and legs pushing his body upwards, showed off the contour of Troy's lean, hard muscles. Definitely not a difficult subject to look at through the lens, she thought.

He was roguishly handsome, even more so than Eryn remembered from the party. He was definitely not a suit man. Outdoors was his element, among the water, the cliffs, and the sun.

She couldn't deny he was attractive and that he had a certain amount of charisma, but there was also something about him that bothered her, something she couldn't quite put her finger on. His smile was smooth and persuasive, his eyes cool and calculating with a hint of malice. With his good looks and endless charm, though, she had no doubt he could seduce a woman into instant submission if given the chance.

"Oh, I think you'll like what I got." Eryn turned and began packing up her flashes and stands. "You're a natural."

"You just bring out the best in me." He was suddenly behind her, giving her little room to move between him and her camera case.

Startled, she turned quickly and lost her footing in the soft sand. She cursed softly, struggling to maintain her balance.

He caught her around her waist. "Gotcha."

For the longest moment they stood inches apart, his hands firmly on her hips, holding her steady. She felt the smoldering heat from his eyes as they traveled down the length of her neck, pausing when he spotted her wildly beating pulse in the soft hollow of her throat. A satisfied smile played upon his mouth. Suddenly, she *did* feel like the prey. Oh, he was good.

"Yes. I think I definitely need to hire you again," he murmured. "Maybe a family portrait."

So, he is married after all, she thought with relief. Eryn gently grasped his wrists and took his hands off of her while carefully stepping sideways. Somebody had to keep this professional. She guessed that would be her.

"Sure. Anytime. How many children to you have?"

"One, if you can count my dog as a kid." His eyes crinkled at the corners as he gave her a knee-weakening grin.

She wondered if he practiced that or if it came naturally. That smile probably got him everything he wanted.

"Sometimes that's all a couple needs," Eryn said. "A dog, I mean."

"Couple? No, it's just me and Duke, living the bachelor life."

"So you're not married?" She realized that came out with a little too much enthusiasm.

"Why, are you interested?" he teased.

"No," she said quickly, not wanting him to get the wrong impression. "I have a friend. She was at the party last night."

"I'm pretty sure I checked out all the women there. You were by far the most attractive."

He's relentless, she thought, shaking her head. She squatted down to put her lenses in the case and then snapped the case closed. Standing up, she faced him. "And very married."

"That doesn't make you any less attractive to me." His attention drifted over her shoulder to something behind her. "Hey, Bryce. Here to watch your wife in action?" He winked at her.

Eryn spun around, feeling a cold sweat pop out of every pore on her body. She should have known Bryce couldn't stay away, but his timing could not have been worse.

Tension throbbed in Bryce's clenched jaw. "How's it going, Troy?"

Troy turned and walked to his gear. "You've got quite a wife there, Bryce. She's a real professional." He stuffed the ropes and other gear into his bags and slung them over his shoulder. "Call me when you have those ready," he said to Eryn. "I'd like to look them over with you."

He's tormenting Bryce on purpose, Eryn thought, flashing Troy a warning glare. She could almost *hear* Bryce's muscles tighten up.

"Take it easy, man." Troy slapped Bryce's shoulder as he turned to leave.

Bryce managed to muster a grunting noise as they watched him walk to his truck and sling his bags into the back of it.

"I don't like him." There was finality to Bryce's tone. He looked somber, hands shoved in his pockets, head turned downward, with a scowl on his face.

She almost felt sorry for him. Eryn went to him and slid her arms around his waist, lifting her face to say, "Why don't you help me get this stuff to my car and then I'll treat you to happy hour?"

He stared down at her, his expression dark.

"Come on. Like old times, remember?" Stretching up on her tiptoes, she softly kissed his neck and flicked her tongue just below his ear. She smiled to herself when she heard a catch in his breath and felt his chest beneath her hands tense.

~ ~ ~

"Here, let me top that off for you." Eryn poised the bottle over Bryce's cup.

"No, I'm good. I have a..."

"I know, I know, a meeting in the morning." She put the bottle down and twisted it into the sand next to the soda. Like old times, but this time they didn't have to pilfer the bottles from their parents' wet bar before sneaking down to the beach to party.

The evening was perfect, with the sun still high enough above the horizon to warm the shore. They settled on a spot next to a cliff in a protected cove, shielded from the off-shore breeze, away from wandering eyes. The seagulls were starting to huddle together on the beach in clusters, having spent the day scavenging for food. All was quiet, except for the soft lull of the waves.

Eryn leaned up against Bryce's shoulder, feeling his body relax against hers, his elbows resting on the blanket that covered their knees. She traced the line of Bryce's muscle along his arm and smiled as he flexed it in response. What would it be like, she thought, if he would just turn to her and kiss her, with no other reason than to show her he loved and wanted her? What would it be like if he held her face in his hands, pressed his mouth hotly to hers, and tasted her lips? Was there such a thing as two people so in love, that just being around each other made it impossible to keep hands off one another?

She closed her eyes against a headiness that started to inch its way up her neck and glide over the top of her head, like millions of tiny fingers kneading through her memory. She felt strangely detached, stuck somewhere between here and there. The sound of voices and laughter was suspended somewhere in that space, too. Her mind was awash with white before *his* face came into focus. Her breath caught in her throat. He was so close. If only she could reach out and touch him this time…

His lips came painfully close to hers. She dared not move. She so desperately wanted to feel his lips upon hers.

He hesitated a moment before he drew closer and softly kissed her cheek. His fingers traced the softness of her lips, marveling at their fullness. "May I?"

"I pray that you will hesitate no longer," she whispered. Her breath was lost as his kiss consumed her, the hot silk of his tongue smooth against hers. Never before had she been kissed so thoroughly, so passionately, and with such abandon. She discovered she was not a fragile flower that would crush under the weight of such passion, but a woman who could give as much pleasure as she took. Boldly

*she threaded her fingers through his hair, pulling him
closer, arching her back as his lips traveled down her
neck, grazing the edge of her gown...*

Eryn's senses screamed. Both her mind and
body were on fire, erasing the boundaries between
them, blurring the line between dreams and reality.
Her eyes flew open and her body instantly stiffened. It
was so fast, too blurred... and then it was gone, leaving
her heart pounding in her chest.

Bryce leaned away, his startled, cool gray eyes
staring into hers. "Are you all right?"

She shivered. Her dress, perfect for the warmth
earlier in the day, gave little protection in the cooling
air. "Uh, yeah. I'm...I'm okay." She ran her hands
over her face. "I just thought I heard some voices."

"Come here." Bryce lay back and tugged her
down beside him, pulling the blanket over their bodies.

With her hand on his solid chest, the beat of his
heart against her cheek, and with Bryce's arms firmly
around her, she should have felt secure. But instead
she was unsettled. Okay, so maybe their marriage
wasn't perfect, but he was here, sharing his life with
her every day. Shouldn't that be enough? She wanted
so desperately to say yes, but now something was
starting to come between them - or *someone*, she
corrected herself. This was the third time the man in
her dream had penetrated her psyche, totally getting
into her head. He seemed to be calling her. She
shivered again.

"We'd better go," she said, pushing herself up.

They packed what was left of their drinks and
with the blanket wrapped around her, they walked back
towards the car.

Bryce gestured down the beach at a campfire. "They're probably not even old enough to drink."

She stopped and stared at the smiling faces illuminated by the flames. Bursts of laughter mingled with the popping of the wood, as the group around the fire tipped back bottles of beer and wine. Was Bryce kidding? Maybe the heat rising off the fire distorted their faces. To her they all looked way older than twenty-one. She blinked and then rubbed her eyes.

Her body tensed and the shivering began again, this time uncontrollably.

"Come on. Let's go home." Bryce held her close and pulled her towards the parking lot, leaving the fire and laughter behind.

Chapter 10

Their horses slowed to a stop just beyond the still-quiet village. Catherine watched the ships in the port rock lazily in the rippling waters while their crews set about their morning duties.

To her dismay, the breeze coming off the ocean barely managed to stir the air's heaviness and her grip on the reins tightened as she fought the onslaught of heat. Memories of her meeting with Jonathan swirled inside her, and some instinct told her the heat she felt was not from the sun. Thoughts of him were sending a fever surging through her body.

"Master Jonathan is up and about early, milady," Emelie said, pointing to *La Helena.*

At the base of the plank leading to the ship, Jonathan moved, opening boxes, inspecting the contents, and putting out goods. His discarded shirt lay on one of the cargo boxes beside him. Catherine followed the line from his broad shoulders down to his trim waist. She bit her lower lip. *This would be so much easier if he would simply keep his shirt on.*

"Quickly, milady," Emelie urged her. "He is alone now, but the sun rises higher and others will be coming."

Crimson stained Catherine's cheeks as she realized how intently she had been staring. She opened her mouth to say something, anything to deny what she felt, but the words refused to come.

Emelie smiled and nodded encouragingly.

"I am here for no other reason, Emelie, than to spend time away from the castle this morning,"

Catherine protested. "The stench of Lord Oakley was too much for me to bear this morning."

Though her maid lowered her eyes, Catherine did not miss the knowing smile. Ignoring her, Catherine took a deep breath and spurred her horse onward.

The soft plod of the horse's hooves upon the ground disturbed the stillness of the morning air, alerting Jonathan of their approach. Looking up, he tucked his hair behind his ears and he gave her a dangerously beautiful smile.

"Catherine!" he cried. He stood before them, hands on his hips, unaware of the effect his naked chest had on Catherine. Even without moving, the strength in his shoulders and arms simmered just beneath the sun-darkened skin.

Her fingers itched to caress a trail from the soft hollow of his throat down along the ripples of his stomach. She blushed fiercely when his eyes locked with hers, but she could not look away.

He returned her gaze, looking not at the jewels she wore or at the richness of her dress, but at her, *Catherine*.

Jonathan gathered his shirt and slid it quickly over his head, finally releasing Catherine's senses from the intoxicating sight.

"I found the walls of the castle a bit too confining this morning," she managed to say. "I merely wished to pass the time elsewhere."

He nodded in understanding and gestured around him. "And what better place to spend time?" Jonathan turned and called towards the ship. "Cedric!"

A tall, gangly young man, appeared at the top of the plank. "Sir?"

"Come take milady's horses and care for them, eh?"

"Aye, sir!" Cedric hurried down towards them, his mass of curly blond locks bouncing around his boyish face.

As Jonathan helped Catherine and Emelie dismount, Cedric took the reins, hesitating a moment in front of Emelie. He seemed to forget his purpose the moment he looked upon her face.

"The horses, Cedric," Jonathan whispered, a hint of tease in his voice.

Cedric blushed, and mumbling an apology, he led the horses away, stealing glances at Emelie over his shoulder.

Jonathan laughed. "A good man, he is. A bit timid with the ladies, but as loyal a friend as one could wish."

Catherine avoided his gaze, intent on studying the retreating Cedric. She could feel Jonathan looking her. Struggling to keep her face passive, she marveled at how he could make her skin so warm without even touching her.

"Would you walk with me, Catherine?" Jonathan asked softly. There was an intimacy with which he spoke her name, a familiarity that rolled naturally off his tongue. "There is a path I found that overlooks the water."

Catherine looked in the direction he pointed. It was a path she knew well, one that her mother had taken her on many years before. A walk this morning was not what she intended, but why should she not walk? A walk would be perfectly harmless, she told herself.

"Emelie…" She looked to her maid, gesturing her to join them.

Jonathan called over his shoulder. "Cedric!"

Face still blushing, Cedric bounded to his side.

"You are in charge here for a time, Cedric. I trust that you will see to Emelie's needs." Jonathan clapped him on the shoulder.

Cedric pressed his lips together and quickly glanced at Emelie, whose face reddened, too.

"Now," Jonathan said, turning to Catherine. "Let us take our walk. Emelie will be well taken care of." Jonathan leaned closer to her, too close to her suddenly willing lips. "We should hasten, lest Cedric loses his wits."

He extended his arm for her to take, but she refused. Though she yearned to feel the strength of his arm, she feared she would lose her own wits if she did. And if she were to be left alone with him, without Emelie…

"But I cannot leave her here," Catherine objected. "Why, that would be highly improper."

Jonathan cocked his head to one side as if he did not understand. "Do you truly believe that to be so?" When she did not answer, he gave her a smile that weakened her knees. "Come. You will not be disappointed." He turned to lead the way.

"Shall I come with you, milady?" Emelie's anxious tone stayed her.

Catherine looked at Jonathan, standing a few steps away, eyes sparkling, then back at Emelie whose hands fisted in her skirt. Then she glanced at Cedric, who was toeing the ground nervously. No harm would come of this, she reassured herself. She would only be gone for a short time.

Catherine shook her head and sighed. "No, that will not be necessary, Emelie." Turning, Catherine followed Jonathan.

~ ~ ~

"Look at that, Catherine." He stopped to look out over the ocean. "What a sight she is!"

Catherine looked at the man before her. Standing there with his arms crossed over his chest, the breeze played with his shirt and whisked strands of his hair across his face. She reluctantly dragged her eyes from him to follow the direction of his gaze. The sapphire waters stretched forever with sparkling drops of diamonds dancing on the surface. In silence, they watched the gulls floating effortlessly in disorganized patterns, squawking to one another, searching for anything to feed upon. Farther out, a sea lion rolled lazily in the waves, diving under the water only to appear a short time later.

She had never thought much about the ocean before, knowing it only as a border to her father's land, a watery pathway upon which the ships came to port. She looked now at the vastness of it, the emptiness, and the loneliness, and wondered.

"What is it like to sail so far from land?" she asked.

Jonathan smiled broadly. "It is like being cradled in a mother's arms. You must trust you will not be dropped and that you will be carried to your destination without harm." He pointed towards the horizon. "Out there, beyond the comfort of the land, away from the ground's sure footing, one must learn to trust and believe. You learn to depend on one another." His eyes lingered on the horizon for a moment before turning to Catherine. "It makes for a beautiful union."

The vastness of the ocean all at once disturbed Catherine, making her long for the sanctuary and security of the castle. The waters far beyond seemed only too capable of swallowing one's mind and all the memories, replacing it with emptiness. The thought of being so isolated and so far from home sent a chill through her.

"Do you ever get lonely when you sail?" Catherine turned abruptly to Jonathan.

"Lonely?" He laughed and the air came to life with the sound. "Ah, milady, hardly! There are too many of us aboard the ship to be lonely. We fight, work, laugh, and most of the time we are in each other's way."

She frowned. It was strange. He made it sound as though there was no distinction of status between him, the master of the ship, and the crew. Her own castle bustled with maidservants, cooks, stable boys, the steward, but they were there to serve Catherine's family, not to offer companionship.

"Yes, but the crew…they are your servants, are they not?"

The smile faded when he looked at her. "No, Catherine. They are not my servants. Each man came to me out of need, but stayed out of loyalty. They are free to go, but they have chosen to stay. That makes them like family."

Catherine thought about Emelie. She was one household member she could depend on, who actually seemed to be loyal to her, but was their relationship akin to friendship or merely based on duty?

She searched Jonathan's face, still so intent on studying her. She expected to see impatience or pity or indifference, anything other than what she saw.

His eyes were soft, moving over her face as if to memorize it. They held so much patience and acceptance. He seemed to understand the thoughts with which she was struggling.

"We, them, us," he shrugged. "It makes no difference. We are all the same." He touched his palm to hers and held her still with his gaze. "See? Fingers, skin, blood running through our veins. The same."

Time stopped for Catherine as she surrendered herself to her feelings. Her hand seemed to melt together with his, skin on skin, blending as one. His hands, though calloused, felt so soft against her delicate fingers. She looked at the man whose mere touch caused her belly to flutter and her knees to weaken. His lips were so perfect, so sensual. How did she not notice before the long lashes that softened his eyes and the laughter that danced within? Under the caress of his gaze, she felt vulnerable...beautiful...perfect.

Lacing his fingers in hers, he drew her hand to his lips. Her mouth suddenly became dry and she could scarcely breathe as she watched him kiss each finger slowly, deliberately. A flutter stormed in her belly. She gasped helplessly.

"Servant or nobility...we all feel the same emotions. Fear, anger... passion." His eyes turned curious. "Tell me, Lady Catherine, what is it that you feel? What makes you happy?"

She was lost. Somehow, somewhere along this path, she had strayed. The world around her had disappeared and she was standing alone, lost in his eyes, her body ablaze with sensations she had never felt before. She was slipping out of control. She wanted more, of what she could not be sure, but she knew he would give it to her for the asking. It was dangerously easy to forget who she was when he stood so near.

Closing her eyes, Catherine tried to shut him out, shut out everything about him, everything he made her feel. She focused on the sound of the waves upon the sand. *Breathe, breathe.* The tingling subsided and her body cooled in the breeze. Steady once again, she opened her eyes.

"What do I feel?" Her words were clipped. "Nothing at the moment, but the need to walk." She pulled her hand away and turned abruptly. Breaking contact with him eased the sensations consuming her. "As far as what makes me happy," she said over her shoulder, "I enjoy visiting the port and discovering the trinkets you merchants bring."

Jonathan threw his head back and laughed. "Of course, milady! As do most women!"

She smiled in spite of herself. Jonathan's laugh was infectious. Her smile tugged harder at the corners of her mouth until she could no longer restrain herself and laughter spilled fourth. This joyous sound of her own laughter was so foreign to her. How long has it been since she heard it? She knew it had been a very long time. Her hand rose to stifle herself, but Jonathan stopped her, taking her hand in his.

"No. Please do not stop. You are so beautiful when you laugh."

But her laughter faded and was carried away by the ocean breeze. This time when Jonathan held her gaze, she didn't fall into the depths of his eyes, but peered into the amber pools, savoring the beauty, searching for what secrets might lie beneath. But there were no secrets. He made no attempt to hide anything from her.

A bit embarrassed to stare so long, she turned and looked out to the water, watching the gulls fly to and fro. The ease with which he gave, his compassion for others, made her feel wholly inadequate. Her station alone granted her privileges that she readily took. She knew no other way. And until now it had not mattered.

"Do you think me spoiled, Master Jonathan?" she asked hesitantly.

He was silent as he pondered her question. "What I think does not matter, milady." He stood beside her, a comfortable silence settling between them as he, too, watched the antics of the gulls. "We choose who we want to be. What matters is if we are true to ourselves and to our hearts."

But for her, it *did* matter what others thought. The ocean breeze brushed across her face, softening the frown that brought her brows together. "That may not always be possible. There are other things, other people to consider. If we are solely true to our hearts, *that* might be considered selfish."

Gently, he took her hand and placed it over his heart.

Her breath quickened at the feel of his firm chest beneath her palm.

"True happiness flows from the heart's desire, not from bending to the will and expectations of others." He brushed away the tendril of hair that had found its way across her face. "To deny others the right to bask in the light of your happiness, *that* is selfish."

To be sure he speaks the truth, Catherine thought, for the happiness that surrounds him is akin to an elixir to her. When he is near, every part of her is intoxicated. No, he could not deny her that happiness, for that would, indeed, brand him as selfish.

At this moment, her desires battled with her sense of responsibility to Galen. "But if we do not consider others in our decisions, their unhappiness is inevitable."

A knowing smile played upon his lips. "Their unhappiness is only because we are not fulfilling their own desires. Is *that* not selfish?" He released her hand and sighed. "We cannot possibly be responsible for the happiness of everyone, milady."

She shook her head to clear her thoughts. Nay, this whimsical fancy of being true to her heart was just not possible. How could she not think of Galen? She could not deny his devotion to her these ten years past and she certainly could not bear to break his heart. Galen's love for her, his need for her, was there in his every expression. Still, she could not deny her own growing desire for Jonathan. Her fists clenched in frustration. What was she thinking? She was a lady and he was a merchant. Besides, even if their stations in life did not prevent them from a union, did Jonathan not have a woman waiting for his return?

Catherine's sudden twinge of jealously surprised her. "And what of your wife? No doubt your wife shares your passion for sailing?" The words spilled out before she could think.

His brows rose in surprise. "I have no wife."

"I do not understand. If you are not married...but you told the women in the village...then who...?" Catherine blushed as the words died on her lips. Her boldness shocked her, but she needed to know.

He gave her an impish smile. "I merely informed the woman that my lips are for someone *other than her*."

Catherine had not realized she was holding her breath until relief washed it from her lungs. She knew not why it mattered so much to her if he had a woman. She had no right to know and had no reason to know. Her life has already been chosen for her. Their paths may have crossed now, but surely they will part once again when Jonathan sets sail. She looked away, afraid her face would reveal her disappointment.

His hand gently captured her chin and turned her face to him. "Perhaps now I *have* found that someone."

God help me, she thought. The urge to close the gap between them and to feel his lips upon hers threatened to overtake her. She was sorely inexperienced in matters of the heart and body, and her head fought to reason with her. This was a man, beneath her station, a merchant no less! Hardly a suitable match for her.

He leaned closer and lightly brushed his lips against hers, his breath so sweet it took hers away. "Come, milady. Emelie must be wondering where I have taken you." He turned and led the way to the village.

She stood there in shocked silence. His contact with her was so gentle, so quick. The only telltale sign that he kissed her was the slight tingling that lingered on her mouth.

Catherine gathered her skirt and hurried her steps to catch up, watching the way his hair draped over his broad shoulders and the way the muscles in his legs tightened and relaxed with each step he took. *Oh! Why do I keep doing that? I am no better than the women in the village.* She closed her eyes for a moment to shut out the desire that refused to go away. She tried instead to see Galen by her side, and as she did, her shoe caught on a rock in the path.

"Oh!" she cried.

Jonathan was instantly there, his strong arms wrapped around her, keeping her from falling. He lifted her up and held her against his chest. Concerned etched his face, now mere inches away from her own.

"Are you hurt, milady?"

His lips were so close…and so inviting. She lowered her eyes only to find herself taken in by the smooth skin of his chest, the way the muscles blended with those of his strong neck. She straightened herself and stepped back, smoothing down her dress.

"Only my pride, Master Jonathan." She set her chin stoically. "I thank you for saving me from making a fool of myself."

His hands stayed firmly on her waist. "You, Lady Catherine, are anything but a fool." His face grew stern for a moment before breaking into a smile. "Shall we?" With a sweeping bow, he invited her to walk before him.

Catherine stifled a smile as she passed him and led the way.

~ ~ ~

They made their way back to the ships where they found Cedric with his foot perched upon a crate and leaning close to Emelie. She was giggling at something Cedric was saying, oblivious to those around her.

"Well done, Cedric. I see you've managed to take care of Emelie quite well!" Jonathan called to him.

Cedric and Emelie both leaped apart abruptly, faces flushed.

Jonathan was the only one who seemed at ease during the awkward silence that followed.

Catherine was too aware of how close Jonathan stood to her, his arm warm against hers. It was making it difficult for her to think. She just could not stay any longer.

Looking at the sky, Catherine said, "I trust enough time has passed. Cedric, would you bring our horses?"

After a nod from Jonathan, Cedric ran off.

He moved closer still and whispered to Catherine, "I pray I will see you again before I set sail."

When she looked at him, her heart quickened, for his eyes held a promise of his heart, his soul, and whispered silent words of passion, love, and honesty. She savored the moments his lips touched her hand and the gentle squeeze he gave it before helping her onto her horse.

Catherine lost herself in the warmth his nearness enveloped her in. So lost, she did not see the white horse standing in the shade of the trees, the figure of a man hidden by the horse, or the narrowed eyes of Galen.

After a quick look over her shoulder at the people walking about the port, she urged her horse in the direction of the castle. Emelie followed close behind.

"Farewell, Jonathan," Catherine whispered under her breath.

Chapter 11

Eryn wrapped her arms around herself a little tighter and stared into the blackened pit. Last night's lusty blaze was just a memory. All that remained of it now were pieces of charred wood, crushed beer cans, and an empty bottle of wine. Just remnants of a few friends having a good time. So different from the blaze it held last night that was so alive, *so real.* But the disintegrating pieces of wood were now void of any energy, as dull and muted as the fog that surrounded her.

It was early. Dawn was barely breaking through the darkness. Not even the gulls were motivated enough to be up this early. She'd hardly slept last night, thinking of the blazing fire, haunted by those she had seen surrounding it. No, she couldn't wait. She had to get out here and see it again up close.

She knew what she had seen, and it wasn't what Bryce had seen, which was a bunch of teenagers having a few beers. No, Eryn had witnessed older, weathered sailors, in shirts with huge, billowing sleeves, pants cropped off below their knees, feet bare. Some had bandanas topping off their long hair, some in ponytails. She saw women she could only describe as wenches, dressed in medieval-type peasant dresses, their breasts nearly falling out of the bodices, hanging all over the men, and laughing at some crude joke Eryn couldn't hear. It was as if she had caught a glimpse of another dimension from which she was separated by a transparent wall. She had felt like an intruder, looking through someone else's eyes, someone else's life.

Another life. My life. The possibility made her heart hammer double time. And if she was going to be honest with herself, it was freaking her out a little bit. *Okay.* She dragged in a lungful of air. *I can have an open mind. Let's just say it was true?* The date on her computer, her dream of the man with the mesmerizing eyes, the vision of the man with the velvety kiss, the boat on the beach, the voices last night, the fire. She recounted each one. They all seemed to fit together like pieces of a puzzle.

Reincarnation. Okay, it was a possibility, wasn't it? *But why me? Why now?* Maybe she was one of those who remembered a past life. One of those case studies psychologists write about.

She puffed her cheeks and let her breath out slowly. Reincarnation. She knew she was grasping for straws, but she needed some sort of explanation for what she had been experiencing.

Eryn willed herself to clear her mind. Just one more vision, one more voice would convince her. "Okay," she said out loud. "I'm listening." She strained her ears for some unusual noise, but the only reply was the sound of the rolling waves. She laughed at herself. What did she expect? A conversation from beyond? For some door to appear in front of her? A door through which she could step into the past and maybe find this man from a life long gone?

She looked around, only slightly relieved when she found nothing had changed. Actually, she was a little disappointed. Whoever this dream-man was, whoever had gotten into her head last night while she and Bryce were on the beach, has gotten her attention. So now what?

She glanced to the horizon, as if the answer would suddenly rise out of the water. Nothing. She turned to face the length of the beach and began her run. The air was heavy, almost palpable, as she cut a path through the moisture-laden fog. She tried to focus on her steps, rhythmic and silent, keeping in time with her breathing, but her mind kept tripping over the possibilities.

"Who are you?" she whispered. A soft rush of warm air brushed past her and then was gone, but there was no breeze. It was more like a sigh that wrapped around her. Like an imprint of a feeling, a feeling long forgotten that hung on the fringes of her mind, just out of reach.

Eryn followed the beach to the cliffs, where the high tide stopped her from going around the rocks. Slapping her hand against the rough surface, she turned and leaned against it, heaving in the moist air. The fog's strength wavered under the glare of the sun, taking on an orange glow. Scanning the beach around her, she took in all the little details. It dawned on her how many little things escaped her notice after living at the beach for so long. Like the way the waves stretched its fingers up the sand before disappearing out of sight. How the ocean's color reflected the mood of the sky, or how each ray of sunlight dropped a single diamond upon the sharp peaks of the water. She felt so small standing on the edge of the ocean's vastness.

She realized she felt more alive this morning than she had in a long time. Her skin tingled with a new awareness of something…more.

"Damn," she muttered, looking at her watch. As much as she wanted to stay, she had to get back. Hugging herself against the cool air, she tried to focus.

There was something hovering just beyond her memory, but she couldn't grasp it. She shook her head in frustration.

A quick sprint helped to shake off the chill settling in her bones. She drew in deep breaths and the moist, salty air moved through her lungs, exhilarating her in a way that brought her to the brink of laughter. When was the last time she did that?

~ ~ ~

More often than not, Brandi spent the evenings at Eryn's house, legs wrapped around the barstool legs, popping olives in her mouth as she watched Eryn cook. It didn't really bother Eryn much. It was as if her friend was part of the décor. Brandi's world rotated around Eryn and Bryce. The two of them gave Brandi firm ground to stand on when her life with her fellow actors and party-goers got shaky. Which was often.

Eryn watched from the corner of her eye as Brandi flipped through the latest tabloid, wine glass in hand. She was grateful Brandi wasn't too talkative tonight, because her own thoughts were bouncing off of each other, hitting up against logic, imagination, and research. A single afternoon at the library gave her entirely too much information for her to grasp in one sitting. She read about encounters with master souls, past life regression sessions, and people transforming their lives because of what they remembered. Eryn started to believe in what she read. It helped explain what was happening to her. The only thing she couldn't figure out was *why* it was happening to her.

She wasn't exactly sure what to do with what she just learned, but she wanted to talk to someone about it. She wanted to hear from someone that she wasn't delusional.

Maybe she could test the waters with Brandi tonight, she thought. Eryn could, and usually did, tell her just about everything. Brandi knew her as well as Bryce did, and perhaps better. Maybe it wouldn't come out sounding too crazy, and even if it did, Brandi was quirky enough that she would probably take it in stride. Before she could talk herself out of it, Eryn asked.

"What do you think about reincarnation?" Eryn tried her best to sound nonchalant as she slid a knife quickly across a sharpening steel.

Brandi's brows came together over an article she was reading.

Maybe she didn't hear, Eryn thought. Maybe that's a good thing. Maybe...

"You mean that living before stuff?" Brandi finally asked.

Eryn didn't realize she had been holding her breath. She let it out, hoping she didn't sound as nervous as she felt. "Yeah. That living before stuff."

Her friend looked thoughtful. "Why would you want to have more than one life? I mean, it would be like watching a bad movie over and over again."

"Well, not necessarily," Eryn disagreed. "What if the movie wasn't so bad in the first place?"

"Yeah, but what if it was?"

"Then you could come back and do it differently."

"Huh?"

"Yeah." In spite of herself, Eryn began to get excited about what she was saying. She put down the knife and leaned on the table eager to share her thoughts. "Like, if you knew you were a mean, miserable person in a different life and everybody hated you, then you could come back and make it right again."

Brandi rolled her eyes. "Oh brother! Now you're starting to sound like those rejects that have those palm reading shops." She thought for a moment. "You know, I remember seeing in a movie once that the Buddhist monks think that even worms used to be someone's mom."

Eryn straightened up, feeling deflated. Asking Brandi had definitely been a bad idea.

Brandi leaned forward as if in conspiracy. "I went to one of those *psychics* a long time ago," Brandi confided, crooking her fingers to form quotation marks. "You know, to find out if I was going to make it in acting or not."

Eryn raised an eyebrow in surprise. Brandi would have been the last person she'd have thought would seek out a fortune teller. She would more than likely sleep with someone for acting jobs.

Brandi straightened her back, her lips curled in a sneer. "Anyway, it cost me seventy-five bucks for her to tell me I had some karmic energy or something that needed to be fixed." She rolled her eyes. "Right. Like I need fixing." She finished the rest of her wine in one gulp, as if to get rid of a bad taste in her mouth. "You're not getting all weird on me now, are you?"

Eryn felt heat rise up her cheeks. She shrugged, deciding it was no use. "I saw a program about it the other day," she lied. "I was just making conversation."

Brandi's eyes lit up as Bryce walked into the kitchen. "Hey Bryce! Guess what? Eryn thinks we're all recycling ourselves." At his uncomprehending stare, she went on, her hands animatedly flipping back and forth. "You know, dying, coming back to life, dying, coming back to life."

Eryn gritted her teeth. She grabbed a carrot and started chopping. She could feel Bryce's unasked question. *What the hell is Brandi talking about?*

Brandi began to giggle. "I think in my next life I'll come back as some movie star's cat and just lay around all day. Or better yet, a dog, so I can just piss on everything." Now she laughed convulsively, slapping the countertop with her palm, snorting with each intake of air.

Eryn wanted to tell her to shut up, to stop her moronic laughing. She wanted to yell at Brandi that maybe she was just too close-minded. And she wanted to do it without bursting out in tears, but she knew she couldn't. Besides, she didn't want either of them to know how much the ridicule bothered her. She took her frustrations out on the carrots, lining them up and chopping at them furiously, not bothering to pick up the ones she sent catapulting across the floor.

Then Bryce was there, taking the knife out of her hand and gently pushing her away. "Here, let me do that. Why don't you get me some garlic?" He nodded his head in the direction of the pantry.

Eryn grudgingly complied, throwing open the pantry door and staring into its depths, not really seeing. She wanted to believe what she was going through was just her imagination, but she couldn't shake the feeling that it wasn't.

"Don't you have to go to work?" Bryce directed a cool look at Brandi.

"What, you're kicking me out?" Her laughing faded.

"Of course not," he said smoothly. "I just didn't think you wanted to be late."

Not catching the sarcasm in his voice, Brandi she looked at the clock on the wall. "Oh, shit. It's later than I thought." She swung her legs around and stood up. "Oh well. I'll just let my manager grab my ass and he'll forget what time it is."

When Bryce and Eryn just stared at her, she protested, "What?" Brandi looked from one to the other. "Hey, it's not my fault he's easy to distract." She grabbed her jacket and keys off the table and headed towards the door. "Hey, Eryn! Still on for lunch tomorrow?" she said over her shoulder.

"Yeah, sure," Eryn said with enthusiasm she didn't feel. She went back to staring inside the pantry.

"Great. See you tomorrow then," Brandi called from down the hall. The front door slammed shut.

It would just be nice, Eryn thought, if Brandi were supportive for once…just once.

"Garlic. Second shelf down. Basket with onions in it."

Eryn hadn't realized she was still staring at nothing until Bryce broke through her thoughts. She grabbed a bulb and snapped off a clove.

"Why do you still keep her around?" He scooped up the cut carrots and dropped them in a bowl before lining up a handful more.

Eryn tossed the clove onto the cutting board. Why *did* she keep her around? She sighed. "We've known each other for a long time. Habit, I guess."

"She could have been a little more supportive," he commented.

"What, you believe in reincarnation?" Her head snapped up in surprise.

"Is that what she was talking about?" he said, not looking up. "No. I just didn't like the way she was giving you a hard time."

She shrugged. "It didn't bother me."

Bryce stared at her, the knife stalled above the carrots. "Eryn, you almost cut your finger off."

He was right and they both knew it. Brandi had pushed her too far and Eryn let her get away with it. Again. Eryn wrapped her arms around his waist and snuggled close to his chest.

They stood in silence, dinner forgotten for the moment. Bryce draped his arms lightly around her back.

The embrace was nothing to cause an inferno, she thought, but it would have to do.

Chapter 12

Catherine sat alone near the cliffs that bordered one side of her father's lands, not far from the castle walls. It was here, on this side of the castle, where the waters raged the fiercest and were the most ominous. These cliffs were the barriers that softened the blow, tamed the current, and protected the beach and port farther to the south so that the ships could safely anchor.

She studied the ocean stretching to the horizon. Very rarely did she venture here. It usually unnerved her, the distance from the rocky edge to the water below, and the realization of how a slight breeze could mean the difference between life and death. But now she was drawn to it, focusing on the beauty of the water, the rich blues and greens of its depths. The peaks of water drifted up and down over the lazy roll of the swells that eventually found their way to the sharp rocks below. An odd longing tugged in the pit of her stomach, an unrest that contrasted sharply against the soft breeze that drifted up and over the edge of the cliff, carrying the scent of salty seawater to her nose. She lifted her face to feel its caress along her cheeks, welcoming its calming touch.

Though only seventeen summers old, she felt as though she had lived a lifetime. In a few months' time her father would host a festive ball to herald her eighteenth summer. How much, she wondered, had she really lived? She laughed often when her mother was alive, but that part had retreated to lie undisturbed, and until now she had felt no reason to seek it out.

Jonathan had caused the laughter to stir anew, bringing with it memories of happier days at the castle.

Her mother had the ability to cast rays of light to any dark corner and enjoyed a disposition that tamed even the stormiest of nights. Her mother loved life and held it tightly to her breast. She insisted her daughters join her for galloping rides upon the beaches, searching for caves along the cliffs, swimming naked in the waves on moonlit nights. She laughed in the face of propriety. Life was for living, she often told them. She dared to test the limits of life and at the same time, the patience of her husband, but he truly loved her and all that she was.

Her mother's death had devastated Catherine. She vividly recalled the pain that ravished her heart, the tears that would not cease, the days and nights she spent in her chambers, inconsolable, and then the numbness that spread through her body allowing her peace at last. Though the pain finally subsided, the protective cloak that she had donned still remained.

Until now. This merchant, a man of the seas, had ripped a hole in that cloak. He caused her to question herself and made her feel things that confused her, sensations she found disturbing…yet pleasurable. She smiled wryly. Around that man her body had betrayed her. His look, his touch, his mere presence overcame her reasoning. She closed her eyes to conjure up the vision of Jonathan, his muscular shoulders bronzed by the sun, his flowing hair, his lips as he touched them to her skin, and his eyes that gave her soul peace and made her smile.

A noise brought her back to the cliffs.

Emelie fell into a deep curtsey. "Milady, Sir Galen approaches."

Galen was, Catherine admitted as she turned and watched him stride confidently toward her, a devastatingly handsome knight. He was tall and strong, with his long golden hair framing a face that many a maiden undoubtedly dreamed of. His eyes, steady and serious, were only for her.

He sat down next to Catherine, placing his sword at his side. "I've been looking for you, Catherine. I hardly thought to find you here."

Aye, I am surprising myself these days past. She sighed.

"It's so beautiful out there, isn't it?" she said, her eyes never leaving the diamond-tipped waters. The ocean rolled rhythmically beneath the surface, lifting the tiny crests and putting them down gently in its wake.

Galen eyed her with curiosity before turning his attention to the ocean. "Aye, that it is."

They sat in silence for a moment before he added, "But never can it be as beautiful as you."

She glanced sideways at him. He was a good, kind man, and completely unaware of his own fine looks. His steel blue eyes harbored intense passion and his strong chin held determination.

He had shown his loyalty to her family many times, protecting what he considered his own. If she were to accept Galen to be her husband, she could be happy. He was her champion and her friend. She could not ask for a more perfect match. And he was here with her now. Jonathan would be setting sail in the morning and would be gone, possibly never to return.

"Did you see Lord Oakley this morning?" Galen plucked at the grass beside him, averting his eyes.

"No," Catherine answered. "I could not have possibly stomached another moment around him."

He nodded, but still would not look at her. "I saw that your horses were gone. Where did you go?"

Galen was behaving oddly, she thought. He never questioned her whereabouts, knowing well that she frequently rode her horse freely across her father's lands, often being away for hours.

She would not lie, but she chose her words carefully. "Emelie accompanied me to the port to pass the time until Lord Oakley left for hawking with Father."

Again he nodded, raising his head to look before him.

Catherine could see him struggling with something, his jaw rhythmically clenching, his eyes looking at the water, but not really seeing what was there. She could see the indecision in the way he ever so slightly rocked back and forth, his breath quick and shallow.

Then abruptly he turned to her with determination. Gently capturing her chin in his hand, he whispered her name and ignoring the servants' stares, he kissed her. His lips were soft on hers, hesitant and questioning.

Catherine surrendered herself for only a moment before pulling away.

Not put off by her retreat, he looked at her through brooding eyes. "I love you, Catherine, and have since I first lay eyes upon you. I believe you know that."

Yes, she knew. She saw it every time he looked for her across the great hall. She felt it every time he touched her. She heard it when he spoke her name. She knew his love was strong and undying. How could she not love this man? She watched the breeze blow the golden strands of his hair onto his face and the sunlight dance upon his hair. Her fingers trailed along the line of his jaw. He was everything a woman could want. Why was she unable to return the love he so freely gave?

He held her hand against his cheek, closing his eyes as if to absorb her touch. "I will wait for you, Catherine. Forever."

Her brows furrowed together. Valiant, controlled, fierce, and commanding. To others Galen was all of these, but only Catherine knew the depth of his vulnerability and passion.

"Forever is a long time, Galen. You could grow tired of waiting for me."

He took both her hands and held them between his own. "I have naught but time." The passion in his eyes had dimmed a bit, tempered by concern. "Pray tell me. What is it that upsets you?"

Secrets had never been held from one another, but today she could not bring herself to share her uncertainty. How could she explain the feelings she had for another man?

She shook her head. "Tis nothing. I was thinking a bit about my mother."

She could not look at him, lest he see another truth in her eyes.

Galen said nothing, but seemed to accept her answer.

She leaned against his arm and settled her head upon his shoulder. They sat together in silence, their thoughts separate from one another.

~ ~ ~

Catherine hardly expected to find herself standing on the deck of the *La Helena*.

After the evening meal tonight, feeling entirely too restless, she had claimed a headache and begged to retire early. After instructing Emelie to lock Catherine's chamber door, stay there, and not let anyone in, she had slipped out the kitchen, saddled her horse, and rode out the gates to the ocean. She felt compelled to go, her body and soul begging to see Jonathan one more time.

This can never be, her mind had argued. *What of Galen?*

Her body, still remembering the sensation Jonathan's touch brought fourth, nudged her soul to speak. *He makes me feel so alive. Do not deny me one more night.* The battle had raged within, rooting her feet to where she had stood, under the trees, just beyond the port.

As if he sensed her presence, Jonathan stood on the deck, looking in her direction.

She had needed no further invitation to join him.

"I had never before realized how beautiful it is!" Catherine now stood against the ship's railing, looking out over the ocean, its borders spreading beyond her imagination. The golden glow of the sun's setting rays warmed her face and a light breeze caught wisps of her hair, the strands teasing the edges of her face. "I understand why you love it so."

Jonathan, leaning on one elbow against the rail, studied her. "Aye, she is beautiful." He gently pushed the loose tendrils away from her face. "She holds many mysteries and many moods. Sometimes predictable, most often times not, but she is what she is. That is why she is so enchanting."

Whether his words were speaking of her or his beloved sea, she could not be sure, but it was his intimacy that brought a blush to her cheeks. His strong hands, accustomed to heavy labor, were surprisingly gentle as he touched her face. Her mind, still struggling to gain control, refused to give in to her desire to take his hands in hers. She stepped just out cf his reach, breaking the bridge of heat that was growing between them. She focused on the expanse of the water. "Why do you sail, Jonathan? Why a life at sea?"

Jonathan's gaze lingered upon her a bit longer before he faced the ocean again. He stood with his arms braced against the rail, contemplating her question.

As the silence grew, she dared to look at him. He looked beyond the water, seeing something she could not. She mentally traced the straight line of his nose and the strong line of his jaw. The breeze held back his hair, revealing his smooth, sun-darkened skin. For the first time she noticed the small loop that adorned his ear. Tonight he wore a shirt dyed of black to match the only other piece of jewelry he wore, a simple gold ring in which was set a black stone.

He finally broke the silence. "Perhaps to be closer to what I love, far from that which I prefer to avoid." He turned back to her and challenged her with

115

his own question. "What of you, Lady Catherine? Have you traveled far from your father's lands?"

"I have never had a desire to," she admitted. "I have my home, my family…" *And Galen*, her mind added. She sighed. *What is it, truly, that makes me hold on so?* Her eyes searched the waters below as if to find an answer there, but in her heart she knew the truth. She spoke in a voice so quiet, even she was unsure she said it. "Perhaps I am afraid."

Jonathan moved to stand behind her and wrap his arms around her waist. Her body tensed as she felt his powerful chest against her back, coaxing the heat to rise once more.

"Look out there, Catherine," he said against her ear. "Breathe it all in. Freedom is yours for the taking. The sea gives so freely and asks for nothing in return." Fierce passion gripped his words. "Take it Catherine! She will give you life!"

Catherine's chest swelled as she closed her eyes and breathed in deeply. She imagined the warm salty air flowing through her veins, awakening a need within her she thought had died long ago. She had the urge to laugh, to cry, to dance, to live!

She was driven back to the moment by Jonathan's kiss. His lips brushed her neck and her shoulders, tender, inviting, and promising. The smoldering heat now exploded into a flame, weakening her knees - and her will. A strangled protest died on her lips, singed by the very fire that consumed her now, as she melted deeper into Jonathan's arms.

He tightened his hold around her as he whispered, "Do not be afraid, milady. Please. Never be afraid."

116

Chapter 13

Eryn was disgusted with herself. A glutton for punishment, she thought. Not only was she still annoyed at Brandi for being so obnoxious last night, but she was even more annoyed with herself for not canceling lunch today.

Sitting across from Brandi, Eryn watched her friend rattle on about all the injustices the world dished out, making her existence so difficult, waving her fork to punctuate each word. Eryn glanced at her watch. They had already been here an hour and Brandi's plate was still half full. Eryn sighed.

The sound of the pounding waves was muted by the windows that stood between the outdoor patio and the beach. Out there, under the glare of the sun, Eryn mused, life rolled out moment by moment, in perfect rhythm, with no pretences. The seagulls stole food, sandpipers poked deep for sand crabs, and beachgoers used their bodies or boards to mold with the waves. Absolute perfection.

On this side of the glass, it was a different kind of perfection. Conversation hummed with polite, meaningless words, napkins dabbed at meticulously painted lips, and glasses were filled with imported beers and wine. This was the place to be seen. A place where people paid just as much attention to others in the room as to themselves. It was all about image.

Eryn noticed a new arrival at the door. "Well, look who's here," she murmured, straightening up, relieved by the distraction, regardless of who it was.

Brandi whipped around in her seat to look and turned back even quicker, recognizing him right away. She swallowed her food and wiped her mouth with the cloth napkin. "Not married, right?"

Eryn shook her head.

"Good. Do I have any food in my teeth?" Brandi leaned forward and bared her bleach-white teeth.

Giving her a cursory glance, Eryn again shook her head and looked back at the door.

Troy stood in the doorway, scanning the room. It didn't seem to matter where he was or what he wore, Eryn thought. He always looked so comfortable. So sure of himself. No, she corrected herself. Smug is a better word to describe his attitude.

When he finally saw Eryn, his face broke into a smile. He wasted no time in getting to their table. "Hey, how's my favorite photographer?" Leaning in, he kissed her cheek and whispered, "Beautiful as ever."

Eryn ignored his comment. "Troy, you remember Brandi from the party, don't you?" She gestured across the table.

As if realizing for the first time there was someone else there, he looked at Brandi and tilted his head a bit, trying to remember. "Oh yeah. You were with Dylan Branson, right?"

"Not really *with* him. Just *talking* with him." Brandi quickly made the distinction, but Troy didn't seem to notice.

He grabbed an empty chair from the next table and placed it between the two women and sat down.

"Will you excuse me a moment?" Brandi grabbed her purse and with a lingering look over her shoulder at Troy, she sauntered toward the bathroom.

118

Troy leaned back in his chair, lazily roaming his eyes over Eryn. He smiled approvingly.

"So." Eryn broke the silence. "Did your mother like the canvas?"

He blinked and politely focused on her question. "Absolutely. So much so that the picture got the best position in her office." He held up his hands, indicating a place up high. "Now she wants that family portrait we talked about to hang above the fireplace at the house." His eyes brightened. "Looks like I'll have to hire you again after all."

"Sure, no problem." Her answer was a reflex, but then she wondered how Bryce would handle it. She twirled her wedding ring on her finger unconsciously. How could she tell Bryce without causing a riff in their lives again? "Your family. Just you and your dog, right?"

"Why? You interested in changing that?" He leaned forward and placed his elbows on his knees, his blue eyes filled with suggestion.

That unnerving feeling of being hunted sharpened her senses. She ignored his implication. "I just thought if you weren't seeing anybody seriously, you might want to ask Brandi out."

He looks over towards the door where Brandi had gone through, looked back at Eryn and shook his head. "Not really my type. Actually, I'd rather ask you out."

Eryn's mouth dropped. She held up her hand to show her ring. "Hello?"

That little detail hardly put him off. "Oh, yeah. Bryce. My foe." He reached for her hand and inspected her ring, then gently guided it back to the table. "He doesn't like me too much, does he?" He leaned back in his chair, contemplating Eryn "He has every right to be concerned. He has a prize worth protecting."

Before Eryn could say anything, Brandi appeared and plopped herself back in her chair, looking back and forth between the two, her eyes wide with curiosity and anticipation. "So, what did I miss?"

Troy was the first to react. "Hey, Brandi, are you doing anything Friday night?" His eyes never left Eryn, a mischievous grin growing.

She felt a sense of impending doom.

Brandi brightened up, oblivious to the fact that Eryn and Troy were still staring at each other. "Friday? I'll have to check my schedule, but I'll be sure to free it up."

Troy glanced at Brandi, taking a moment to look her over before nodding. "Maybe we could double date." He turned back to Eryn, his brows raised. "Eryn?" It seemed more of a statement than a question.

Now they were both staring at Eryn, waiting for an answer. The doom wasn't impending any more. It was here and now.

Eryn looked at her friend, who could barely control the pleading in her eyes, and at Troy. *Damn him! He knows that if I want him to take Brandi out, I'll have to agree to the double date.*

Brandi was already grabbing a scrap of paper out of her purse and scribbling her number on it.

"I'll have to check with Bryce." Eryn hedged, giving her some time to figure out exactly what she had gotten herself into.

Chapter 14

"Sir, a young lady is asking to see you."

"Lady Catherine?" Jonathan stood up from where he was crouched on the deck, coiling thick braids of rope. He glanced down the wide expanse of the ship's deck.

The pale blue sky held streaks of soft orange and red from the rising sun, creating a ceiling over the still sleeping waters of the blue-green sea. A morning breeze was gaining strength, promising a strong hand for the crew of *La Helena.*

"Nay," said Cedric. "I believe…"

"You are truly leaving, Master Jonathan?" Catherine's sister stepped out from behind Cedric.

"Sara?"

Cedric's hands splayed in a gesture of helplessness. "My apologies, sir. She was insistent that she needed to speak with you." Cedric turned and scowled down at Sara. "She said it was important."

"It is fine, Cedric." Jonathan clapped Cedric's shoulder. "I will see her. You go on below with the rest of the men."

"Are you alone?" he asked when the crewmen had gone.

She looked behind her and dramatically exhaled. "Yes. Everyone has been so busy entertaining Lord Oakley they seemed to have forgotten about me." Her bottom lip pouted.

"Forgotten about you? I find that hard to believe," he laughed.

She sidled up beside Jonathan, leaning close enough to touch his arm. Her eyes glistened with moisture. "Oh, but they do. They dismiss me so thoroughly that sometimes I wonder if I can be seen at all."

Jonathan looked down at Sara, a skeptical grin playing at the corners of his mouth.

She stood wantonly close, her shoulders thrust back, her bodice cut dangerously low.

He stepped back. "Why are you here, Sara?"

She reached up and patted her hair that she had so meticulously piled upon her head. "Because I believe we seek the same thing. We are lonely and we need someone to love us."

"I do not believe I ever said I was lonely, Sara."

"There is no need to be coy, Jonathan. I know we need each other." She reached up to trail a finger down the front of his shirt. He deftly grabbed her wrist and held it away.

Anger flashed in her eyes and she sneered. "If my sister cared for you, would she not be here? Mayhap at this moment she is enjoying Sir Galen's touch." She smiled, pleased when she saw Jonathan's jaw clench.

She stepped closer and stared into his eyes, lowering her voice to a whisper. "I am here, Jonathan. She is not. We are both lonely. Please, take me. Let me sail with you." She seductively touched the lace of her bodice, enticing him to look, but his eyes never left hers.

"Sara, as tempting as your offer is, it will never be that way for us."

Batting her eyelashes, her eyes wide with innocence, she said, "Do you not find me attractive, Jonathan?"

"Indeed, Sara, but..."

122

Without a word Sara flung her arms around his neck and kissed him hard, her lips pressed fiercely against his.

Jonathan immediately grabbed her wrists and pried her off, holding her at arm's length. No longer were the lines around his eyes soft and laughing. "As I was saying, Lady Sara, you are most attractive, but there is more to it than attraction. Pleasures of the body must be paired with the longing of the heart."

Her glistening eyes betrayed her hurt and frustration, and her small bosom rose and fell with her angry breaths. She yanked her wrists from his grasp and stood glaring up at him, hands clenched in tight fists at her sides.

Jonathan continued, "You deserve someone who will love you, not just bed you, and that someone cannot, and will not, be me."

Tears spilled over, staining her cheeks. Her foot came down hard on the deck. "No one will love me. Everyone loves dear, sweet Catherine. I will just grow up to be an old spinster."

Jonathan wiped away the tears that trickled down her face. "I doubt that very much." His voice softened again. He tilted her chin up so she would look at him. "You will find someone."

"No, I will not!" she spat out. "Oh! Catherine will live to regret this!" She spun away and ran across the deck, her slippers pounding.

Cedric and three other crew members scrambled above deck.

"Sir! Is everything alright?"

Jonathan sighed and nodded his head at Sara's departing figure. "Cedric, follow her at a distance to see that she arrives to the castle safely. I do not want her to do something foolish."

~ ~ ~

"You said once that you thought me to be beautiful." A deep breath steadied her voice. Do you still believe that to be true?" Sara stood in the doorway of the hawk mew. Her silhouette filled the doorway, her hair now flowing around her shoulders.

Lord Oakley slowly turned around at the sound of her voice. Facing her fully, his eyes slithered hungrily down Sara's body, digesting the implication of her unexpected presence there.

"My dear Sara," he said with velvety smoothness. He extended his hand, inviting her to approach him.

She stepped into the room and placed her hand in his.

Drawing her closer, he reached behind her to close the door.

Her thin body startled at the sound of the latch sliding into place. The mew was dark with only the early morning sunlight seeping through the windows high above. She fought the shiver that ran up and down her spine and glanced at the bolted door. She was trapped now.

No, she reminded herself. Not trapped, for this is what she wanted. This is why she came here, was it not?

Lord Oakley turned her face towards him, his fingers light on her chin. "I meant every word then as I do now." Gathering a handful of her hair, he placed it to his nose and inhaled deeply. "So fresh." He fondled it between his thin fingers. "So soft." He reached for the lace of her bodice and lingered there, reveling in her slight tremble. "So very, very...womanly." He whispered the last word with the smooth voice of a hunter knowing his prey was within his grasp.

Sara looked up sharply. "Womanly?"

A wicked smile crawled across his face as he drew her further into the darkest part of the room, backing her into a corner. "I find you very beautiful, Sara," he whispered. "Much more beautiful than your sister."

Sara's face lit up in triumph. Before she had a chance to respond, Lord Oakley's lips fell eagerly upon hers, devouring their innocence.

"So beautiful," he murmured as his lips raked against her neck and her throat. His hands were everywhere all at once, wrenching her dress down to her waist.

She gasped at the sudden coolness of the air upon her naked breasts and Lord Oakley's wet tongue as he dragged it across her nipples. Her fingernails bit into her palms as her hands clenched in response. She felt helpless against his power, revolted by his foul breath, yet she was determined to stay still.

She heard him curse beneath his breath as he fumbled with his breeches and chuckle as he set himself free. She found strength by envisioning her sister's face when she told Catherine her little sister was now a woman. With a satisfied smile, she allowed him to lower her to the dirty straw-covered ground and closed her eyes against his grunts and groans, prepared to endure his intrusion.

~ ~ ~

Catherine awoke feeling devilishly happy. Thoughts of her time aboard *La Helena* brought a blush to her cheeks. She touched her lips, remembering how

125

Jonathan had so gently taken them. She could scarce remember a time that she had given in so completely to her desires. She relived the pressure of his arms around her, the feel of his hair tangled in her fingers, the beating of his heart against her breast. She had not known what a kiss could be until then. She smiled to herself, feeling a little bit wicked. *So unlike you, Lady Catherine. What would they all think of you?*

She laughed out loud as she reached above her head in a cat-like stretch. Pushing the bedcovers away, she got out of bed and padded to the window. The sun was already making its way up the sky. Jonathan would have set sail by now, she mused. So be it. The passion they shared last night would sail away with him, their secret tossed to the wind and scattered across the waves. The kiss she shared with Jonathan was the beginning of something new for her. He found a passionate woman inside of her and skillfully coaxed her out. Now she was certain that her relationship with Galen could be so much more and she was determined to bring the same spark to life between them.

The sound of clashing swords and the shouting of men in training made its way to Catherine's window. Below, Galen came into view carrying swords and lances towards the training ground. Catherine leaned out of the window, "Galen!" she called to him.

He looked up and smiled. "Good morrow to you, Catherine! It is almost midday! I trust you are rested?"

She leaned forward a bit more, letting her hair cascade around her shoulders. She smiled with satisfaction when she saw him pause, taking in her beauty and the sheerness of her nightgown.

126

His smile promptly faded as he looked quickly around him and then back to her. "I pray you dress yourself, Catherine, with haste, lest you attract unwanted attention!"

Catherine laughed as she withdrew. She summoned Emelie to draw a bath and turned her attention to selecting her gown, humming to herself as she rummaged through her trunk and then her wardrobe, ignoring the maid's curious glances. When the bath was steaming, Catherine abandoned her search, undressed, and lowered her body into the rose-scented water. Like a lover's touch, the water inched its way up her legs, over her thighs, up to the cleft between her legs, the place that only just last night burned with need. She sank lower to feel the caressing water cover her hips, her stomach, and her breasts before she finally leaned back, fully immersed. The feel of Jonathan hands on her waist, his fingers stroking her back and arms was still etched in her mind as she smoothed the scented water over her ivory skin. *Why have I not felt like this before?* Her mind was alive with questions. *How can a kiss, a mere touch, make me feel so alive?* She took extra care to wash her hair until the rich color glimmered. Perhaps all she needed was to be awakened to such sensations. Yes, she was positive she could be with Galen and feel excitement and passion with him. She would be happy to be his wife.

She quickly stood up and took the towel Emelie offered her as she stepped out of the tub. She smiled. *Naughty Catherine.*

Catherine rejected the dress Emelie had placed on the bed, choosing instead a gown fashioned in deep green fabric that fitted snugly about her waist. The neckline scooped low to reveal the tops of her full breasts.

Emelie brushed Catherine's hair and fluffed it until it was dry, fanning the locks over her shoulders and down her back.

Confidently, Catherine went to watch Galen and the other men training as they engaged in mock attacks.

Unaware of her presence, Galen's face was focused, intense, utterly engrossed. His stance and his movements were smooth and graceful, but his muscled legs, wide shoulders and chest held restrained force, ready to react at any moment.

One by one, the men stopped their maneuvers and started at her, their jaws slack and eyes round. Galen, about to reprimand the men for stopping, saw Catherine and quickly turned to face his men. "Rowan, stand in my stead. The rest of you, carry on!"

Giving his sword to Rowan, his second in command, Galen quickly closed the distance between him and Catherine. He stood before her, taking in the full length of her, his eyes reflecting a mix of approval and confusion.

Realizing the exercises had not yet resumed, he turned and cried, "Carry on, I said!" Taking Catherine's arm, he led her towards the garden.

"Such a beautiful day, is it not, Galen?" she asked, her voice lilting. The sky, so brilliantly blue and the sun so gloriously bright, were no match for Catherine's disposition this morning.

His eyes narrowed in response. "You are in a fine mood."

They walked a few minutes in silence. She could feel Galen's burning gaze on her, but she would not look at him. She rather enjoyed seeing him a bit confused.

"What brought you to the training?" he asked. "Is something amiss?"

"Do I need a reason to watch the men train?" She looked at him with wide, innocent eyes.

He pondered her question. "Nay, but you have never shown an interest before."

"Then it is far past time I should, Galen. After all, they are part of the family."

"Family?" Raised eyebrows betrayed his surprise.

She shook her head. "Pay no mind." She hooked her arm through his and they walked in silence.

"I daresay the men saw a different Lady Catherine today," he ventured at last. "It seems your beauty had them mesmerized."

"Hmm, I cannot say I noticed." *'Tis unladylike to flaunt yourself,* her mind chided. Her heart paid no mind. *Ah, but you must admit that the feeling is simply delicious!*

Galen stopped and turned her toward him, studying her face and hair. His eyes followed the lines of her neck down to her shoulders and to her bodice. She felt her body respond to his attention, with a quickened pulse and a tightening in her belly. She lifted her chin with invitation.

His brooding eyes locked with hers, searching for an explanation. Catherine did not miss the flicker of uncertainty that flashed before it melted into desire. The way he cradled her face in his hands, so strong, so tender, took her breath away.

He touched his lips to hers, gently at first as if afraid he would hurt her, and then harder when he felt her respond.

Her lips parted when his tongue sought entrance, seeking the warmth inside. She gripped his shoulders and waited for the passion and abandon to come, the spark to ignite her flame still smoldering within her. Though Galen's kiss was gentle and loving, she could feel him hold back; unlike Jonathan, whose spirit seems to know no bounds, whose kiss was simply...fire. Hot and burning, consuming everything in its path.

Galen abruptly pulled away, resting his forehead against hers. His voice was ragged, his breathing fast. "Catherine... I pray you forgive me..."

"Hush." She smiled. She took his hands in hers and waited until he looked into her eyes. "There is nothing to forgive." She wrapped her arms around his waist and put her cheek against his chest.

With time the passion would grow between them, she thought. She now knew what it felt like and what she was capable of feeling; how a man could make a woman lose all sense of reason, for one night and quite possibly for a lifetime.

Chapter 15

Eryn's thumb moved over the keypad of her cell phone. She scowled at the text messages, all from Troy, asking for the same thing. Weren't his two messages from that morning about another portrait session enough? Granted she had not yet been able to get back to him to set a time, but his persistence was to the point of annoying.

"Tell me again why we're doing this?" Bryce's form filled the bathroom doorway, his shoulders nearly touching the sides of the frame. Midnight hair, slicked back off his face, dripped water down his still-wet body, droplets rolling teasingly downward from his chest over his rippling stomach and into the towel wrapped snugly around his waist.

Eryn closed her phone and looked up. She blinked and swallowed hard. How can he radiate hot sex when his eyes are like ice? She shoved away the urge to go to him. If the set of his jaw was any indication, he was definitely in no mood – for anything.

Putting down the phone, she focused instead on fastening a pearl necklace around her neck, pondering his question. Why did she ever do anything for Brandi? It was just the way it was since the day they met. On the first day of high school, Eryn happened to be walking past Brandi in the parking lot. Brandi was bent over, trying to get her nose to stop bleeding, muttering profanities. Apparently Brandi had mouthed off to a couple of seniors - who found a quick way to shut her up. There Brandi stood, blood running down her face, spattering the front of her shirt. How could Eryn not offer her the extra sweatshirt she had brought for gym class? She had even walked Brandi to the bathroom and helped clean her up. Thus began the pattern between the two of them.

Eryn couldn't figure out why she felt compelled to take care of Brandi even though she knew her friend took advantage of her. Maybe it was time to start drawing the line, Eryn thought. She was starting to feel an inkling of resentment. *Maybe if Brandi starts depending on someone else, she'll get a life of her own...and get out of mine.*

Bryce arched a brow, waiting for her answer.

"Because Brandi needs to hook up with somebody, and I'm thinking Troy might be the one." She shrugged. "I'm just trying to be a good friend," she said as she went into the closet.

"You're way too tolerant of her, Eryn."

"I know, I know," she muttered, emerging from the closet a holding a red, capped-sleeve cocktail dress with a scooped back and matching heels.

"I'm doing this under duress, you know," he said, still not moving.

"I know that. But listen, maybe if they like each other we can see less of the both of them." Tossing the dress and shoes on the bed, she wrapped her arms around his waist. "I really appreciate this."

His hair fell over his steel eyes as he looked down at her, his jaw still firmly set. Letting out a deep breath, he gave in, kissing the top of her head before pushing her away.

~ ~ ~

The drive home was quiet except for the radio playing low. Eryn thought dinner went relatively well, but the rhythmic tightening of Bryce's hands around the steering wheel signaled to her that he thought

132

otherwise. She nervously bit her bottom lip as she ran through, for the third time, everything that happened tonight. During dinner Bryce was cordial enough, though not offering much to the conversation, and seeming more than happy to let Eryn do the talking for the both of them.

The conversation over dinner had steered itself through neutral territory, touching on the most scenic places to rock climb, college life, latest building projects Troy's uncle was drumming up, and Brandi's acting career. Troy was a bit full of himself, but that seemed normal, and Brandi, although seeming a bit agitated at times, for the most part was content to hang on Troy's every word and touch him whenever she got the chance.

"Doesn't it bother you?" Bryce's sudden question snapped in the air.

Eryn cringed. She didn't like the way that sounded.

"Doesn't what bother me?" She stared out her window. What was she missing?

He turned his head sharply in her direction. "You really didn't see it?" His brows were drawn together so tightly it was obvious he thought she was completely blind or an idiot or both.

The confusion she felt must have clearly shown on her face because he let out an exasperated breath and shoved his hand through his hair. The oncoming headlights lit up his face as he focused on the street again. His jaw muscle clenched tight.

"That bastard was hitting on you."

"What? He talked, I responded. Somebody from our side of the table had to keep up with the conversation," she said defensively. She sat back further into the seat and crossed her arms across her chest. "You certainly weren't helping." She immediately wished she could take that back. It was she who had dragged him along tonight, knowing full well he didn't want to go. But he still did it. For her.

"No, Eryn, it was more than that." Bryce shook his head, dismissing her interpretation of the evening. The car came to a smooth stop, idling at a red light.

"I think I would have noticed if Troy was making moves on me."

Bryce shook his head, like it couldn't have been more obvious. "I wasn't the only one who saw it."

Maybe it was Bryce's imagination. Maybe his dislike of Troy twisted the way he saw things tonight. That had to be it. She thought she had done a great job of putting Brandi and Troy together. They were a good fit. But she didn't argue with Bryce. They obviously didn't see it the same way. Eryn sunk lower in her seat and scowled.

Bryce was silent as they pulled into their driveway and waited for the garage door to slide up. Whatever it was that was bothering him, it was because of her. Eryn knew he was going to retreat to whatever place he needed to go to be away from her emotionally.

"I'm sorry. I won't ask you to do this again." She wanted to touch him, to bring him back, but she knew it was already too late.

"Good." Bryce shut off the car and continued to stare out the windshield. He waited until the garage door slid shut before turning to her. Though the anger had dimmed somewhat, his eyes held something that bristled her nerves. He opened his mouth to say something, but apparently thought better of it. Instead he leaned over and kissed her. Hard. It was almost dangerous the way he held her face to his, unyielding fingers threaded in her hair, demanding she meet his passion. His tongue swept inside her mouth, seeking hers.

She winced at the pressure of his lips and his demanding intrusion, but didn't fight him. She wasn't about to stop him now after what she put him through this evening.

His breath became ragged as a surge of intensity overcame him. Grabbing her hand he guided it to his growing erection and pressured her fingers to wrap around it.

"Shit." He abruptly pushed her away and in one swift motion shouldered open the car door and got out, flinging it closed behind him.

In confused silence, Eryn watched Bryce skim around the front of the car, his eyes never leaving hers.

Pausing at the hood, he turned to face her fully. Polished to savage perfection, dressed in head-to-toe black, his gleaming reflection off the car doubled his presence within the confines of the garage. Straight black hair framed a face with smoky eyes that voiced *You are mine.*

Eryn shivered under the glare that pierced her through the windshield, pinning her back to the soft leather seat. Tonight pushed all the wrong buttons in him, she thought, and had thrown him into possessive overload. Hot pins of dread pricked their way up the back of her neck.

The length of the hood was hardly an effective buffer against this intense, focused, dominating male, who seemed to be contemplating his next move. She instinctively gripped the door handle when he strode with purpose to her side of the car and wrenched the door open.

He gripped her arm and pulled her out, slamming the door behind her. A solitary moment was all she had to watch the lines around his eyes and mouth harden before the overhead bulb quit, draping them in darkness.

A soft *humph* escaped her mouth when Bryce pushed her against the car and delivered another punishing kiss, his tongue tangling with hers and drawing it deeper into his mouth.

He draped her arms around the back of his neck, slid his hands over her shoulders, down her back, and closed his palms on her ass, squeezing, pulling her hard against his bulging shaft, shifting his hips in small erotic thrusts.

Eryn could hardly breathe. It felt like he was sucking the life out of her, stealing the air from her lungs. She was smothered by his need to possess her. Protesting was out of the question. She was no match for this kind of intensity. He overwhelmed each and every one of her senses. Her mind fought against this primal taking, but her body was embarrassingly aroused.

He backed up, pulling her along with him and turned her around, yanking her back against him. The thin silk of her dress did nothing to protect her from his rough caresses, the kneading of her breasts, and the plucking of her nipples to evoke a response. And, against her will, they responded, straining against the fabric of her dress.

She closed her eyes against he pain of his teeth raking and biting her neck and shoulders. An agonizing moan, part frustration, part ecstasy, slipped from her mouth. In a matter of seconds, he had her dress hiked up around her waist. His arm was a vice around her waist as he shoved his hand into her panties, fingered apart the soft folds, and caressed the wetness inside.

She hated being taken this way. She wasn't some territory for him to piss on or a battlefield to conquer and lay claim on. *Damn it, Bryce! You don't need to prove anything!*

She inhaled sharply as he slid his fingers into her, thumbing her clitoris into a swollen, throbbing *thing* that completely took over Eryn's mind.

"Say it." He demanded quietly against her ear.

"Wha…?" Her heavy breaths deafened her ears, the smell of sex saturated her nose.

"Say you need me," he demanded. His voice was seductively rough. "Say it's me that you want and no one else."

Not like this, she wanted to argue back, but she knew damn well it was useless. He would have her any way, any time. Where was her backbone when she needed it? Thrust up against a wall of hot, determined, masculine, domineering passion, that's where.

"I want *you*, Bryce." Her words choked out between little gasps. "I *need* you." Her climax came to a complete standstill midair and came crashing to earth, splintering into shards when his fingers abandoned her.

She found herself pressed down, cheek flat against the hot, smooth, black shiny metal of the hood, held there while he quickly unzipped his pants.

Bryce's fingers bit into her hips, shifting her firmly before him. He entered her fully with one deep thrust, filling her completely. The harsh rush of his breath echoed off the walls as he ground his body into hers, driving into her relentlessly.

Her hands pressed against the hood to steady her body against the back-and-forth motion, letting him bury himself inside her. She tried reaching for that place to feel, to finish her orgasm where he had left off, but couldn't and from the sound of his breathing, he was beyond helping her.

His body stiffened as he slammed his release into her, once, twice, three times, before he collapsed, pressing his weight on top of her. His breaths were shuddering gasps, hot on her neck.

Eryn closed her eyes. They couldn't have been further apart than they were at that moment.

He shifted his weight and stood up, pulling her up with him. Neither of them spoke as they adjusted their clothes.

She didn't bother to turn around because she knew there would be no cuddling or murmurs of love. He had taken her on a hard ride on the very boundaries of his tolerance. She stared straight ahead, listening to his footsteps as he walked around the car towards the door.

Hand poised on the doorknob, he stopped and said over his shoulder, "This is between Brandi and Troy, Eryn. Don't drag us into their world."

Bright light from the kitchen illuminated the garage for a moment before he let the door close behind him, leaving her find her way in the dark.

Chapter 16

The freshly-penned words stared back at Catherine. They were words to a man who might never see them. Words to a man who unbeknownst to him held her heart in his hands. How could he know? She herself had only realized this.

After Jonathan set sail, she had opened herself to Galen and gave to him what she could. Galen fully embraced the hope that blossomed within him. His touches were bolder. His whispers were sweeter. He courted her with gifts and stories and constant attention to her needs, yet still a small piece of her heart remained untouchable and unreachable.

I have tried. Her eyes closed against the anguish. *God help me, I have tried.*

She slowly opened her eyes and again gazed at the letter before her. These words were for Jonathan. It was the only way she knew to ease the ache that had settled in her heart.

She blew softly on the paper. Satisfied the ink was dry, she carefully folded it and pressed the edges until they lay flat. Rising from the chair, she went to the trunk at the foot of her bed and kneeled before it. Taking one more look at her letter, she lifted the lid and reached beneath the folded dresses, easily finding the opening in the fabric she had cut on the bottom of the trunk. She slid the letter in with others she had written and pressed the dresses over it. Smooth once again, they shielded that part of her heart that yearned for Jonathan. The part no one must know about.

She looked around her room. Normally it was a comfort to her, but this day she found herself to be restless. She rose slowly, drawn to the bright sunshine outside the window. The azure skies and the sound of laughing children were at odds with the melancholy mood that blanketed her spirits. She shivered and rubbed her arms against the chill she felt.

She would ride, she decided. Yes, she would slip from underneath this grayness and ride to where there were no barriers, where she could feel free. At least she would feel better, if only for a brief while.

Making her way to the stables, she granted the barest of smiles to those she passed. Jarrid, rubbing down her father's horse, made haste to saddle Catherine's mare when she entered the stables.

"Shall I saddle a horse for Emelie as well, milady?"

"No, Jarrid. That will not be necessary. I do not intend to be long."

He bowed in acknowledgement and helped her to mount her horse. Within moments Catherine was galloping beyond the gates, following the well-traveled trail that lead to the rolling hills to the west. She slowed as the path wound upwards to a knoll. From here she could see the endless hills of honey-colored grasses that rolled to the south and west and to the majestic blue-green water of the ocean to the north and east that bordered her father's lands.

She often came here to bask in the serenity that permeated the air and to listen to the peace whispering in her ear. Here the breeze skimmed over the hills unchallenged, taking with it her troubling thoughts. With the softness of a mother's embrace, this place had the power to wrap around Catherine's heart and once again make her world secure.

But this day Catherine would find no comfort. She bent down to stroke her mare's blonde mane, unable to fight the emptiness that plagued her. Sadness had ridden with her here, a feeling of emptiness in her soul.

She could deny it no longer. Her heart was lost to Jonathan.

She sat upon her horse, not knowing what to do or where to turn. Behind closed eyes, she let her mind drift with the breeze, and let her thoughts scatter where they may. She did not want to go back. Perhaps she could just ride. Somewhere. Anywhere. But where could she go to escape the loneliness that overcame her? She clutched her fist to her chest. As much as she wanted the pain to be gone, she knew it was too late to feel any differently. Nor, she admitted, did she want to. It was but a bittersweet gift, meeting Jonathan. Because of it, she had found a part of herself she did not know she was looking for.

She drew in a breath, summoning strength. She would go on. She could not willingly hurt Galen, though she knew it was inevitable. Even if she were to agree to marry him, she could not give him her heart. And he would know.

Reluctantly, she drew the reins to turn her horse around, but seeming to sense Catherine's reluctance, the mare resisted and began a slow canter away from the castle, across the expanse of hills before them.

Catherine made no effort to stop her, and instead leaned forward, urging the mare to run and chase the wind.

Chapter 17

Eryn took her time editing this little girl's portrait, because it was the average person, especially children, she really liked working with. Unlike some of the upper-crust adults she'd shot, children's eyes didn't reflect the greed for money or power.

This little girl, Ashley Miller, was a photographer's dream. Big green eyes that projected innocence, long dark hair that draped along her cheeks, bangs framing a face of soft ivory skin, and pink lips that curved into a smile. Eryn tilted her head to the side, staring at the image. She wondered if she really needed to do much with it at all.

Then, in an instant, the rich color of Ashley's hair turned dull, the sparkle in her eyes burned out, the sharpness of the entire image blurred, and the colors bled with one another. Eryn blinked to refocus her eyes, but the haziness grew until another image lay over Ashley's.

Rolling hills of wheat-colored grass lazily pushed against the horizon. The weather was warm, making her feel a bit uncomfortable in her binding gown. The breeze lifted the few strands of hair that had escaped her braid and brought them around to her face, but she did not raise a hand. Her mare grazed complacently while she sat upon the animal's back, contemplating her surroundings. Reaching down, she stroked the blonde mane hanging loosely down the horse's sleek neck...

Then it was gone. The face of little Ashley Miller stared back at Eryn as if nothing happened, as if time didn't just skip a beat. Eryn's heart, seemingly sensing it had to slow down to almost nothing, beat heavily in her chest. Her emotions started to build, swelling like a tidal wave and overpowering Eryn before she knew what was happening.

Pressing her hands hard on her face didn't stop the tears forcing their way out and the steady stream didn't relieve the tension that had built up in those few moments. Eryn knew what had happened. She felt it deep inside her. She had just experienced a memory of herself in another place, another time. She had distinctively felt the horse beneath her and the reins that she held loosely in her hands. She had heard the breeze that whispered through the grasses, had seen the hills rising and falling before her. She had felt the ruby velvet of her dress weighing upon her body as oppressively as the indecisiveness that lay upon her heart.

Pushing away from her desk, Eryn stumbled from her chair and dried her face with her sleeve. She needed to get out into some open space. Her heartbeat sped up, as she grabbed her keys and her jacket, and headed out the door.

She was barely aware of the short drive to the beach, her mind still reeling. She eased her car into the first empty parking space and jumped out, slamming the door shut as she ran towards the water. Once on the sand, she kicked off her shoes and dug her toes into the gritty sand.

Oh, it felt good to be here, breathing in the salty air! Breathing in deeply through her nose, she pushed the air out hard through her mouth. Doing that five times finally had her in control again.

She raised her hand to shield her eyes against the glare of the sun. The beach was as it always was, unchanged from day to day. Time was consistent from one moment to the next, as it should be. But her own moments were not so predictable, with the past bleeding into the present and the rhythm of time skipping beats. It was as if a closet crammed full of stuff had opened and everything was spilling out.

The dream, she thought, shivering. *That was the starting point. I'm remembering the middle of a story somewhere else, sometime else.*

She walked a few feet, then plopped down in the sand when her legs wouldn't stop shaking. *It was another life, one in which a man loved me like no one else ever has.* Pulling her knees up, she wrapped her arms around them tightly, rocking back and forth.

It was hard to imagine there could have ever been someone else. It had always been Bryce. In fact, she never so much as considered anyone else. Except, maybe, that one time long ago. Funny that she thought about the guy once in awhile, for it had been a chance meeting, nothing more. She rested her chin on her knees.

It was the summer after high school graduation.

Eryn trailed after Bryce and his friends. They were at Solstice Beach and she and Bryce had just had a fight. She had threatened to break up with him – again - and really meant it that time, or at least she wanted to mean it. The heat of the sand beneath her feet was nothing compared to her anger as she struggled to keep up with Bryce's long strides. He and his friends finally stopped. They formed a circle and began hitting a volleyball around, shutting her out completely.

Oh, how he frustrated her, she remembered.

"I could just walk away. I don't have to put up with him," she mumbled to herself as she turned away. *But she knew she wouldn't leave him any more than he would break up with her. Whatever their differences, there was something that kept them together. Rather than let him see how upset she was, she walked toward a volleyball game farther down the beach and sat down to watch.*

From the back row on the other side of the net, one of the players made his way towards her, signaling to the others to keep playing.

"You okay?" He kneeled in front of her, hands on his hips, and waited for her answer.

One look at him and she was speechless. His sun-bleached brown hair barely brushed his wide, muscular shoulders. Her eyes drifted down his bare chest and rippled stomach and stopped where his bathing suit laced. She quickly looked up. If he noticed her suddenly flushed cheeks, he graciously pretended not to. Instead, he looked in the direction of Bryce. A flicker of irritation reflected in his face for an instant. He looked back at Eryn and asked, "Are you going out with that guy?"

Bryce, she saw, was still ignoring her. She stared down at the sand slipping through her fingers. "Yeah, sort of. I guess." She wondered if she sounded as pathetic as she felt and she looked back up to see his reaction.

He just nodded. And he looked at her, seeing past the frown on her face and her lips that were pressed together in a tight line. He seemed to see deeper than that.

She took in a breath as he gazed at her so intently, for in those aware, perceptive eyes, fringed with the thickest lashes she had ever seen, she could see everything she was reflected back at her. It unnerved her, but at the same time, she knew she was safe.

The silence between them was unhurried and comfortable. For reasons she couldn't explain to herself, she felt totally at ease with him. It was as if every unasked question she ever had was answered. She thought that if she just reached out and wrapped her arms around his neck and buried her face against his chest, he could make it all better.

She pressed her lips together harder to suppress the sudden urge to ask him out. It would be so easy. Make a clean break. It wasn't like she was married to Bryce or anything like that. Hell, they weren't even engaged. She could do it. She should do it. Her mouth opened to ask him, but she snapped it shut. As much as she wanted to, she couldn't bring herself to ask. She just wasn't ready to give up on Bryce yet.

She could tell he wanted to say something, but he apparently thought better of it and just smiled - a warm, understanding smile. He accepted her silence without question. With one last look at Bryce, he nodded and said, "Okay. I'm going to get back to the game."

A chill ran the length of Eryn's spine as she thought back to that day. His eyes still haunted her. She has never been able to shake the feeling that when he looked at her, he was trying to tell her something, but she had twisted herself into too big of an emotional knot to understand it, though. She wondered what would have happened if…she stopped herself from going any further. What if's didn't do anybody any good.

She let a big breath. "Okay, so now what?" she said aloud. She needed to know more about who she was, who she had been.

Eryn only remembered that there had been a time when she wore dresses of velvet, rode a horse across the empty hills, and stole kisses on the beaches with a man who made her feel loved and protected.

God, he must've been something incredible. She started to believe she actually *felt* something for him. "This is nuts," she whispered. Already she was feeling an ache of loneliness for him.

It would be easier to let this reincarnation stuff go, to forget what had happened, but she knew it was too late. She was in too deep.

~ ~ ~

By the time Eryn got home, a roaring curiosity had taken over. She sank into her office chair, excited all over again about the possibilities.

The plain brown envelope from her brother still lay on top of her in-box. She leaned forward and took the envelope in her hands, turning it over a few times as if making sure there wasn't some clue on it somewhere that she missed. The necklace, still wrapped in paper, slid out of the envelope onto the desk. The cord felt light as she wrapped it around her fingers, the stone heavy upon her palm. "Cornwall." She flipped the stone back and forth. Why *did* he send it?

She sat down at her desk and wiggled the mouse to bring her monitor to life. Ashley Miller still waited for her.

"Sorry Ashley. Something came up." Getting to the search engine, she typed in Cornwall 1501. Nothing. She wasn't really sure what she was searching for. "Castles Cornwall," she whispered to herself, typing the words. She clicked on a few entries, studying the images of castle ruins. They were so majestic. Even with their now-crumbled walls, she could see that power they had once held. Picture after picture clicked by and with one, the familiarity grew along with the chills that made her shiver.

She searched for something that would tie it all together. The man had been dressed in pirate clothing. Maybe he was a sailor? Rowboat, fires on beaches, velvet dresses, horses, rolling hills. She stared out the window. What exactly was she doing? Her fingers tapped impatiently on the keyboard and she straightened up.

"Let's try reincarnation again," she said aloud as she typed out the word. She scanned the multitude of entries, focusing on bits and pieces of information. *The rebirth of the soul...physical being...expanding self...lessons learned for soul advancement.* Rubbing her eyes, she followed link after link. *Souls travel in groups...serving different roles in each physical life...help one another to learn...soul splitting...one half stays in non-physical plane while other half assumes physical form...twin flames...guides...debts to be paid.*

She hadn't realized how much time had passed until she heard the garage door slide up. She quickly shut down her computer and rubbed her face, eyes tired from the glare of the screen.

Walking to the kitchen, she grabbing a bottle of wine from the bar on the way, still mulling over the information she read. *Souls travel in groups. We are attracted to those that we recognize. Lessons learned. Past events still influence current relationships.* She felt like she must have missed something. If events in the past carried over to this life, wouldn't she still have the man she once so loved? What else happened? And who exactly was in her soul group?

"Are you going to open that or were you waiting for me to do it?" Bryce looked tired, standing with his hands in his pockets.

"Um…" She looked down at the wine bottle, corkscrew tip already buried into the cork. "Oh. Yeah." She quickly finished opening the bottle and poured the Merlot into two glasses.

"Carl Michaelson dropped by the office today," Bryce said.

"Oh yeah?" She held out his glass.

He hesitated a moment before he crossed the kitchen.

Eryn watched as he lifted the glass to his lips and drank deeply, then added, "He said Troy has a long list of pictures he wants you to take."

Eryn's back stiffened.

"He found it amusing that Troy will have you busy for the next 12 months." He finished his wine and set the glass down. "I'm going to bed."

They locked eyes for a brief moment before he turned away. He showed no emotion. Only the sharp edge to his voice let Eryn know his patience was wearing thin.

~ ~ ~

The light from the window was too bright. Scrunching her eyes closed, Eryn pulled her pillow over her head to shut out it out and to try to reel her dream back in. Fragments lingered, flitting in and out of her memory. She wasn't ready to let it go.

"Hello?"

The room was completely empty with nothing to mar the walls. She kneeled on the floor and clutched the receiver, her knuckles as white as the walls that boxed her in. She wanted to crawl inside the black plastic that she pressed hard against her ear, just to get closer to the voice it held.

"Hello." One word, spoken so softly, wrapped seductively around her. It swirled like a mist, moving silently across her face, drifting like fingers through her hair.

She sighed. "I've waited so long for you to call."

The receiver lost its shape and became translucent, before dissolving in her fist. Frantically, she searched the room, palming the floor around her, looking for the one thing that connected her to him.

"Look behind you, love. I've always been here."

Scrambling to her feet, she spun around towards the voice.

The space between them closed with a few gliding steps. Willing arms wrapped around each other, giving them what they needed – comfort, rest, and a place to come home. Heated love reached out, capturing her breath.

"I've missed you." His lips brushed her hair and her temples before he held his cheek to hers.

She clung to him, not understanding the sadness in his voice. His arms tightened around her. And then he was fading.

An echo of his voice haunted her. "Please do not turn me away."

The dream was getting harder to hold on, slipping away like mercury on glass. It was no use. The harder she tried, the more it eluded her. With a groan she slammed her fists into the bed.

"You're awake."

She sat straight up, the pillow landing in her lap. Bryce stood at the bathroom doorway rubbing his hair with a towel, another one tucked around his waist. She shivered, but it wasn't at the sight of his taut stomach or the way his broad chest and strong shoulders seemed to fill the room. It was the way he was looking at her, a potent mix of strength, power, broodiness, and control. He walked to her, his eyes smoldering with possessiveness, each step purposeful.

His eyes held hers for a moment before he reached for the pillow and put it beside her. Towering over her, he leaned in and pressed his lips against hers, his breathing quick and hoarse. The towel came open as he slid under the sheets with her, leaning her back, trapping her with his body. He pulled back just long enough to smooth his thumb across her lower lip, then quickly covered her mouth with his, sweeping his tongue inside. The invasion should have been sweet, but instead he fought with her, leading her with hungry urgency.

Starved for intimacy, Eryn clutched at his corded shoulders, pulling him closer, feeding him the sweetness of her mouth.

"Eryn," he groaned, heavy with need.

Rolling her towards him, he shifted her hips to shed her of the scant fabric that was the barrier between them.

152

"I need you, Eryn. Right now. I need you."

That statement, that small admission from Bryce, slammed into her. He had never admitted to needing anything or anyone. She moved her hips against his, encouraging him, but when his fingers stroked her flesh, when he nudged her thighs open, when they fell into rhythm, she remembered again.

"Please do not turn me away." As if ice had been thrown on her face, Eryn cringed. Her hands clenched the sheets. She suddenly felt like such a traitor.

Pushing the dream away, she surrendered herself to Bryce and took all that he gave, giving what she could. For now, she had Bryce. For now she would not hurt him.

Chapter 18

My Dear Jonathan,

I had no knowledge how difficult it would be to let you go. When we parted, I knew not if I would see you again, and told myself it was not of great import. Though you made me feel so alive, showing me the true woman I had locked deep inside, I grudgingly convinced myself we could go no further, being that our lives are so vastly different. I had hoped that our kiss would be a new beginning for me, but in the time that has passed between us, I have discovered it was merely an end.

Since the day you set your sails, I had allowed my mind and body to rule without restraint in my quest to feel the same passion that I felt in your arms. The notion that it would be fruitless without the participation of my heart had never occurred to me. I convinced myself that my heart would eventually follow, but alas, I was indeed mistaken.

Now I pass each day with a stillness I have never known before. Food passes my lips barely noticed. The colors of the roses in the garden seem less brilliant, their aroma less fragrant.. The laughter of the children sound less joyful to me.

Oh, Jonathan, I am lost! Although, I suppose it would not be difficult to find me, for the path to the beach is well-worn from the many times I have walked upon it. I find it impossible to stay away from the sea, finding some solace in my memory of our walk along the same path.

Many a sail have appeared upon the horizon when I am there, raising again and again my hopes that you have returned. But when I see the ships that approach our port are not La Helena, I feel painful loneliness and sadness. Often times I will stay and watch until the sun settles beyond the sea, finding a strange comfort in the emptiness the night brings. I can almost hear the sun sigh as its last rays find their way to my heart, a peculiar sorrow that I embrace. I yearn to be the sun that falls slowly behind the water's edge, for surely it closer to you than I.

My mother once told me it is best to live in the moment, for we do not have the past or the future. But, Jonathan, if I were given the choice of which moment to live in, I would be hard-pressed to decide. Any moment with you would be heaven.

What I found with you leaves me bittersweet memories, but I have no regrets. If the saints are punishing me for my lack of restraint, I will gladly pay penance until the end.

Chapter 19

"Troy wants to double date again. You up for it?"

"No, not really." The hard sound of ice against glass gave emphasis to his flat words.

Brandi thought for a moment, leaning against the wet bar as Bryce poured himself a drink.

"Probably just as well." She stared down at her own drink, swirling the ice cubes in circles. "I think the only reason why he wants to double is because of her."

Bryce shot her a sidelong look, eyes narrowed in question.

Brandi glanced at him for a moment before looking back down at her glass. "Well, he never really comes out and says it. It's just in the way he looks at her."

Bryce's jaw tightened in response, a gesture that didn't go unnoticed.

She pushed it further. "I think he has a thing for her and Eryn won't do anything to stop it."

Bryce turned his back to her, putting some distance between them.

Brandi was relentless. "She hasn't been around all that much, has she? Where is she now?"

"Out," he said quietly.

Emptying the rest of her drink, she gently put the glass on the bar. Stepping closer, she trailed her nails down his back, hooking onto his belt. "Well, *I'm* here, Bryce." She leaned into him seductively, brushing her breasts against his back.

"Get away from me." His mouth snarled with disgust. He walked across the room and sat down, eyeing her warily.

Brandi stared after him, unbelieving. Moving to stand in front of him, she planted her fists on her bony hips and demanded, "What the hell is wrong with me? What has she got that I don't?"

His icy stare matched hers. "You've got to be kidding," he laughed. "You really want me to answer that?"

The hall echoed with the sound of the front door slamming shut, cutting off Brandi's response. She straightened her shoulders and stepped back, throwing Bryce a smug look, mouthing *"Your loss, asshole."*

"There you are, Eryn." Brandi said as Eryn rounded the corner towards the kitchen. "We were just wondering where you were."

Eryn looked between the two, sensing something was off. Judging from Brandi's smile and the way Bryce was staring into his glass, she figured Brandi had gotten under his skin somehow, which was hardly new. She shifted the grocery bags in her arms.

"I didn't realize anyone was waiting for me." She turned and walked to the kitchen with Brandi not far behind.

Putting the bags on the counter, Eryn started pulling things out and putting them away. "So how's Troy?"

"Oh, he's fine." Brandi poked around in the bags. "You forgot chips." She shrugged and added, "Me and Troy are going out tonight."

Eryn turned to stare at her. "Then why are you here instead of at home getting ready?" Brandi's constant presence there was definitely getting on her nerves.

"Troy said he would pick me up here. He wanted me to get you guys to go out with us."

Eryn grabbed a bag and headed to the refrigerator. "We can't go."

"I know," Brandi said. "I'm glad. I don't think I could deal with it again."

Eryn frowned. She turned, bag still in hand. "What do you mean? Deal with what?"

Brandi rolled her eyes. "Oh, please. He's got a thing for you and you just encourage him!"

"I don't understand," Eryn protested. "I haven't done anything."

"No, of course not." Brandi was suddenly tense, her arms crossed over her chest. "You never do anything. That's the point. You're just...*you*." She spat out the last word as if it was a repulsive taste on her tongue. "When was the last time you tried to get a guy *before* they just fell at your feet?"

Eryn was still trying to follow the direction the conversation was heading when Brandi pressed on.

"Don't you see how hard it is for me to find a really nice guy? I think I have a chance with Troy and you're messing it up."

"*I'm* messing it up?" Now she was completely lost. "What exactly do you want me to do?"

Brandi's fists clenched at her sides. "Leave him alone. Stop taking pictures of him and his fucking dog!" Suddenly she was on the verge of tears.

"But that's my job, Brandi. It has nothing to do with..."

Brandi cut her off. "It has everything to do with it!" Her voice started to rise, punctuated by a foot stomp. "Just for once I want to have a real relationship with someone who isn't some loser. Let him go, Eryn. He's mine!"

Brandi looked different tonight. There were subtle changes Eryn hadn't noticed before. Usually so nonchalant about things, Brandi was beginning to look resentful and spiteful and at the same time so pitifully insecure.

"Okay," Eryn said slowly. "He's yours. I won't do anything to come between you." She raised her eyebrows and waited to see if that was what Brandi wanted to hear.

Brandi nodded and sniffled.

Bryce came around the corner and leaned against the wall, hands in his pockets, staring at Eryn.

Oh, God. Not you, too. Eryn could only guess he heard everything and, given the hardness in his eyes, shared the same opinion as Brandi.

Brandi pulled her cell phone out of her pocket and started pushing buttons as she turned and walked past Bryce, leaving the couple to stare at each other.

Bryce was accusing her without saying a word. There was no sympathy, no support in his eyes.

Frustration squeezed her throat. "Do you really think I had any part of this?"

"I told you I didn't like him."

Brandi's voice filtered in from the next room. "No, it's just us tonight. They're busy. No, I *don't* know what they're busy with. They're just busy. Yeah. I'll meet you outside."

Brandi appeared behind Bryce, purse in hand. She looked at the two of them still staring at each other. Brandi's mood had shifted back to happy again.

She had gotten what she wanted. She nudged Bryce in the back.

"Hey, lighten up you guys," she said before turning and walking out. The front door slammed behind her.

Bryce's stare was unwavering, his eyes smoky beneath dark brows. "So what's it going to be?" There was a slight edge of anticipation in his voice.

So this was it. She could see in Bryce's eyes what he expected her to say and she knew what would happen if she didn't. Of course, he would get his way.

~ ~ ~

Eryn squinted at the clock on her dresser. Eleven o'clock. She strained through the darkness for the sound that had woken her up. It was the low hum of a motor. Brandi was back, she thought. A car door slammed and the engine cut out. Hushed laughter and voices drifted up to the open window. The creak of another car door announced its opening and closing and then there was silence. When neither car started up again, Eryn groaned inwardly. Looking over to see that Bryce was sleeping, she slid out from under the covers and tiptoed to the window. Brandi's car was still parked in the driveway where she left it earlier, but now Troy's truck was parked behind it. In the dim glow of the porch light, Eryn could detect some slight movement in Brandi's car. The car windows were already steaming up.

Eryn curled her lip in disgust. She knew this little display was Brandi's way of making a point.

"Grow the hell up, Brandi," she spat out softly. Eryn slowly slid the window closed and rolled down the blinds, then padded quietly to the bed and crawled back under the covers.

She pressed her fingers to her eyes, squeezing her them tight. In the morning she would finish editing Troy's pictures . After that she'd let him know there would be no more photographs. She had to, if she was to make everyone happy again. If that was even possible! Why did things have to be so complicated? She shivered in spite of the warm night and moved closer to Bryce. His breathing remained deep. She pressed her back to his and hugged her pillow hard against her chest.

Tears trickled out of the corners of her eyes, slow and hot. She felt so lost, so defeated. Beside her Bryce was quiet and his steady breathing infuriated her. *Damn you, Bryce! Why won't you take my side on this?*

It was after midnight by the time she heard the cars start up and drive away. She pulled the covers over her head and finally drifted off to sleep.

She walked slowly on a long stretch of white sand. It was quiet here. Serene. The ocean was calm with the waves gently rolling onto the shore, leaving whispering secrets in the sand. A lone figure stood on the edge of the water further down the beach, hands in pockets, looking out at the ocean, looking for something or someone. His black pants and white shirt billowed in unison and his hair was swept back by the ocean breeze. Her heart quickened. She had found him! Or did he find her? In a moment she was standing beside him and without a word he took her in his arms and held her close. She felt comfort there as she buried her head on his shoulder. She knew he understood her. She closed her eyes, feeling protected and secure. She had no desire to leave. Ever. She was home.

~ ~ ~

Eryn woke up gradually the next morning, savoring the peacefulness that blanketed her. The dreams were becoming more and more real. She could feel his arms around her, feel her cheek against his chest.

She tried to make sense of it. These dreams were a part of her now, connecting her to a past with this man. Memories of long ago intertwined with her present in one continuous strand of events. When she was dreaming, it was just the two of them. With him, she felt whole. No words needed to pass between them. Though he was quite possibly the most beautiful man she has ever seen, the attraction went beyond the physical. It was as though their souls blended. *One half of a whole. Twin souls.*

The sheets next to her were cool now, the heat of Bryce's body long gone. But it didn't matter anymore. She was tired of his distrust. Tired of the distance he put between the two of them. It doesn't matter how much she tried, because he certainly wasn't.

She drew a long breath and let it out quickly. She had some very unpleasant business to take care of today. She pressed her hands to her face, slowly drawing them across her eyes and to her temples and rubbing them in anticipation of a headache that undoubtedly would attack soon. How was she going to tell Troy she was dropping him as a client?

She dragged herself out of bed, shuffled out of the room and went downstairs, letting her feet land with a thud on each stair.

Once in her office she found Troy's phone number and picked up the phone. She hesitated with every number she touched, wondering what she was going to say. She pushed the last number and held her breath.

Each passing ring upped the notch of tension in her neck. Would he understand? Would he try to convince her to stay on as his photographer? Probably. When the ringing stopped and his recorded message began, she let out her breath, relieved.

"You chicken," she muttered and then said out loud, "Hi, Troy. This is Eryn. I have a few pictures left to edit and then I'll get them to you right away." She bit her lip before going on. "I need to cancel next week's session…and I can't reschedule. I'm sorry for the short notice." She pinched the bridge of her nose between her fingers. There was nothing more she could say. "Goodbye, Troy."

She hung up. She just knew that her message wasn't going to be well-received.

Chapter 20

The darkened room lit up briefly as lightening slashed through the night sky, illuminating the heavy drops of rain that splattered down upon the soaked ground. Galen breathed in the moist air. In spite of the disturbance outside, he had never felt more at peace. Of late Catherine had seemed more open and more responsive to him. She was less reserved and smiled more these days past. He joined her on frequent rides over the hillside or shared a meal at the cliffs, and evenings passed quietly in the great hall reading poetry or telling stories.

He was able to dismiss his haunting vision of the merchant kissing Catherine's hand, now that he realized his concern was for naught. He had seen Catherine and Emelie ride fiercely out of the gates the morning after they dined with Lord Oakley, and thinking perhaps Catherine was upset by the events of the evening, he had followed them when they did not return right away. He had stood in the shelter of the trees beyond the port and watched with growing unease as Catherine - his Catherine! - and the handsome merchant stood too close together and exchanged words he could not hear. Jealousy had raged within him, but when he saw no response from Catherine, Galen quelled his desire to challenge the man.

Now he laughed out loud, relieved that his fears were unfounded. Catherine was his and always had been, he thought. She just needed more time. He straightened his tunic and smoothed back his hair.

There was a frantic knock and the door flung open before Galen could move.

"Oh, Galen!" Sara closed the door, and stared at him, her eyes wide.

Sara had become dramatic of late, he mused, and this could very well be another performance. Still, he was compelled to ask. "What is it, Sara?"

She threw herself in his arms. "Galen, I was so scared!" She clung tightly to his waist, her face pressed to his chest.

Wary now, he reached behind his back and released her grip. Though she held tightly, she was no match for his strength. He distanced himself from her, eyeing her closely.

"What frightened you?"

"There was a noise beyond my wardrobe. It was a horrible scratching noise!"

He rolled his eyes. "Tis likely nothing more than rats you heard scurrying about, Sara," he said, trying to hide his annoyance.

Hands clasped tightly together, she gazed at him from beneath her eyelashes. "Do you really think so?"

A crack of light, followed by a thunderous boom, shook the air.

With a shriek, Sara flung herself at him, wrapping her arms around him once again. "Please hold me, Galen." She looked up at him through fluttering eyelashes, lips slightly parted.

A poor performance after all, Galen thought. Sara was anything but a frightened girl. In fact, he had never known her to be afraid of anything. What was she playing at?

He pushed her away from him and said as softly as his mood would allow, "I am not a pawn in whatever game this is, Sara. You know where my heart lies. I will always be true to your sister." He scowled at her. "You would do well to remember that."

Her thin hands dragged across her face, wiping away tears that were not there. "Think you that she pines for you?" Her voice turned soft as she reached out to touch his arm. "You speak of loyalty, but that is a word Catherine does not understand, not as I do."

Galen flinched, drawing his arm back. "And you know of this word, Sara?" he said with disbelief.

She added, softer yet, "I would pledge my life and my body to you, Galen." Stepping closer, she whispered. "Let me show you."

His gray eyes turned stone cold. "You show your loyalty by trying to seduce me?"

Sara squared her shoulders and stepped back. "She plays you for the fool, Galen. You did not see the way they looked at each other!"

"They?" Galen growled. "What do you mean?"

"The merchant," she spat out. "The captain of *La Helena.*"

Galen grabbed her by the shoulders and turned her around. "I will not discuss this with you, Sara." He thrust her towards the door. "Go join the others in the hall. I will be down shortly."

He quickly closed the door, but not before he saw the look of satisfaction on her face. Leaning hard on one hand against the door, he closed his eyes firmly against the doubt, which like a faint mist, settled in the corners of his mind and in his heart. Could he believe Sara's words? No, he thought firmly. Sara was a manipulative little chit and what she said could only have been born from the resentment she seemed to have toward Catherine.

Galen pushed himself away from the door, shoving his hand through his hair. Catherine held his heart. There would never be another woman for him, and he was fair certain she now felt the same. He swung the door open and made his way to the great hall. He would see her tonight and show her how much he cared.

~ ~ ~

Catherine stood at the entrance to the hall, smiling at the gaiety within. This night was in honor of the people of the village. Her suggestion to hold such a gathering had been met with some hesitation by her father and Galen, but she had persisted. She insisted the villagers should reap the benefits of their lord's generosity, if only for one night.

The hearth was filled with cut wood, the flame within blazing tall, chasing away the dampness with its heat and light. She looked around the great hall, satisfied to see that tonight they were as one. After such a dreary day of constant rain, a night of festivities would lift everyone's spirits.

Her father and Galen had already seated themselves at the high table and were flanked by the knights who had pledged themselves to her father. Galen sat with quiet reserve among the others, who laughed and raised their tankards in unison, clearly enjoying one another's company.

Catherine's gaze fell upon Galen. This evening he had taken much care with his appearance, perhaps more than usual, she thought. His chosen color of deep blue did well to contrast with his golden hair that hung loosely about his shoulders. She could find no fault in him. The fault truly was with her. How could she fail to be stirred by a man such as he? He gave her his heart and soul as well as his protection. His kisses had lost their hesitancy and grown more daring, more passionate lately, but still they could not rouse a flame within her. Each time when she pulled away, could he not feel dissatisfaction? Though she enjoyed being in his arms, she knew she failed to return as much passion as he gave.

As if sensing her, Galen's watchful eyes roamed the room and when they lit upon Catherine, he transformed. His eyes shone and his face relaxed. He rose quickly and crossed the room, his eyes focused only on her.

"Catherine, you look beautiful tonight." He took her hands in his and lightly kissed her forehead. "Come. Allow me to escort you." He tucked her hand in the crook of his arm and led her to the table, seating her next to her father. Galen joined in more fully now with the conversation before them. His smile reached his eyes, as it always did when she was by his side.

After a simple fare of wild boar, quail, bread, and much ale, the floor before the high table was cleared for the entertainment. The walls were lined with knights, servants, and villagers, all laughing and clapping with anticipation. A troupe of performers, seeking shelter from the storm, entered the hall. Dressed in rich, bright colors and head coverings of green, yellow, purple, and red, the troupe of men and women danced and somersaulted their way into the hall. An exotic beauty, dancing seductively with swaying hips that were swathed in flowing skirts, was followed by a younger, but taller man. His hands moved swiftly as he juggled four knives at once, tossing them in the air with breathtaking speed. His bright yellow shirt with billowing sleeves was cut open to his navel and his muscular thighs strained the fabric of his breeches. Straight ebony hair was captured at the nape of his neck, accentuating the strong line of his chin. For one moment that lasted an eternity, the room and all within seemed to fade as he captured Catherine's attention. Visions of Jonathan assaulted her mind as the dark eyes of this man seemed to penetrate her thoughts.

Laughter, tangled with the sound of breaths being caught, broke the spell.

Feeling certain all in attendance were witness to her thoughts, Catherine's eyes darted around the room, but the performers were the center of attention, not she.

Even Galen seemed thoroughly entertained. She managed a smile for him. The warmth of Galen's hand upon hers only fueled the guilt coming to life within her. She could no longer deny the feelings that grew within her heart, but those feelings were an obstacle she would have to overcome if she and Galen were to be together.

Suddenly too tired to pretend another minute, she bid her father good night and kissed his cheek before turning to Galen. "Forgive me, Galen. I grow weary." As he rose, she stayed him with her hand on his shoulder. "Please, stay and enjoy the evening. I only wish to retire."

His smile faded as he captured her hand in his. "Are you certain, Catherine?"

She stroked his cheek gently and nodded. How could it be, she wondered, that she alone had the power both to make him smile and to take that happiness away?

She summoned Emelie to follow her and made her way to the door. Once outside the hall, she turned to her maid. "Draw a bath and await me in my chambers."

Emelie curtsied and ran towards the kitchen.

Catherine then made her way to the stairs leading to the walkways. The stone walls were too confining tonight and the air was too stale. She needed to breathe the air outside where she could be alone.

The storm had receded a bit, pulling away the darkest of the clouds, gifting Catherine with glimpses of the crescent moon and a handful of stars that pulsated with life. She held her breath, listening for the sound of the ocean. Jonathan was out there, somewhere. He had given her a gift, one that she could not seem to share with anyone but him. A gentle breeze caressed her cheek and brushed across her lips. She closed her eyes to the sensation, summoning the vision of Jonathan. Would he be thinking of her tonight?

"Catherine." The voice behind her was strained, the word spoken with uncertainty and perhaps a little fear.

Catherine turned to face him. Galen knew, she thought. She could hear it in his voice. She had not fooled him. His very soul lay naked before her, and her heart ached at the pleading in his eyes.

With two steps he closed the gap between them and gathered her in his arms with the desperation of a man realizing what he loved was slipping away. His strong fingers threaded through her tresses, bringing her face to his.

She wrapped her arms around his neck and pulled him closer, giving him what she could, taking everything that he offered. Tonight they both could feel things were changing, and they clung to what remained for them. Their past and future tangled together in this one kiss. She could feel the heat in his lips, his desire to possess her, and his need to claim her for his own. No, she would not deny him this kiss, for she needed him right now as much as he needed her.

Chapter 21

Thumping on her chest with her fist didn't relieve the ache that burrowed inside. Eryn finished putting her hair in a ponytail, leaned against the balcony rail, and took a deep breath. Focusing on the ocean only seemed to make it worse. Eryn hardly noticed it at first, but the ache started to swell, and she couldn't ignore it anymore.

She sat down. Maybe it was time she faced it. This wasn't happily ever after. The emptiness shot like a bolt through her chest. *No.* She shook her head. *We're supposed to be together. We've hung in there all these years for a reason, didn't we?*

She leaned back and thought hard about the possibility of leaving Bryce. No, she couldn't quit! He needed her.

But what was it she read about the unresolved issues from past lives? *We all have dominant traits that we need to overcome and if we don't overcome them, we carry them over to the next life.* What were her unresolved issues? For one thing, she was forgiving to a fault. She tended to be everyone's doormat, trying to keep everyone happy.

Oh, damn! She needed to get out of here and the beach was the best place to connect with her past. Maybe she would come up with answers there.

Ever since dinner with Troy, Bryce has been watching suspiciously. He was even resorting to going to work later these days, and sometimes he worked at home instead of going to the office, just so he could keep an eye on her.

She closed the doors to the balcony and made her way to the back of her closet. Grabbing her shorts, she hurried to pull them on. She lost her balance, catching her foot in the shorts, and slammed her shoulder right on the edge of the closet door, sending a sharp pain through her back. "Damn!" Recovering her balance, she winced as rolled her shoulders to loosen them up.

Her cell phone chimed the arrival of a text message. Hurrying out of the closet and sweeping the phone off the dresser, she glared at it and spat out, "Shit." It was Troy again, demanding she call him. *What part of my message didn't you get, Troy?*

The aroma of fresh ground coffee drifting up the stairs should have had enticed her, but instead it hovered like some sort of warning.

"Why is he still here?" she grumbled. A glance at her watch told her Bryce wasn't going in to work.

Maybe she could sneak out and avoid having to explain herself to Bryce – again. Pulling her sweatshirt on and grabbing her shoes, she hurried towards the stairs, pausing at the top. There was no way she could sneak out. It would be too obvious. She'd have to pass right by the kitchen. She groaned. The sound of coffee cups clinking together could only mean he was in the kitchen. She crept down the stairs, holding her breath. Maybe he would take his coffee and go into his office and get busy. Then she could just run out the door and wave on the way out. Maybe this morning would be different. Maybe today she wouldn't feel the guilt or the resentment.

"Eryn?" he said, coming out of the kitchen.

She took a deep breath. "Mmm, smells great!" Her forced smile made her cheeks ache as she made her way down the stairs. She tucked her shoes under her arm and reached for the steaming cup, ignoring the scrutinizing look he gave her. She slid past him into the kitchen to place her cup on the counter before putting on her shoes.

Bryce's cup slammed onto the countertop with a little more force than was necessary, his agitation clearly showing. "Going to the beach…again?"

"What do you mean? I always go running," she said, not looking up.

"It seems you're getting more out of it than exercise."

It amazed her how quickly he could go from cold to glacial. His gray eyes were like shards of ice now. She stiffened at his accusing gaze.

"What exactly is that supposed to mean?"

"I think you know."

She rolled her eyes. Whatever his issue, it would have to wait. She just wasn't in the mood and suddenly the house was feeling too small. Pulling tight on her shoelaces, she took a few sips of her coffee and headed out the door.

Outside, the morning was clear, the air heavy with the tang of saltiness. She made her way to her car parked outside the garage, patting her pockets in search of her keys. The sound of jingling stopped her short. *How could I be so stupid?* Pressing her lips together, she forced a smile before turning around to face Bryce.

"Can't get far without those." She mustered a small laugh. "Here, toss 'em."

"Come and get them," he tempted, holding them out. His smile never reached his eyes.

"I could just run down to the beach," she countered.

175

"You could, but if I leave, you'd be locked out of the house." He leaned against the door jam in satisfaction, one eyebrow raised.

The tension in her neck started to throb, renewing the pain in her shoulder. Okay, she thought, two can play this game. Taking a deep breath and letting it out loudly, she feigned defeat. She tried to keep her steps light when she went to him.

He hid the keys behind his back when she reached for them. "Come inside with me." His gaze burned hot and promising.

"After my run," she said.

His eyes glinted steel when he spoke. "Who are you meeting every morning, Eryn?"

She blinked in surprise, and couldn't stop the laugh. "Meeting? Are you kidding?" He couldn't further from the truth – or closer to the truth.

She sighed. "I'm not meeting anybody." Was dreaming about a man from another life the same as meeting someone? "Since when is it a crime to exercise?" She put out her hand. "Come on, I won't be long."

He shrugged his shoulder away from the door and tossed her the keys, his eyes never leaving hers. He turned and went inside without saying a word.

She backed up a few steps before she turned on her heel. *Damn him!*

Inside the car, she didn't look at the house. She hit the steering wheel with her palm, torn up with guilt.

But beach was calling to her. "I know, I know. I want to go," she whispered. Pulling out of the driveway, she chanced a look at the bedroom window. Her eyes locked with Bryce's for a split second, then he was gone.

She sped down the street, feeling like she was pulling the thread that was slowly unraveling their marriage. But she was compelled to go, to somehow connect with this man with whom she shared a life with centuries ago. Jonathan. *A twin flame. The other half of my soul. The ultimate union.* What lesson did she have to learn to get to him?

The parking lot was empty. The off-shore breeze blew past unobstructed, freely sweeping the sand into random piles. Seagulls hovered, wings frozen in mid-flight, balancing on the wind.

With her hand poised over the keys, she couldn't bring herself to turn off the engine. "I should go back." She shook her head at her own words. "No! I can't be responsible for his happiness. I have to take care of me!" She leaned her head back on the headrest and closed her eyes as her mind and her heart warred.

I have to go back. I have to fix things. Her mind started.

No, I have to walk. Her heart countered.

Not now. Tomorrow.

No. Now. Please.

"I'm sorry," Eryn said out loud. She put the car in reverse. "Old habits die hard." Tears pooled in her eyes, hovering precariously on the edge. All she wanted to do was get out and put her feet in the sand and walk to the water's edge for a little while, but she knew if she did, she would likely keep walking.

She pressed hard on the gas.

"Hey!" A hand slapped the side of her car.

She jammed on the brakes, horrified she hadn't even looked before backing up.

"Oh my God," she muttered. "I am such an idiot."

She smiled apologetically at a group of surfers walking past her door, some indifferent, some scowling. But only one existed in her world. He kept the front of his body to her, turning as he walked, keeping his eyes locked with hers. His smile made her forget everything. More precisely, she realized, it made her remember.

She shouldered her door open and scrambled out. Her heart and mind clashed as they met in her throat. A thousand years could pass and still she would remember him. He hadn't changed, really. He was just bigger, more mature, and if all possible, even more good looking. Her jaw went slack as she took in his wide shoulders, tapering to a narrow waist and muscular legs held tightly underneath the black rubber of his wetsuit. And all that glorious, thick wavy hair, teasing the tops of his shoulders. The flash of his smile blasted her like the sun ricocheting off a mirror, straight to her heart.

One of the others called over his shoulder. "Come on, dude. Let it go."

He lifted his hand to wave before finally turning to catch up with his friends.

She melted against the car door, watching his retreating back as the group made their way to the water.

"Wow," she whispered. How ironic. This was no different that it was ten years ago at Solstice Beach.

Upset with Bryce.

Moping at the beach.

An angel in disguise.

The impact was no less intense than it had been that day. Understanding and comfort rolled off of him, surrounding her like a warm blanket, making her feel protected and cared for.

History tumbling around in the recycling bin.

She dragged the car door open and fell behind the wheel. For the second time in her life, she watched him walk away, while she clung pathetically to Bryce She revved up the motor. This time looking around her, she backed out and headed for home.

~ ~ ~

She closed the door quietly behind her, listening for sounds that might lead her to Bryce. The soft clang of iron and heavy breaths led her to the room off the patio where their home gym was set up. Kicking off her shoes, she tiptoed over and stood in the doorway watching.

Bryce sat with his back to her, elbow braced against one knee as he curled the weight to his biceps. His t-shirt strained over his muscles as they worked to contract against the heavy iron, his breaths coming out in short bursts.

"Hey," she said softly. "I'm can soap that sweat off you."

He stopped mid-rep and said without turning around. "That was fast."

"I didn't go running. I decided to come back instead."

"You shouldn't have bothered. I'm busy now."

She stood up straighter. It wasn't supposed to go like this. "Well, you have to take a shower some time. I just thought…"

He put down the weight with a thud and stood up. Her smile faded as he walked past her. "Like I said, Eryn, I'm busy now."

He could have thrown ice water on her and it wouldn't have been more biting than his words. This time it was him that was pulling the thread of their marriage.

She knew it would do no good to go after him, but she followed him anyway.

A knock on the front door saved her the embarrassment of groveling at Bryce's feet, something she would have hated herself for doing.

A split second after flinging the door open, she felt the color drain from her face. Her first impulse was to just slam the door shut, and she would have, had her body not frozen up on her.

Troy stood on the step, but his eyes weren't friendly.

"Troy," Eryn managed to choke out. "What are you doing here?" She looked back inside the house, and seeing that Bryce wasn't close by, she stepped outside and closed the door behind her.

"What exactly did you mean by your message?" He shoved his hands in his pockets and stood expectantly, waiting for her answer.

"Oh." She pressed her lips into a tight line. She cringed at the anger that simmered in his eyes. "Please understand. It's nothing personal."

"It sure feels personal," he shot back.

"No, really, it's not." She struggled for an explanation without bringing Brandi into this.

"What is it then? Maybe you have bigger jobs now? You don't have time for me?" he asked tightly. His eyes narrowed and a muscle twitched in his jaw. "If that's the case, I'll pay you double what you normally get."

"No, no…" How much should she say? She tried to choose her words carefully. "It's just that there seems to be…um…kind of a conflict of interest." In the seconds that stretched she had to remind herself to breathe. She felt as if the air had turned thick and her lungs strained against the effort. She wasn't sure if it was the heat of the sun or her own nerves that caused sweat to trickle down her back.

Troy's jaw tightened and released rhythmically, his eyes hardening as he contemplated her meaning. "Well, that could only mean someone is less than enthralled with our arrangement." Suddenly his eyes softened and he smiled. He took his hands out of his pocket and spread his hands out to his sides. "I'm sure there's a misunderstanding. Which one is complaining?"

Eryn didn't respond.

"Is Bryce home? Let me talk to him…" He began to reach around her to ring the doorbell.

"No." She grabbed his arm to stop him. The last thing she wanted was to have Bryce involved. It was already complicated enough. "It's not…" She stopped.

Troy's face was inches away from her. He had tricked her and smiled with the knowledge. His piercing blue eyes bore into hers before they slid down to stare at her lips. She released his arm and stepped back.

"I'll deal with Brandi. I'll make her understand," he said.

This definitely was going the wrong way. Eryn had to stop this, and right now, before it got too far out of hand. "There's nothing to deal with. I just can't do it anymore."

"And if I don't agree with you?"

She stared at him, incredulous. "You have to."

He grabbed her arm and leaned in. She grimaced at the force of his hand and the warning in his face. He started to say something, but stopped when the front door opened and Bryce stepped out.

"Get inside, Eryn." His words held a dangerous edge.

Troy now looked past her and glared at Bryce, his face lined with hatred.

Bryce pushed her behind him, back into the house.

She closed the door behind her and leaned on it hard. Low voices volleyed back and forth behind her in threatening tones.

"Damn it." She whispered. She really thought Troy would warm up to Brandi, but maybe Bryce and Brandi were right. Troy really *was* dating Brandi to get to her. She hit her fist against her thigh again and again, completely frustrated with herself. How could she have been so stupid?

Finally, there was silence on the other side of the door followed by a car door slamming shut, tires squealing on the street. She ran to the kitchen, not knowing if seeing Bryce right now was such a good idea.

The front door opened and closed. Bryce's footsteps echoed. The sound of ice dropping in a glass was followed by the splash of liquid. No, seeing him now was definitely not a good idea.

Chapter 22

"Milady! Milady!" Emelie's voice was just above a whisper, but the urgency it held cut through Catherine's slumber and her lashes fluttered open. She had been dreaming again.

She stood alone on the cliff in nothing more than her nightshift, her toes placed boldly along the ragged edge of the rocks with arms spread out to her sides, face upturned to bathe in the light of the moon, her skin cooled by the ocean breeze. There was never any fear for her there, no anger or hurt. But there was also no love. It was a place of emptiness, a place she could hide from the guilt and indecision. Nothing, she found, was sometimes better than something.

Catherine groaned. "I trust you have an excellent reason to wake me before the sun has had a chance to rise, Emelie." She had not been so inclined to wake early in the months past. Sleep had been her savior, allowing an escape from her ever-present restlessness. She had told herself she could wait for the passion to grow between her and Galen. But time had passed with no such promise. She now had to admit defeat. Galen, though handsome, strong, and passionate, just did not stir within her those feelings she experienced with Jonathan.

A part of her resigned herself to this fact. Though her life lacked passion and laughter, she was well cared for. There were many marriages that had little to do with love. Why should hers be different?

But the rest of her refused to forget. She had tasted passion, relished the fever that ran through her blood and heated her skin. She knew the sensation of being free, her emotions unlocked by one man alone.

"The ship is here!" Emelie was trembling with her hands clasped tightly together. "Master Jonathan has returned!" she said with barely-controlled excitement.

Catherine bolted upright, fully awake now. Her heart beat frantically in her throat. "How do you know of this?"

Emelie stared at the floor and she shifted uncomfortably from foot to foot. "I have been watching every morning, milady, for their return."

Catherine's tilted her head to the side, looking at Emelie through narrowed eyes. "What reason would you have to…" Catherine's words drifted as the answer dawned on her. "It is Cedric." She peered closer at her maid's face. "You are smitten with Cedric."

Turning bright crimson, the maid clutched her skirt in tight fists. "Oh, please do not be angry, milady!" she pleaded.

How simple it was for Emelie to love so freely, Catherine thought. No one would condemn Emelie for following her heart. For the first time, Catherine felt pangs of envy for her maid's simple life.

But then the realization that Jonathan was so near sparked a fire through her blood, rendering her helpless to stay away from him. She had missed him more than she knew. He had taken her heart with him and now he has returned to make her whole once again. The fact that seeing him was wrong simply did not matter to her. She *would* see him, and her stomach fluttered at the thought.

"Are you certain it was his ship you saw?" she asked eagerly.

Emelie's eyes lit up with excitement and she nodded.

Catherine placed her hand to her heart, feeling it beat faster still. She desperately wanted to see him again and she needed to know if he felt the same. Throwing off the covers, she scrambled out of the bed.

"Then we must hurry! See that the horses are saddled."

Emelie ran to the trunk at the foot of the bed and began rummaging through it. "It is done, milady," she said breathlessly. "I took the liberty of having that done this morning..." She broke off, looking worried. "I assumed milady would be anxious to see Master Jonathan."

Catherine gasped. Had her feelings, then, been so very apparent? She thought of the man who made her forget everything that was proper. She could not stop the smile that slowly spread across her face. She suddenly laughed. "You are but a hopeless romantic. Come. Let us hurry."

Together they selected a deep purple gown with an underskirt of white and a bodice that clung her slender figure. The sleeves dipped just off of her shoulders and scooped deep in front.

After tying silk ribbons in Catherine's hair, Emelie went to open the door, but Catherine silently motioned her wait. She kneeled before her trunk and retrieved the folded letter she had hidden within the lining and then tucked it into her sleeve.

~ ~ ~

By the time they arrived at the harbor, the sun was making its ascent up the sky, splashing the water

185

with crimson and yellow. A few villagers milled about, shouting up towards the ship.

The familiar face of Cedric appeared from amongst the crew unloading the cargo. His boyish grin stretched across his face when he saw that Emelie was there and he sprinted toward them, and did not stop until he stood before Emelie, grasping her hands in his.

Catherine's heart softened when she saw the look of bliss on Emelie's face. Her maidservant clearly adored Cedric, and his love-struck face made Catherine smother a laugh behind her hand.

A few moments passed before either one of them realized they were not alone. Emelie was first to break the silence.

"Forgive me, milady." She pulled her hands away.

As if seeing Catherine for the first time, Cedric blinked at her as if trying to remember something. As realization struck, his eyes widened.

"Oh, milady!" He bowed low. "Master Jonathan wishes to see you, if you will." He pointed in the direction of the ship's railing.

Then she saw him. Jonathan was leaning on the ship's railing, chin in his hand, looking at her. She could not stop the erratic flutter of her heart when she imagined his arms around her, holding her to his hard chest. Her fingers touched her mouth, remembering the feel of his lips upon hers. It no longer mattered to her the difference in their stations. Nothing mattered to her now that he was here.

Jonathan disappeared behind the rails only to reappear moments later, running down the plank. He wove his way to her, through the people who stood between them. Then, deeply serious, he bowed low before her.

"Milady."

Her heart sank. Perhaps a smothering embrace and a crushing kiss was a bit too much to have asked for, but she certainly had not expected such formality. With so many months between them, maybe he truly did not feel the same as she. Feeling foolish for allowing herself to open her heart, she straightened her back, and closed her eyes to hold back the tears that she knew would come.

"Why so serious, Catherine?"

The tease in his voice made her catch her breath. Hope flickered to life, urging her to look at him.

The sparkle in his eyes danced as he leaned toward her. Suddenly his arms wrapped around her waist and the world became a blur as he spun her around, making her laugh with delight. Ah, she had lost herself again! He made her feel so reckless and alive. At this moment she was not the Lady of Elderidge, but just…Catherine.

His voice was soft and his breath was warm, tickling her ear. "Please tell me you have missed me as much as I have missed you."

She held strong to his shoulders, for her knees went weak. He could not have spoken sweeter words.

His cheek was smooth against hers as he slowly pulled away, kissing a path from her ear, until his lips found hers. His kiss was gentle, but too brief, taking in her full lips and drawing back, leaving her breathless. He gently placed her feet on the ground and held her at arm's length, his hands firmly on her waist. His brows rose in anticipation of her answer.

Her lids were heavy with desire and her breasts rose and fell with quickened breaths. What she truly wanted to do was to shout to the sky how she felt, to throw her arms around his neck and kiss him with all the passion that raged inside.

"Yes," she whispered. "More than I could possibly say."

"Cedric," Jonathan said, never taking his eyes from Catherine. "I am sure you and Emelie have much to talk about."

"Aye, sir." Cedric understood Jonathan's words and began to guide Emelie away, but the maid protested.

Jonathan held up his hand to silence her. "I am perfectly capable of tending to the needs of Lady Catherine." He looked back at Catherine. "Unless, of course, your mistress objects?"

Catherine looked at the three before her. Emelie wringing her hands, Cedric begging with his eyes, and Jonathan challenging her with an arch of his brow.

Object? She hardly thought so.

"I could prove to be quite demanding," she warned.

Emelie's worried look was eased when Catherine gave her a quick wink.

Catherine's heart was lighter than it had been in years, as if something inside her had been cut loose to run free.

Jonathan stood straighter, in mock resolve. "Well then, I am ready for the challenge, milady." With that, Jonathan dismissed Cedric.

As Cedric and Emelie walked away, Cedric began animatedly explaining something of obvious interest to the maid.

Catherine watched them, thoughtful. An unfamiliar feeling of compassion towards Emelie settled around Catherine. It was an unlikely friendship that was being forged, a relationship defying what she was raised to believe. Never before had Catherine looked upon Emelie as a confidant, but here they were, two women, stations apart, with a shared purpose.

"Where have your thoughts taken you?" Jonathan asked softly. The touch of his fingertip as he gently traced the curve of her jaw coaxed her back to him.

She was speechless as she gazed upon him. He had tied his thick locks at the nape of his neck with a thin leather thong, exposing the golden ring in his ear. His impossibly thick lashes lined eyes that were lighter in the morning sun, a golden brown. His eyes held so many emotions all at once, interchanging and blending so swiftly that she was compelled to watch in fascination. Her mouth went dry and her breaths turned shallow. She touched her tongue lightly to her lips.

A lopsided grin slowly formed on his lips. "Ah, milady," he sighed. "You test my strength of resolve." He took her hand and pressed it to his lips, closing his eyes tight. "I could think of little else but you while I was away."

His words caressed her heart, melting away any reason to ignore her growing passion for him. But this was all wrong for so many reasons, she reminded herself. Wrong for her, for Jonathan, and for Galen, but her heart refused to listen. It wasn't so much who he was, but how she felt when she was around him. Inside she felt free, unbridled, and strong. Jonathan had transformed her into a woman who could play with the sun and dance with the moon. She was a woman willing to take a chance. But words that would say as much died in her throat. She freed her hand from his grasp and stepped back, realizing her own control was waning.

"And I thought much of you as well." She took a deep breath. "In truth, I tried to forget you after you left." Her fingertips touched the parchment still tucked in her sleeve. "But it seems as though I have failed quite miserably."

Continuing after a deep breath, she stammered, "I penned a letter when I...when I realized my life would not be the same after that night." She slipped the letter from her sleeve and held it in her hands, her fingertips grazing the folds. Though the gray-white paper felt weightless and appeared harmless, in truth, she knew, the words it held could well cause pain for the both of them. "Perhaps this is best forgotten," she said quietly.

"Please." His voice slid over her like silk. "May I read it?"

Looking into his eyes was her undoing. She wanted him to know. She *needed* him to know. He has changed her, and like a flower catching the light of the sun, her feelings would only continue to grow. Slowly, she handed the letter to him.

He looked at her and waited for her approval before unfolding it.

Catherine nodded.

My Dearest Jonathan,

I write this to you with the hope you will read it one day. I know not where your ship sails, but you have taken my heart with you. The gray skies stretch out endlessly, casting gloom upon me. I shiver. Not from cold, but from fear. I fear for your safety. I fear my heart will break. I fear I shall go mad if you do not return soon. At day's end I see the sun fall slowly behind the water's edge. I watch as the sun burns a hole into the sea, burying itself, to lie in wait for morning so that it may shine brightly once again. The sun is much like my feelings for you. They have burned a hole in my soul, buried there, waiting, until your ship brings you back to me.

She watched his face as he read. Now he would know he held her heart in his hands, but she had no regrets.

Jonathan pushed his hand through his hair, staring a moment longer at the letter before his eyes rested upon hers. A smile curved his lips.

She had not known how much softer his eyes could become.

"These words were written so long ago, Catherine. Do they still hold true?"

She felt her heart would burst. Never before had she felt this way. The wall around her heart was crumbling, exposing feelings so new, so raw, it hurt. Catherine hesitated before slowly nodding.

"Aye, they are still true, Jonathan." She took a deep breath and looked over at Emelie. How she wished she were free to love whom she pleased as was her maid. "But I know they are wrong."

She could not look at him now, so great was her confusion. She only knew she did not want to cause him pain.

"It can never be wrong if it makes you happy, Catherine." He stooped, leveling his face with hers.

"So you say, Jonathan." She sighed. "But I know there is no help for it." She raised her eyes, unashamed. "I have written others letters, but they remain hidden away."

He lightly touched her hand. "I should like to see them."

"Should like to see what? What have you hidden, Sister?"

Sara stood with her hands on her hips with Elizabeth peering around her, eyes wide with curiosity.

Sara's snarling lips distorted her face. "What is that?" She nodded at the letter Jonathan held.

Casually Jonathan tucked it into his boot. "Sara!" He brought her hand to his lips. "Is it possible for you to have grown lovelier since I last saw you?"

At once her face softened and she looked at him from under her eyelashes.

Catherine turned to her sister, smiling sweetly. "Sara, you delight us with your presence so early this morning. We usually do not see you until midday."

Sara glared at Catherine. "Are you unescorted?" she demanded.

Catherine's forehead tightened. How dare Sara challenge her thus!

"Emelie escorted your sister, Sara." Jonathan said, calmly. He gestured to where Emelie and Cedric stood. "It seems as though she has found favor with Cedric."

Sara's face twisted with fury. "You are indulging your chambermaid? Since when have you gone soft with the servants?"

"Take care with your words, Sara. Your tongue seems to be sharp of late."

The air between the two was palpable as they faced each other.

Sara broke the silence, glancing between Catherine and Jonathan. "Father was inquiring as to your whereabouts this morning. He wanted to speak about some plans he had for you."

"And did you tell him where I was?" Catherine felt a cold sweat creep along her spine. If her father knew where she was, then so would Galen.

Sara's distain for her sister was etched in every movement of her face. "How am I to know where you scamper off to from one moment to the next? I did not know where you were, nor did I care. But had I known," she added, turning to Jonathan, "mayhap I would have come sooner."

Catherine rolled her eyes. Catherine's wish to share time with Jonathan was dashed the moment Sara appeared. Even if Catherine were successful in sending her away, it would only be a matter if time before her spiteful sister would tell Galen where she was. Catherine cursed the knowledge that she must leave while Sara would undoubtedly stay...with Jonathan.

"Come, Sara," Catherine said tightly. "We must be taking our leave. I am certain Father will want to see you and I both."

Sara dragged her eyes from Jonathan and looked around the port. "No, Catherine. It is you he wishes to see. My morning is my own." Sara looked between her sister and Jonathan and, as if struck by a sudden thought, her lips curled upwards in a smug grin, her eyes alight with mischief. "Besides, I have things to attend to." She lifted her chin and turned on her heel, her hips swaying invitingly.

Catherine glared at Sara's retreating figure, fuming at her sister's smug expression and the hint of maliciousness that had danced in her eyes. What, pray tell, was her sister up to?

She turned to Jonathan, her eyes full of regret. "I must see what my father bids of me, Jonathan."

"Of course you must." Jonathan's smile was encouraging. His fingers traced the line of her jaw. "I do not set sail for another two days. We will see each other again. *That* I promise you," he said meaningfully.

She nodded. His eyes told her all she wanted to know.

Jonathan turned and whistled to Cedric, then took her hands in his and brought them up to his lips. "Do not look so forlorn, Catherine. If we so will it, nothing can stop us from being together."

Her smile dimmed. She wished she were as certain as he.

Chapter 23

His humming sounded neither happy nor sad. It was almost like a small motor, the only thing that kept the old man alive. The steady drone kept time with his meticulous poking and sifting through the trash in the cans that dotted the beach. Peering into crumpled bags and Styrofoam containers, he ignored Eryn, who stood next to him, lining him up in her viewfinder. Against a backdrop of a surfer cutting across the face of a wave, her shutter captured the calm determination of the old man, his face weathered by the elements. The flash of the bright yellow surfboard, as its rider flipped it up over the crest of the wave, provided an interesting contrast for Eryn.

Young and old. Freedom and imprisonment. Life and death.

Eryn looked at the plastic bag the old man gripped his gnarled fist. It held a few cans. Hardly worth his effort. She walked to her backpack she had placed in the sand and pulled out a paper bag. She smiled. It would ease his hunger and ease her conscience. The Have's and the Have-Not's.

"Excuse me, sir." She gently grasped his hand and placed the bag in his palm.

His eyes, set deep within wrinkled folds of his aged face, searched hers suspiciously.

"Please," Eryn said softly. "Enjoy."

His crinkled smile was reward enough when he realized what he held. He nodded and smiled, and kept smiling, as she turned and walked away. Eryn found his smile contagious. She picked up her beach chair and backpack, and walked further down the beach, past the pier, and found her place of solitude.

Her chair sank into the sand as she settled herself into it, and pulled out a pad of paper and pen from her backpack. To her right the ragged cliffs jutted out onto the water, the rock stubbornly rigid against the waves. To her left the beach stretched out endlessly, interrupted only by the pier that cut a path over the water. Joggers usually turned around at the pier, so, except for the occasional walker, this spot on the beach was relatively private.

She watched as an older couple made their way silently in her direction, stopping every few steps to pick something up and then throw it into the water. An occasional shell found its way into their pockets.

She took a deep breath and let it out slowly. *Where to start?* She tilted her head back and closed her eyes against the sun. Any other time the whisper of the tide creeping up the sand would be soothing to her, but not today.

She had to sort things out. With each new dream he was becoming more and more real. It was a wakeup call, but she had no idea how to answer. With resolve, Eryn straightened up and stared down at the blank sheet of paper in front of her. It seemed to wait patiently for her to gather her thoughts.

"This is nuts," she said out loud, looking again to the water. "How can I feel so strongly about someone I can't see?" She shook her head. It really didn't matter how. Her dreams held enough passion to bleed into her reality. The way he made her feel was real.

She turned her attention back to the page, her pen poised. *Okay. Here I go.*

196

Her pen moved slowly at first as the words struggled to flow, but gained momentum as she realized they were words she needed to write.

You made me remember, and I'm not entirely sure I like it. My life may not be happy, but at least I am happy not knowing how unhappy I really am, if that makes sense. But then nothing does anymore. This just complicates things, and I don't do well with things that complicate my life. I have always felt there is a part of me missing, and now I know why. I can feel what is between us. It is a love that has followed me through time. It feels so good and at the same time, it's so painful. Good because I know love like that does exist. Painful because I don't have it. All I know is that you make me whole. You are the other half of me.

There, she'd written it. Her words were true, coming from her heart. She drew a deep breath and let her pen flow over the paper again.

I dreamed of you the other night. You were on the deck of a magnificent ship, sparkling waters all around. You were standing on the rails looking out, squinting into the sun to see the horizon. I knew you were going away. I told you that if you forgot me it would break my heart. Then you were gone. I tried to find you, but I was lost. No one could or would tell me where you were. I miss you. I need you. Don't leave me to be alone. Stay with me. I am forever yours.

Eryn read her words again and again. The feelings were so vivid now, imprinted on her soul. He wouldn't let her forget. He had reached across the centuries and made her remember.

But now, in this life, she had Bryce. It wasn't always so bad. Bryce loved her and always stood by her side. Sure, he had a hard time showing he loved

197

her, but she could do a whole lot worse than a marriage without passion, right? *Besides, he needs me. Deep down, he needs me. He told me so.*

But her soul wouldn't accept it. *You're always trying to make everyone happy. What about you? When are you going to make yourself happy?*

Eryn drew in a deep breath. She wasn't so sure she could be happy knowing she made him miserable. She needed to try to make this work. She would still have her dreams. Though her heart belonged elsewhere, her mind and body belonged to Bryce.

The struggle ceased, but even with the decision made, she had a hard time holding back the tears.

~ ~ ~

The hollowness in her chest was forgotten the instant Eryn saw Brandi sitting against the wall by the front door, beer in one hand, cigarette in the other, eyes closed. Even as Eryn pulled the car onto the driveway, Brandi didn't open her eyes. Not a good sign.

It had been a couple of weeks since Brandi had been around. It had been pretty nice, actually. Eryn had called, but Brandi's phone had been disconnected. Now, the sight of her friend, looking a little more than defeated, brought on the guilt Eryn had managed to ignore. She hadn't tried hard enough to find out why Brandi hadn't been coming around or why her phone was out.

Eryn watched as her friend tipped the bottle to her lips and finished off the beer. She sensed that this was more than Brandi not getting a part in a movie. Something was really wrong this time.

She turned off the engine and got out of the car, shoving her keys in her pocket. "Brandi? You okay?" She knelt in front of Brandi and took the empty bottle from her hand, placing it into the carton with the other five empty bottles.

"Hey," Eryn coaxed.

"He broke up with me," she slurred. "Asked me to move in with him and then he kicked me out."

Eryn sat up straighter. "So that's where you've been? At Troy's house?"

"At least he paid for the abortion before calling me a whore and throwing my shit out the door."

"You were pregnant?" The words stuck in her throat. "God, Brandi, how could you be so careless?"

Brandi laughed. "I thought that would make him happy. Stupid me." She hit her head against the wall behind her a few times.

"Bastard." Eryn spat out.

Brandi sat up straighter and opened her eyes. Usually so careful with her appearance, her eyes were puffy and without makeup, her cheeks stained from crying. "Don't be too hard on him. I knew he never really wanted me." She sounded resigned, but there was an edge of hardness in her voice. "I thought by getting you out of the way it would help us, but I think it just pissed him off."

Eryn remembered her last conversation with Troy. Yeah, pissed off was a fairly accurate description.

The glassiness in Brandi's eyes disappeared as she stared at Eryn. "It was you he really wanted."

There it was. Brandi was blaming her for this and she wasn't going to let Eryn off the hook.

"I have nowhere to go," Brandi said matter-of-factly.

Eryn returned her hard stare. She should just get up, go inside, and close the door between them. It was always going to be like this. She was never going to make Brandi happy.

A group of neighborhood kids filtered out from the house next door, kicking around a soccer ball, their shouts filling the air. The sun bore down directly overhead, heating up the roses lining the front of the house, sending out their potent fragrance. But Eryn wasn't aware of any of it. The coldness and the blame in Brandi's eyes made her shiver. Now Eryn had no choice. She had to fix it.

"You can have the guest room for as long as you need it."

Brandi nodded her satisfaction. She pushed herself up and held onto the wall for support. The two looked at each other and in that moment Eryn could feel their friendship die. But Eryn didn't care anymore. She was tired of being blamed, tired of being the one to pick up the pieces. As soon as Brandi got herself together, as soon as she was able to move out, Eryn would finally walk away. Until then...

"How do you feel?" Eryn asked.

"Like crap."

Eryn nodded. She unlocked the front door and held it open for her new housemate. She sighed. Bryce wasn't going to like this.

Chapter 24

"Catherine, what say you?"

Together they walked through the gardens. The roses were in full bloom, gracing the gardens with their intoxicating fragrance. Galen picked a brilliant yellow rose and presented it to Catherine.

She absent-mindedly inhaled the sweet fragrance of the petals, but his question did not penetrate Catherine's mind, so filled was it with her own musings.

Tonight a ball would be held in honor of her eighteen summers. Months ago, invitations had been sent out. In recent days, hunting parties brought back game, fresh flowers had been cut, tapestries cleaned, floors swept, and rooms aired. The castle was bustling with last minute preparations.

This had been an evening she had played out in her mind a hundred times. She would be dressed in her finery, jewels adorning her hair and slender neck. Galen would be by her side, staving off advances of potential suitors. So many months ago she told herself that if true love had not yet found her, then this night would mark the beginning of their courtship. She would accept her future with Galen.

But true love did find her, and in its wake left her yearning for a man she could not have. How she longed to ask Jonathan to attend the ball, but that, she knew, would never come to pass. Her father would never allow it. Nor would Galen.

"Will you have me?" Galen's voice held a note of pleading.

The meaning behind his words finally took shape in her mind. He was again asking her to be his wife.

She could not respond.

Quickly he said, "I do not wish to rush an answer from you." He raked his fingers through his hair, his laugh shaky. "I fear my desire to have you as my wife far exceeds my patience." He took her hands in his and his thumbs smoothed across them. "In truth," he said, not looking up, "I would wait a thousand lifetimes for you."

His hair draped down like a curtain, hiding his face, but it could not hide the quiver in his voice.

Though his words spoke of forever, Catherine wondered if he truly would wait. Would he not grow weary and marry another?

When he finally raised his eyes to hers, she saw the truth. There was not the slightest shadow of doubt that he wait…forever if need be.

She looked away to hide the tears that burned. Her soul was being torn apart between two men. Two men who were so different. Galen could offer her a life to which she was accustomed to, yes, but Jonathan would show how to live it with passion.

She sighed. This marriage was inevitable. So why did she fight the fates? She squeezed her eyes tight. She fought for whatever moments she could have with Jonathan. She fought for the smallest hope that she had a choice.

She still spoke no words, but she knew Galen was intensely aware of her inner turmoil, though she was certain he knew not the cause.

They walked in silence through the gardens. Catherine pressed the velvety rose petals to her nose and inhaled their heady fragrance. She dared not look at him for fear she could crumble under his gaze.

"Do you wish to visit the port before the ball?" he asked.

Catherine shot him a sidelong glance, shocked. *Is it possible he knows?*

He smiled. "That was a foolish thing to ask. Of course you already have everything you need." Galen looked straight ahead, taking a deep breath. "Those merchants have quite the life, have they not?"

Catherine stiffened. "Whatever do you mean?" She feigned boredom, while her heart pounded mercilessly against her chest.

"I wonder how they become accustomed to having no place to call home, what with their travels from port to port." He paused, looking lost in thought. "I could only imagine none of them have families, save perhaps the bastards they undoubtedly leave behind."

Was this idle chat merely a coincidence? Jonathan's words flooded her mind. *They are free to go, but they have chosen to stay. That makes them family.* She bit her tongue. As for bastards...No. She dismissed the possibility from her mind. Not Jonathan.

"She shrugged. "Who is to say 'tis not the perfect life for them?"

Galen stopped mid stride and grasped her shoulders, gently turning her to face him. "What of you, Catherine? Would you find a life with me as your husband not so perfect?"

She could feel his desperation, but how could he speak of the rest of her life when she was not even certain of this moment?

"You need not answer that now, Catherine." He took her hand in his and led her back to the castle.

At the doors to the great hall, he turned to face her. For a moment, neither said a word.

Galen was the first to break the silence, his voice thick with defeat. "I shall take my leave, Catherine. I must see to my men." He kissed her gently on her forehead. "Until tonight." He backed away a step or two, his gaze lingering before he turned and walked away.

Chapter 25

Good. Eryn stood quietly inside the hallway listening. *Nobody is home.* Bryce usually *was* gone, but unfortunately her new housemate rarely left and was fast becoming an obtrusive part of the décor. It had only been a week and already it was too crowded with the three of them living in the big house.

Eryn bounded up the stairs two at a time thinking of what she would like to be doing. *Maybe I'll soak in the tub. Or maybe I'll pull out that yoga DVD I picked up...* "Oh!" She pulled up short just inside her bedroom door. "Geez, you scared the hell out of me!"

Brandi lay flat on her stomach across Eryn's bed with a bag of pretzels and a book open in front of her.

"I had no idea anybody was home. Where's your car?" Eryn asked.

"Does Bryce know about this guy?" Brandi continued to turn the pages, not bothering to look up.

Eryn's heartbeat sped up again as she realized what Brandi was referring to. With a few quick steps, she reached the bedside and ripped her journal from Brandi's hands and slammed it shut.

"That's *private*, damn it!" Her jaw ached, she was biting down so hard. "And it has nothing to do with Bryce. It's just a story idea I had. There is no 'guy'."

Good one, Eryn. Eryn chided herself. *Never mind the fact that you've never written a thing in your life.*

"Hey, it makes no difference to me if you're seeing him or not." Brandi rolled over onto her side and leaned on her elbow. "I can keep a secret."

Brandi's gaze completely unnerved Eryn. She could be calculating and Eryn couldn't risk having her get any ideas. Casually, Eryn opened the journal and pretended to be reading her entries. "Listen, like I said, it was an idea I had and I didn't want anyone to know about it until I had something more substantial to show."

On second thought, I could be a budding author. Maybe it's a hidden desire of mine. Eryn smiled at her creativity. Then, like the journal wasn't a big deal anymore, she tossed it on a chair out of Brandi's reach.

"So, what were you doing in my closet, Brandi?" She kicked off her shoes and made for the closet to put them away, wanting to see for herself what else Brandi had gone through.

"I was going to borrow a dress for tonight. There's a party at The Slam."

Eryn rolled her eyes. A newly-opened nightclub, The Slam catered to a younger crowd, where money, music, and drugs blended seamlessly. Oh yeah, perfect for Brandi.

"That sounds like fun." Eryn's voice was calm and sounded interested, but inside she fumed. She had kept her journal wrapped in a towel in her running bag that was tucked in the corner behind some bags of clothes headed for the thrift store. Not typically the place one would look for a cocktail dress. Everything had been pushed aside. Brandi didn't even care if she was discreet about it or not.

Eryn grabbed the first dress in her sight. "How about this one?" She held up an emerald green halter dress with a neckline that plunged to the navel. Eryn hated that dress.

Brandi's expression hadn't changed, but Eryn pushed on. "This is a great cut for you and the color would be fabulous against your skin." After another moment of no response, Eryn added, "You'd definitely turn heads."

That seemed to snap Brandi out of wherever her thoughts were going. Her vanity was too deeply embedded to ignore a comment like that. "Yeah, you're probably right." She finally got off the bed, not caring that the bag of pretzels had overturned, spilling crumbs onto the bed cover.

Eryn didn't care either. She just wanted to get Brandi out of her room.

Handing the dress to Brandi, Eryn went back to the closet and grabbed matching shoes and put them on the floor in front of Brandi who was now standing in front of the mirror. "See? Perfect match."

Brandi was now fully focused on herself, engrossed in her image.

"Okay," Brandi said, apparently satisfied. "I'm going to take a hot tub before I get ready. What about you? You want to sit in the jacuzzi?"

Yeah, right, Eryn mentally rolled her eyes. *I can't even be in the same room as you.* She mustered a smile. "No, I think I'm going to do some yoga. Do you want to join *me?*" She knew she was safe with that one. Brandi and yoga? Never.

Brandi snorted. "Yeah, right. That's for granola junkies and tree huggers." She draped the dress over her arm. "My idea of relaxation is a cocktail and a hot tub." She turned to leave.

Not quite out the door, Brandi turned. Eryn's skin bristled with Brandi's smug smile and parting words.

"By the way, Eryn, you're not a very good liar."

Chapter 26

Tonight, Galen vowed, he would make certain Catherine knew how much he loved her, how much he wanted her for his wife. She would give him the answer he has waited so long to hear. Galen drank deeply from the tankard before filling it up once more. It would serve him well to be bold tonight.

The door swung open and Sara breezed over the threshold, not bothering to wait for an invitation to enter.

Galen scowled at her over the top of his tankard. It appeared she intended to be noticed tonight for she had chosen to wear a scarlet red gown with bell sleeves and a square-cut neckline. The laces that ran across the front of the bodice pushed her small breasts upwards enticingly.

She stopped close enough for him to look down upon her. Coyly, she batted her eyelashes and thrust back her shoulders.

Galen shook his head. "Nay, Sara. 'Twill not work. Not now, not ever." Not bothering to hide his annoyance, he set his tankard onto the table and crossed his arms across his broad chest. "Say what you will and be gone."

With one blink, her eyes changed to anger and defiance. "Galen, it troubles me to tell you this, for I know you do *so* love my sister." She paused a moment before going on. "I thought it would be best for you to know that the merchant has just arrived to attend the ball."

Only a tightening of his jaw revealed his emotion. He favored her with a stony gaze. "The merchant, you say?" He turned away and busied himself with the fastening of his belt. "He is of no import to me."

Sara was silent for a moment, eyes narrowed, and then she shrugged. "Be that as it may, I did not wish for you to be caught unawares."

Every muscle in his body tightened. He was angry with this merchant, but more so with this meddling chit standing before him. He knew she had something to do with the merchant's appearance tonight, for Catherine would not have invited a commoner. She would not dishonor her father or him by extending such an invitation.

Quelling the pain that ripped through his gut, he glared down at Sara. "Your concern is touching."

Satisfaction spread across her face as she turned to leave. "Oh, and I might say" she said before slipping into the hallway, "that he looks even more handsome than usual this night."

His long strides swallowed the gap between them and he pushed the door closed behind her. His hand gripped the handle, turning his knuckles white with rage. Slowly uncurling his hand, the rage that burned hot gave way to icy chills. He looked at his palms. Strong, with the ability to wield a sword with ease, warrior hands that would crush an enemy. But now they were of no use for he felt Catherine slipping through his grasp.

Laughter drifted in through the window behind him, drawing him to it. He stood there, gripping the sill, not even noticing the brilliant colors splashing across the sky as the sun made its descent. Torches lined the walls of the courtyard, the flames dancing in the fading light, but the brilliance was blurred by the tears stinging Galen's eyes. His heart twisted in sadness. There was nothing he could do. With the merchant here within the castle walls, Galen would be expected to treat him as a guest.

"Would that I could throw him out myself," he said through clenched teeth.

He walked to his bed and picked up his sword. He slowly unsheathed it, his practiced eye admiring the newly-sharpened blade. After tonight, he thought, he would suffer the merchant's presence no more. He returned his sword to its sheath and belted it around his waist. He would find Catherine before she found the merchant. Flinging open the door, he walked resolutely toward the stairs, his footsteps echoing off the walls.

~ ~ ~

"Enough. Enough." Catherine pushed Emelie's hands away, suddenly impatient with the fussing. "How could it be that he is here?" She found herself quite breathless with excitement after Sara's announcement. "Certainly he would not be so bold as to come uninvited?"

"Well, 'tis of no matter," she answered herself.

Catherine bit her lip. This could prove to be complicated, she thought. To have Jonathan so close and to not be with him would be unbearable. But, would she not be expected to dance with a guest? But of course! By her father's decree, all in attendance must be made welcome. She brightened at the thought and her stomach fluttered in anticipation. Perhaps they could slip outside unnoticed and he would hold her in his arms, cup her face in his hands, and place his lips upon hers...

"Milady, it is time." Emelie stood at the door.

Blinking a few times, Catherine cleared her thoughts. "Yes." She took a deep breath and pressed her hand to her stomach. "Yes, it is. I…I am ready."

Her steps hastened once she emerged from her chambers. She could scarce believe he was here.

"Catherine!" Galen's voice echoed off the stone walls.

She stopped at the top of the stairs, pleading silently. *Not now! Please, not now!* She bit back her shame, for she had forgotten Galen the moment Sara spoke Jonathan's name. She took a deep breath and turned, hoping her smile would hide her impatience.

"Why Galen, I expected you to be in the hall. I fear I am already late." She smoothed her dress to help hide her trembling hands.

"Catherine." His eyes swept the full length of her. "You look radiant."

She was uncertain of what to say. An awkward moment of silence stood between them until he broke it. "I wish to have a dance with you this night."

At one time such a request would not be necessary. There would have be an understanding that he would be at her side. But tonight that had changed.

"Of course, Galen!" Catherine reached out and squeezed his hand. "But now I really must greet my guests."

As she turned to go, he grabbed her arm, pulling her towards him. He ignored the small gasp that escaped from Catherine.

He brought his lips close to her ear. "Your 'guests,' Catherine? Do you not mean one guest in particular?" His grip was firm, almost biting. "He will not do for you, milady," he said through clenched teeth. "He is a mere merchant. He cannot give you what I can."

Frightened by the harshness of his voice, she looked into his eyes and saw the desperation and anger that simmered beneath the surface. How did he know Jonathan would be here? She herself had heard only a short time ago.

When she gently touched his cheek, she heard his breath quicken. "I do not know what you are talking about, Galen," she lied. Never before have untruths been told between them and it hurt her more than she could have imagined.

He grabbed her hand and pressed it to his face, closing his eyes, absorbing her warmth.

"Please, no," she breathed. She pulled away quickly and ran to the stairs, not daring to look back.

From the bottom step, Catherine searched the faces of the guests milling about. Her pulse quickened at the sight of Jonathan, standing patiently, looking about with mild interest. He seemed not to notice the giggles and coy glances from the young ladies as they brushed by him. Had she not remembered his easy stance, had she not dreamed of him every night, she would not have known it was him. The red undershirt with slashed sleeves revealing a shock of gold fabric was a dramatic contrast to the velvet black doublet, fitted tight against his waist. The doublet blended seamlessly with the black breeches that clung to his long, muscular legs. His flowing mane of hair was held at the nape of his neck with a leather thong. His mannerism and confidence would rival any nobleman she knew.

When he turned his focus in her direction, his eyes blazed gold, and his smile challenged the sun.

Catherine's legs felt utterly useless when he looked at her that way, and so she just stood there, unable to move.

But he was there in an instant, taking her hand and bringing it to his lips. "You take my breath away, Catherine."

As you do mine, she wanted to say, but she did not trust herself to speak. She had not realized how she ached to hear his voice.

The spell was broken by a sound at the top of the stairs. She looked over her shoulder to see Galen watching the two of them, his jaw tightly clenched.

Her heart gave a lurch of anguish and she closed her eyes to the assault of guilt. She abruptly pulled away from Jonathan. "I am sorry, Jonathan, I cannot..."

"Hush," he said, placing his finger to her lips. "You can. We choose from here," he said, tapping his chest. "This is *your* choice.

The decision weighed heavily against her. By turning her back on Galen, she risked pushing his patience too far. She sought reassurance in Jonathan's face, but he was looking past her, up the stairs.

With his lips pulled into a tight line, Jonathan's slight nod reflected acknowledgement of Galen's place in her life, but he made it clear, without question, he would not relinquish his position by her side tonight.

Jonathan did not have to touch her for Catherine to feel his protectiveness, and a delicious warmth weakened her. She would follow him anywhere. Like a thief, she would steal whatever time she could with Jonathan and later make amends to those she offended.

Jonathan tucked her hand in the crook of his arm and led her to the hall, not giving Catherine the chance to look back at Galen. Of that she was glad, for she knew the hurt and fury in Galen's eyes would be too much for her to bear.

She smiled pleasantly at the other guests and ignored the whispers and stares that followed in their wake.

"I can hardly believe that you are here, Jonathan." Catherine fingers curled tighter around his arm.

"How could I not be here, after your invitation?"

Catherine stopped walking and turned to him. "Invitation?" She blushed. "I did not...I mean, Sara told me..."

"Do you not wish me to be here?"

She saw a flicker of uncertainty in those beautiful eyes. She wanted desperately to touch him, to soothe the furrow of his brow, and to trace the soft line of his face.

"Nay, you are indeed most welcome here," she said softly. "In truth, there is nothing I could want more." And that *was* the truth of it, Catherine thought, no matter what had brought him here.

Music filled the air as the musicians began to play. Amidst the ever-growing number of stares, she placed her hand in his and they began to dance.

~ ~ ~

Galen paused at the entrance to the hall, searching for Catherine. There she was, laughing so freely, something he rarely saw her do. His jaw clenched until it ached and he damned himself for allowing this to happen.

"It appears you are incapable of keeping our fair lady's attention, Sir Galen," Lord Oakley said.

Galen stiffened and instinctively he grasped the hilt of his sword.

Lord Oakley sighed loudly. "Must I take care of this for you?"

Galen's mood turned dangerous. "You know as well as I there is naught I can do while he is under this roof. But rest assured, I *will* take care of my own."

Lord Oakley huffed his disagreement. "That has yet to be seen."

The two men stared at each other, locked in an unspoken challenge, until the fragrance of lilacs surrounded them. Sara's eyes were alight with satisfaction. She was clearly enjoying the tension.

"It appears to me the true threat stands not here, but over there, with him. *Master Jonathan*." Sara gestured to Catherine and Jonathan who were talking quietly, their heads close together.

Galen broke his icy stare at Lord Oakley and glared at Jonathan. Perhaps there was a chance he could be rid of the merchant, he thought. A small one, but a chance nonetheless. As Lord Oakley and Sara watched, he walked around the crowd to the high table where Lord Roberts sat with his trusted counsel at his side, presiding over the festivities. Lord Robert's attention was focused upon his daughter and her unexpected escort.

Galen leaned close to Lord Roberts' ear. "Shall I escort him to the gate?"

Lord Roberts studied the couple for a few moments before responding. "I do not know who extended an invitation to him, but the man is a guest here, Galen, and I will not have guests mistreated. We will let it be for now." He withdrew a dagger and sheath from his belt and handed it to Galen "I cannot deny his presence here. He has shown due respect by sending a gift ahead of his arrival."

Galen took the dagger and examined it. The hilt was thick and heavy, fashioned in the likeness of a dragon, and inset with rubies and emeralds. Once unsheathed, the blade glinted fiercely in the light that radiated from the torches that illuminated the hall. Such a fine dagger would slide nicely into the heart of an enemy, he thought, transfixing his gaze upon Jonathan.

Lord Roberts laughed and held out his hand. "Give me the dagger, Galen." He looked between Galen and Jonathan. "Competition is a good thing. Makes the fire run through a man's blood." He winked. "Winning the heart of a woman, Galen, should never be so easy."

Chapter 27

The turnout for her gallery reception was a lot better than she had hoped for. Eryn was pleased with the attention her latest work was getting. Lately she had been driving around to the seedy little pockets of the city, seeking out the faces of the homeless, the runaways, and the children - the nameless faces the rich found so easy to ignore. These were the people who didn't have the advantages and money that she had, but they were no different. She had decided to let the Haves get a good look at the Have-nots.

Yes, this was definitely good, she thought, unable to hold back a smile.

She glanced around the gallery. No sign of Bryce yet. It wasn't like him to be so late. Eryn sighed. Would things ever be right with them?

"Great crowd." Melissa, the owner of the gallery and Eryn's friend, appeared beside her, obviously pleased. "I think you found your niche."

Eryn had to admit that stepping out of the stuffy corporate boardroom and into the real, gritty world outside really had made a difference in her photography.

"There was a man here asking about you, but he didn't tell me his name." Melissa said, eyeing the crowd.

Eryn groaned. *Troy.* Who else would it be? It would be so like him to start it up again. "Blonde?" Eryn asked, her senses now alert, scanning the crowd.

"No. Dark brown, actually, and long. This guy was *extremely* sexy," Melissa said with a deep sigh. "Shoulders like this." She held her hands out, indicating wide shoulders. "Butt like this…" She started to demonstrate how tight his backside was when Eryn laughed and stopped her.

"Okay, okay! I get the picture. He was gorgeous!"

"I would take him in a heartbeat," Melissa said, nudging Eryn with her elbow. "You've already got one of those at home, don't you?"

Eryn's laughter faded. "Yeah, I do, don't I?" She looked at her watch. So where was he?

"Oh! Oh! There's the guy who was asking about you!" Melissa grabbed Eryn's elbow and nodded towards the right wall of the gallery. "Damn, he is yummy!"

Eryn's attention shot over to the section that featured her images of the homeless men and women who found shelter along the beaches, and she felt her jaw go slack.

"It's him," she said in a barely audible whisper.

"You *know* him?" Melissa's brows shot up.

Eryn straightened up, shaking off her surprise. "Sort of," she said. "I first met him a long time ago." She looked at Melissa and let out a laugh of embarrassment. "And then a few weeks ago I almost hit him with my car at the beach."

Melissa laughed, looking back at him. "Well, it looks like he's forgiven you."

"Yeah." Eryn bit her lip. "Maybe so."

With his hands shoved in his white linen cargo pants pockets, dark blue Tommy Bahama shirt hanging loosely on his muscular frame, he was leaning in close to one of the photographs, a faint smile pulling at the corners of his mouth. He stood back, head tilted, and his smile grew. He nodded in satisfaction before moving over to the next picture.

Eryn stood, unbelieving, watching him sweep his attention over each one of her pictures. He was *really looking*, actually taking in the details, and seeming to appreciate what he saw.

Bryce would have barely given her work a glance. Maybe he would have said a courteous "nice work" before moving on to something that truly mattered to *him*. But there was no doubt this man was interested.

He had pulled his hair back in a leather tie, giving Eryn full view of his profile. Smooth sun-tanned skin graced his straight nose, high cheek bones, and solid jaw and chin. Full, sensual lips curved up in a smile. His eyes, under dark brows and thick lashes, narrowing once in awhile, took in everything before him.

Maybe it's time I introduced myself, Eryn thought. After all, this is the third time he has popped into my life. The only thing standing between friends and strangers were names, right? She swiped her hands nervously down her hips, realizing her palms were sweating. Would he remember her from ten years ago? Would he know it was she who almost hit him and his friends with her car?

Eryn hadn't realized Melissa had left until her friend flanked her again, this time in the company of two older patrons. The man was tall, dressed flawlessly in an Armani suit and polished shoes while his wife, much shorter, was covered in folds of silk, fashionably hiding her round figure. Both looked eagerly towards Eryn.

"Get that glazed look off your face and close your mouth a little," Melissa whispered out of the corner of her mouth. "Eryn," she said louder. "This is Richard and Cynda Carleton. They own a gallery in Beverly Hills and they'd like to talk to you about featuring your work there."

Eryn was about to drag her eyes from the man when he turned and locked his gaze with hers. His smile told her all she needed to know. Yeah, he remembered.

Melissa gave Eryn's hip a bruising pinch. "Mr. and Mrs. Carleton have a special interest in the runaways and homeless, particularly in Hollywood. They'd like to showcase your work as part of a project that they're having a fundraiser for."

Obligingly, Eryn focused her attention on the couple and put on her warmest smile, extending her hand to the couple. "It's a pleasure to meet both of you. I'd like to hear more of your project."

"Good," said Melissa, relief evident in her tone. "I'll take care of your clients, Eryn." With a quirk of her brow in Eryn's direction, she left.

Eryn tried to position herself so that she could discreetly keep her eye on the room, but eventually got caught up in the conversation. She was thrilled to meet someone with money and status who was actually going to use it for the good of the less fortunate.

When the older couple finally took their leave, Eryn searched the room, hoping Mr. Tommy Bahama was still there. She felt foolish, though, to think he would wait around all night for her.

She wandered over to the picture she had seen him stare at so intently. It was the image of the old man she had given her lunch to. Eryn had transformed the picture into a black and white image, with the only color in the picture being the bright yellow surfboard shooting across the face of the wave behind the old man. She looked closer, seeing the deep wrinkles on the man's face, his wispy hair escaping the confines of his filthy baseball cap, and, just beyond his shoulder, the surfer. She stood back, and then stepped in close again.

"No way," she whispered. "No friggin' way."

"That's him in the picture." Melissa appeared behind her. "And he liked it so much, he bought it. That and a couple of others."

Eryn spun around, eyes wide. "He bought *three* photos?"

Melissa laughed. "All cash. I told you I'd take care of your clients."

Unbelievable, Eryn thought. Even with total access to her work, Bryce has never asked her for a picture to hang on one their walls. Speaking of which, where the hell was he?

~ ~ ~

"Do you mind?" Bryce growled at Brandi, standing in the open doorway that he distinctly remembered shutting a few minutes before.

Brandi smiled, not in the least bit deterred by the fact that he was standing there in his towel, his chest flexed and tensed under her gaze. "On your way to see her show?"

"Yeah, and if you were half the friend you pretend to be, you'd be going, too." He turned towards the closet and disappeared inside it.

"Nah," she said, following him. "She probably wouldn't even notice I was there. Or you, for that matter."

He clenched his jaw. He was so sorry he'd allowed Eryn to talk him into letting Brandi stay. The woman was poison in its most potent form.

Brandi moved in closer. "She has some guy on the side, you know."

He spun around, eyeing her dangerously. To his disgust, it seemed to excite her.

Brandi licked her lower lip seductively.

Bryce grabbed her arm, half in rage, half in fear that her words held some truth. Eryn has been pulling away from him, but he thought it was because she was stressed about tonight's gallery showing.

"There isn't anyone else. I'd know about it." He let go of Brandi's arm, pushing her away.

Brandi only smiled. "She said there isn't, but I've seen her journal and she writes about him in every page."

He was sickened by the way Brandi seemed to enjoy the turmoil she was inflicting. He could see her thrill at every emotion he knew he couldn't hide: Suspicion, anger, pain, disbelief.

"You lie." Bryce hissed. Eryn was his. There *was* no one else.

"Do I now?" Brandi's voice was smooth. "Think about it." She moved closer and hooked her finger on his towel and stood on tip-toe. "Just think about it," she whispered in his ear. She tugged hard and the towel fell around his feet.

It didn't immediately register in his mind the sensations running through his body as his mind fought to make sense of what Brandi said. He'd once accused Eryn of meeting someone at the beach, but he had just been baiting her. Could she really be having an affair? Was that the real reason why she was pulling away from him? He was suddenly filled with fire, lit by an all-consuming jealously. And from that fire a need was taking root, spreading out of control. A need to strike back.

He looked down, then quickly glanced away, unable to hold back a groan.

Brandi trailed her tongue down his muscled stomach, her fingers down his back and over his hard buttocks. He was disgusted by how aroused he was, but his anger drove him on.

He watched, mesmerized, as she flicked her tongue on him and finally taking him in her mouth. The tension rose until it released a growl deep in his chest. He grabbed Brandi's arms and dragged her up the length of his body.

"No." His voice was strained, but years of resentment that he hadn't even realized was there, was now pouring out of him.

Crushing her against his chest, he assaulted her mouth with his, shoving his tongue through her parted lips. His hands founds the hem of her dress and lifted it up over her head and tossed it aside, hardly surprised she wore nothing underneath. He shoved her in the direction of the bed.

Brandi, only too willing to comply, jumped on the bed and rolled on her back with her legs spread wide. A wicked grin dominated her face as she waited. The wait was short and her triumphant laugh saturated the air as Bryce covered her body with his.

Chapter 28

Galen's stone-gray stallion pawed the ground impatiently, sensing his master's mood. Galen had urged him at break-neck speed, setting his hooves thundering down the path leading to the port, flattening grasses and snapping branches, before coming to a skidding halt a short distance from where *La Helena* was docked. So intent had Galen been to confront the merchant, that as soon as Catherine had retired after the festivities, he had set out.

The stallion's sides now heaved beneath his master's knees. Galen leaned forward to stroke the beast's neck, murmuring praise, but his attention was on the ship before him. The darkness under the trees provided him a shield as he studied the merchant ship.

The glow of lanterns dotted the deck, reflecting the movement of shadows. An occasional shout crossed the distance between them, but none belonged to the man Galen sought.

He swung his leg over the saddle and landed on the ground without a sound. Stepping out from the cover of the shadows, the moonlight illuminated his way as he walked resolutely to the vessel. The high-pitched whistle that signaled his approach did not slow Galen's stride, for he had expected it. A ship such as this would be carefully guarded. The shadows on the deck stopped and turned in his direction.

Galen stopped and called out, "I seek the captain of this ship."

The point of a blade bit sharply into his back.

"And what might you be wanting with Master Jonathan?"

With blinding speed, Galen unsheathed his sword and swung around, his blade clashing against Cedric's.

"What I have to say is for him alone," Galen's voice was low, seething with his rage.

Then around him came the glint of swords and knives, held by six men of varying height and girth, all wearing the same menacing smirks, eager for foul play.

Galen's stance did not falter. "Where is he?"

"He has business dealings and is not to be disturbed." Cedric held his sword firm against Galen's. "And we will ensure his wishes are carried out," he paused, pushing against Galen's sword ever so slightly, "by whatever means necessary."

Galen's anger boiled beneath a stony gaze. The air around Galen seemed to press against him as the others took a step closer.

"Then you will tell your Master Jonathan," Galen said, grinding the name through his teeth, "that his presence at the castle will no longer be tolerated."

Cedric considered his words. "Might I tell Master Jonathan if that is Lady Catherine's desire, or simply your own?" Laughter rippled through the men.

"I speak for all at Elderidge," Galen hissed. "Tell him to abandon his ambitions. A man of his station could never hope to win a high-born lady."

Cedric was taken aback. "A man of his station? And what station might that be?"

Disgruntled mumblings began to swell around Galen. "He insults him, he insults us all! Let us just run him through." Murmurs of approval echoed. They stepped closer still.

Cedric looked around at the men. "Nay, there will be no fighting tonight, gentlemen. We will deliver his message, such that it is." Cedric looked at Galen with bored amusement.

Galen tightened his grip on the hilt of his sword, incensed at the disrespect.

Cedric lowered his sword and signaled for the others to follow.

Galen stared at their retreating backs, anger hardening every muscle in his body. He dropped the tip of his sword and sheathed it, then whistled low. In an instant his stallion trotted to his side, snorting and tossing his head. Galen leaped on its back and at his barked command, his horse bolted back toward the castle at blinding speed, eating up the ground beneath them.

~ ~ ~

"It sounds so beautiful and sad, like many souls crying out at the same time. Or maybe they are singing. I cannot say which." Catherine had never known the ocean to put forth such a melody as she heard tonight. Away from the castle and the endless chattering and noise, she was discovering music that caressed her ears.

The full moon cast a glow on the breaking waves that whispered as they melted into the sand. The onshore breeze was warm as it blew her hair softly around her face.

"Aye," agreed Jonathan. "She sings a sad song when the sun has fallen. Perhaps she is lonely."

The sound of the waves rolling over and over was broken only by the sounds of laughter. Merriment and ale flowed freely among Jonathan's crew, who sat with a few women from the village farther down the beach, around a blazing fire.

"Tell me, Jonathan, what is it about the sea that keeps you out there? What makes you return to her time after time?"

Jonathan sat next to her, legs crossed, contemplating the waters. "She sings the sweet sound of freedom. Out there, she may be the queen, but she will let you have your freedom if you respect her." Turning to Catherine, he went on. "There is power in freedom, Catherine. Freedom is living for yourself, not for others."

Freedom. Catherine thought about he word. She was free to come and go as she pleased. So why did she feel like a captive in her own home? What was it that bound her in chains she could not see? She accepted her responsibilities and what was expected of her. But out here, away from her father, her sister, and Galen, sitting with Jonathan, she felt free. Free to love, free to dream, free to live. What would all of this be without Jonathan? Wrapping her arms around her legs, she put her forehead on her knees.

Jonathan gently traced the line of her arm. "What troubles you?"

She turned her face to rest her cheek on her arms, smiling in response to his touch. Even in the darkness, his face illuminated only by the light of the moon, she could see his concern.

"I know I cannot ask you to stay, but you must know I shall miss you. Already I feel an emptiness that threatens to consume my entire soul."

He brushed away a lock of her hair that had strayed onto her face. "Such beauty should never know sadness. 'Tis a crime."

The way he looked at her, the way he caressed her face with his eyes, made her breath quicken.

230

He leaned close. "I wish that I could stay, but others are expecting my arrival."

She nodded, speechless. She would not make it difficult for him.

He sighed and his gaze searched her face as if memorizing every detail. "I ask that you believe that I will return, for you have my heart, fair lady."

His lips were painfully close to hers. She leaned in ever so slightly, just to feel his sweet breath dance upon her lips.

Jonathan hesitated only a moment before he softly kissed her cheek. His fingers traced the softness of her lips, lingering on their fullness. "May I?"

She would not deny herself. "I pray that you wait no longer," she whispered. Her belly tightened with the anticipation. She reached out and held his arms, feeling the hard muscles respond to her touch. His kiss sent her into a sweet darkness, which then exploded with heat that demanded more. His kiss was slow, deliberate, tasting her upper lip, then her bottom lip. She pulled him to her, craving more, anxious to feed this awakened hunger. A sigh of his name escaped her lips.

Jonathan suddenly pulled away, his own breath coming in short bursts, smiling as Catherine whimpered in protest. "I will escort you home, milady, before I can no longer call myself a gentleman."

"But..."

He placed a silencing finger to her lips. "It must be so. You will be missed if we dally much longer." He helped her to her feet. As they stood with just a feather of space between them, he slid her hands under the folds of his shirt, against the bare skin of his chest and held them there. "Take care of my heart, Catherine, for I give it to you for safe keeping."

The rapid beating pounded against his warm, smooth skin, covered firmly by her hands. As his eyes penetrated her own, she tried to commit to memory every line of his face, the lush lashes that adorned his amber eyes, the curve of his lips, the straight line of his nose, the way he tucked his hair behind his ears. This is the way she would remember him. This is how she would dream of him.

They walked the short distance to her horse in silence, fingers entwined, savoring the last few moments before he would once again bid her farewell.

Chapter 29

"There's no excuse. It was a big, fucking mistake."

Bryce's usually composed features had given way to lines of worry, his brows drawn together tightly over his steel blue eyes. Two days had passed since Eryn's gallery showing. Two days that Bryce relived his betrayal over and over, with Brandi's presence a constant reminder. The sun bore down from straight above, causing beads of sweat to form on his upper lip. He leaned forward, his elbows on his knees, staring into the pool.

"But you needed me, Bryce," Brandi said soothingly. "You were hurting and you needed me."

He turned to glare at her. "Yeah, like Eryn would understand that." He shoved his hand through his hair. "No, it was unforgivable."

Brandi leaned back in the lounge chair, turning her face to the sun, and placing her hand on her belly. "What if you got me pregnant? Are you ready to deal with that?"

He shot her a deadly look. His anger towards her now matched his anger at himself. "I should kick your scrawny ass out of here right now," he threatened.

Her smile, one that had been hovering on her face for the last two days, turned smug. "Ah, but then I would tell her, wouldn't I?"

"Tell me what?"

Bryce stood up quickly to face Eryn, a weak smile barely hiding his anguish. "Hey, you're back." He pulled her toward him, but she resisted.

"Tell me what?" Eryn repeated, looked expectantly from Bryce to Brandi.

"Well?"

Brandi slid her sunglasses down her nose and looked at Bryce and then laughed. "Big surprise."

Bryce put his arm around Eryn and led her towards the house. She tried to shrug him off, but he held tight. Once inside, he turned her face towards him and kissed her, a gentle, lingering kiss that slowly deepened.

Something was wrong, Eryn thought. She could feel it in the way he kissed her. Pushing against his chest, she managed to break free and step back. "What surprise?"

She felt his hardness pressed against her belly as he pulled her closer to him again.

"If I told you, it wouldn't be a surprise, now would it?" he said, dropping light, feathery kisses on her lips. "Let's go upstairs." His fingers whispered a trail, starting behind her ear, down her neck, slipping her strap from her shoulder, his lips not far behind.

Gone was the coldness and demanding persona Bryce always wore as a second skin. Here, thought Eryn, was desperation and an eagerness to please. Did he feel *that* guilty about forgetting her art gallery opening?

He picked her up and carried her up the stairs to their bedroom, locking the door behind them. Two steps into the room and he stopped, closing his eyes for a long moment, but not before Eryn saw the anguish in his eyes. She started to ask what was bothering him, but his mouth crushed her question mid-breath.

He laid her gently on the bed, his eyes raking the curves of her body, before towering above her, his muscular thighs straddling her hips.

Eryn studied Bryce while his fingers fumbled with the buttons on his shirt. Her eyes were intent on the slight tremor in his hands. Once or twice he swallowed as if it hurt, like tasting bile and forcing it back down before it could surface.

His shirt fell open, exposing his broad chest and hard abs that rippled towards his waistband. His chest heaved now with ragged breath when Eryn stroked the length of his stomach.

Something about this was all wrong, she thought, her senses acutely aware of his unease. He was normally too confident to be fumbling with his clothes. Their lovemaking had always taken place on his home field, played by his rules. Now he just seemed lost, like someone had just misplaced the playbook.

"Hey, you guys?" The knock that followed was not a timid one, but one demanding attention.

Bryce cursed under his breath. "No!" That one word said more than "no." It contained anger, frustration, hatred, and pain.

He leaned over her now, fisting her hair, and pulling her closer. His kiss was unforgiving. His other hand pressed unrelenting against her body.

This Bryce scared her. Only when he pulled away did she realize she had been lying there, not moving, and not kissing him back.

"I'd do anything for you." He bent over again to kiss her again, his breath coming quicker. "We need it to be just us. No more Brandi. She's ruining it for us. She always has."

"I know, I know." Her voice was almost a whisper. "It's not that easy though." She wanted to say what he wanted to hear, but she had to fight with her conscience. "How can I kick her out now after I single-handedly ruined her life?"

Bryce let out a labored breath and rolled on his back, his voice now flat. "She did it to herself, Eryn. You don't owe her anything."

"She seems to think I do."

"Christ, Eryn. She thinks everyone owes her." He shoved his fingers through his hair in frustration.

"I know," she whispered. She rolled on her side and laid her head on his chest. Her hands skimmed over the flat plane of his stomach. He felt good. Solid and strong. Maybe their definition of love wasn't the same and maybe they had different ways of showing it, but it was all they had.

"I'll help her get a place to stay," she said. "Then she'll be gone. I promise."

His arms wrapped around Eryn, crushing her closer. "Soon, Eryn," he said quietly. "Please."

Chapter 30

"Our presence is required at Rynonshire." Lord Roberts' chair scraped the stone floor as he pushed away from the table. "There is a bit of unrest there. Some problem between the villagers and the steward."

"*Our* presence, milord?" Galen tensed.

"I have been giving this some thought." Lord Roberts crossed to the window, and stood looking out, hands held behind his back. "It seems as though our good steward is unable to maintain control. There is also rumor he is abusing his station."

"How does this involve me, milord?"

"I am asking you to come with me, Galen," Lord Roberts spoke again, not turning around. "You are my most trusted knight. If I must dismiss him, I would have you there in his stead."

Galen could feel the blood fade from his face, his body suddenly cold. To oversee one of Lord Roberts' many holdings was an honor any knight would embrace, but residing at Rynonshire would mean leaving Catherine behind. That is, if she did not agree to wed him.

Lord Roberts turned abruptly. "Prepare yourself and ten of your men. We leave immediately."

"Is it necessary to leave so soon, milord?" Galen stopped himself from saying anything more. Never before had he questioned a command given to him.

Lord Roberts raised a brow at Galen's objection. "Yes, it is. Either the steward has the spine of a grass blade or is deceitful. Either way, I must discover the cause behind the unrest."

Lord Roberts studied Galen's face with an unwavering gaze, and Galen returned it, his own eyes yielding very little.

"You worry about Catherine."

Galen's fists clenched until his knuckles turned white. What he truly wanted was Lord Roberts' blessing to run his sword through the merchant.

Controlling himself with a deep breath, Galen spoke the truth. "Milord, I love Catherine very much."

"The merchant. You've not been able to fend him off?" A hint of amusement quivered at the corners of Lord Roberts' mouth. "You are slipping, Galen."

"Milord, she is confused as to where her heart truly lies." He let out a breath, defeat weighing on his shoulders. "I know she cares for me. I have been patient, milord. I have given her time. I believe she would have agreed to be my wife had this merchant not interfered."

Lord Roberts slapped Galen on the shoulder. "Whether or not it is necessary for you to oversee Rynonshire, I will ensure that you and Catherine are wed." He turned and walked back to the table to gather his papers. "It is long past time for her to choose."

Galen nodded his head in acceptance, but had no feeling of elation in response to Lord Roberts' declaration. He wanted Catherine to accept him freely, by her own decision. Still, he had no doubt she would be happy with their union eventually. He squared his shoulders and set his chin in determination.

"Thank you, milord." Galen bowed and turned to the door.

~ ~ ~

The courtyard was now quiet as the servants went back inside the hall to resume their duties. Catherine

238

watched as Lord Roberts, Galen, Sara, Elizabeth, and ten knights rode out. Their journey would take them to Lord Oakley's castle for a night, a fact that Catherine did not miss when her father insisted she stay behind. A fortnight they would be gone. A fortnight to be alone to think about her future.

Her father's words before he left had settled heavily on her heart.

"This matter at Rynonshire will be laid to rest quickly, Catherine. I expect I shall be relieving the steward of his position." He had looked hesitant and had then said, *"As much as I loathe to lose his services here, Galen will be of great value to me at Rynonshire."*

"Galen is leaving Elderidge?"

"Not immediately, but very soon."

The meaning of her father's words shook the very foundation of her world. Could she so easily let Galen go? Could she wake up each day knowing she would not see his easy smile?

Out of the emptiness that poured into her heart, emerged the realization this perhaps would give her the time she needed. Time to be with Jonathan and time to convince her father of his worthiness.

Her elation quickly soured. She had no doubt Galen would ask her to accompany him as his wife to Rynonshire. He had selflessly given her the time she asked for and now he would expect her to accept his proposal. She could hardly believe he would so easily leave her behind.

She could deny him, of course, but there was no guarantee her father would approve of Jonathan. Could she defy her father and follow her heart, turning her back on the life she knew?

She looked around the courtyard. All was quiet. She headed towards the stables and ordered Jarrid to saddle her horse. There was no doubt in her mind where she would go. She would seek solace by the water's edge.

As she and her mare neared the water, she saw a few ships lingered in the port, but *La Helena* was already making her way towards the open sea. Catherine wished she could reach out and pull the ship back to her, just to see Jonathan one last time.

She turned her horse to the path leading to the beach. The sun glared over the surface of the water, hiding the horizon from view. She filled her lungs with the salty air and then let it out slowly. Once on the sand, Catherine's horse followed the lazy roll of the waves as they came upon the shore.

Shouts of men drew her attention back to the *La Helena*. Shielding her face against the sun, she squinted through the glare. The ship seemed to be hesitating, then her sails suddenly became limp, flapping loosely in the breeze. Catherine strained to make out the small boat that was being lowered into the water and the three men who were sliding down a rope into the boat.

What was amiss? Catherine wondered, watching.

Her heart began a slow pounding in her chest. *Is it possible one of those men could be Jonathan?* Using her heels and slapping the reins, Catherine urged her horse into a gallop. The boat made its way toward the shore, slicing easily through the water with the rhythmic pulling of the oars.

The steady pounding of her heart turned to a stutter when she saw one of the men was indeed Jonathan.

One of the men spoke to Jonathan, gesturing in her direction. He turned and looked at her, with a smile spread wide across his face.

She dismounted, unable to contain her excitement.

Just inside the wave break, the boat was pushed onto the wet sand by the churning water and the three men jumped out to drag it higher on the beach.

Letting it go, Jonathan turned and broke into a run and in a moment he was there. She screamed in delight as he lifted her and spun around, holding her tight to his chest. Barely letting her toes touch the sand, he buried his face in her hair, his lips brushing her cheek.

"Catherine," he murmured. "I could not leave. Not yet."

She eased her head back, savoring the tingling of her skin where his lips planted gentle kisses along her neck. Her hands tangled in his thick locks, pulling him closer. *How could this be so wrong?* Her breaths came in short bursts now, no longer able to deny what she needed. She slid her hands down to hold his face

His eyes glittered with the same fever she felt rage through her blood. His lips parted in a slow seductive curve.

Pulling him close, she pressed her mouth to his, seeking the intimacy and warmth of his tongue. She relearned the softness of his lips, savoring how they molded so perfectly to hers. She did not understand what possessed her when he was near. She was reckless in his arms and made bold by the freedom she

241

tasted on his lips. She could not, would not, think of anything beyond this moment. She clung to him because that is where she belonged.

Shouts of encouragement from down the beach filtered through her haze.

Jonathan groaned as he pulled away and lowered her gently to the sand. "It seems that my men approve."

"As do I," she said weakly. It was as if she had taken a draught, one that would render her body unable to move, yet she felt incredibly alive.

His finger traced the delicate line of her jaw and down to the soft spot on her neck where her pulse gave away the intensity of her desire.

"Come with me, Catherine. Come sail with me." He leaned closed, brushing his lips upon her ear.

His soft breath upon her skin sent a delicious chill along her spine. Visions of sailing the open waters, her hair catching in the wind, with Jonathan at her side, engulfed her. Then, other visions intruded: Elderidge on the distant horizon. Galen standing on the cliffs, wondering, searching.

Suddenly, the magic was broken. What was she thinking? She knew where her duty lay. She drew a trembling breath and laid her forehead against his chest. "I cannot. As much as I would so desire to sail with you, my destiny still remains here."

His hands moved up and down the length of her back with soothing strokes. "Destiny is what we make it to be. It does not make us." He drew back and lifted her chin. "It is a choice we all have."

She shook her head. "No, you do not understand. You do not know what it is like to have such responsibilities. I am bound by my station. There are certain expectations."

His eyebrows raised, he said softly, "I do understand. More than you realize." He paused a moment before a gleam danced in his eyes. "Come, let us enjoy the day." He laughed, taking her hand and running down the beach. His enthusiasm was contagious as he pulled her along with him.

She ran with him, her skirts clutched in her hand, squealing as she tried to avoid the water rushing upon the shore.

"Am I correct in assuming you have never placed your feet in the water, milady?" he asked.

She stopped, quite out of breath, her face flushed. "I most certainly have," she said with indignation. "My mother brought us here when we were children." She pointed down the beach. "I remember very well gathering shells and exploring the caves hidden in the cliffs."

"Ah, but do you truly remember the feeling?" he challenged. His face was close to hers now, his breath sweet upon her face.

She lifted the hem of her dress and looked down at her slippers and hose, the only things that kept her away from the cool water.

He gently squeezed her hand. "Go on."

Glancing to where the boat had been pulled ashore, she was surprised to see it gone.

In answer to the question in her eyes, Jonathan said, "They'll be back later."

She realized that for this moment, nay, for this day, she was free. No one was about, except her and Jonathan. There were no boundaries. She could not stop the smile that ached her cheeks as she looked at

Jonathan. Just for one day, she would *not* do what was expected of her.

Oh, I may pay for this recklessness, but I will live!

She took him by the shoulders and spun him around. "Hide your eyes." She pushed him gently towards the water. "And do not turn back to me until I say to."

She pulled up her skirt hem enough to remove her slippers and hose, and carefully lay them aside. With her feet now naked in the warm sand, she sifted the rough grains between her toes and looked at Jonathan. He stood at the water's edge, facing the ocean, hands clasped behind his back. His unbound hair, held back by the breeze, flowed freely over wide shoulders, his pants tightly gripping his legs.

Yes. This day is my own.

"Turn around," she commanded, and laughed as she wiggled her foot, showing him her feet were bare.

He beckoned her to the water's edge. "After you, milady," he said, with a most courtly bow.

She inclined her head in response and stood tentatively in the water, her skirts lifted modestly above her ankles. It felt cool against her skin, the small waves swirling sand over her feet.

"Oh! I cannot move my feet!" she laughed, fighting to keep her balance. Jonathan was there in a moment, holding her firm about her waist. Laughing, she spun around and scooped water, splashing Jonathan before he knew what she was about.

He started toward her, feigning a menacing look.

"'Tis not fair play! You cannot accost a lady!" she admonished. She turned and ran as fast as she could, her gown dragging in the water.

"'Tis not fair, you say?" he laughed as he gave chase.

Lunging toward her, he lost his footing and landed in the water. He rolled onto his back, his chest heaving with laughter.

Catherine spun around to face him.

"You are a sprite, milady," he said, panting. He held his hand out. "Pray, have mercy on me and help me rise."

She stopped just beyond his reach and eyed him cautiously, an eyebrow raised, questioning his intentions. He looked at her with such innocence, her caution melted away. She offered her hand, but lost her balance when he pulled her down into the water next to him.

"Now *this* is fair play!" His laughter flowed at her scowl.

"Oh...you!" She lunged at him, but he caught her wrists and held her at a distance, but close enough for her to feel the heat of his body.

She stopped struggling against him knowing full well she was no match for his strength, nor did she *wish* to struggle against him. She was just happy to be so near.

He was too beautiful for words. His hair was tousled, dripping wet about his face and his wide grin revealed perfectly straight white teeth.

She bit her lip, her body already reacting to the knowledge of what it felt like to touch his chest and the rippling lines of his stomach.

Then she giggled, imaging what a sight she must be. Her own hair had fallen about her shoulders, wet with the salty water, and her dress, soaked through, felt tight against her skin. Suddenly, she was all too aware of his searing gaze.

She had one day alone with him. One day to explore the depths of her feelings for him. She wanted, nay, *needed* to be truly one with him. She looked around. The beach, though empty, provided little privacy. There is one place, she thought, that could offer such; a cave, where as a child, she hid to escape the pain of her mother's death.

"Come with me." She pulled her wrists from his grasp and stood.

He studied her with narrowed eyes, twinkling slivers of amusement. "What revenge do you have planned for me?" he teased. "Should I be frightened?"

She considered what she was about to do. "Nay." A blush colored her cheeks. She ducked her head, avoiding his eyes. "It is I who should be frightened."

She turned and began the walk toward the rocky walls that turned sharply to face the ocean, leaving Jonathan to scramble to his feet and chase after her.

"I'd follow you anywhere, Catherine, but might you tell me where you are leading me?"

She glanced sideways at him. The desire in his eyes had cooled a bit, replaced with curiosity.

"A place I went as a child when I wanted to be alone. 'Tis there, around those rocks. I do not believe many know of it."

"And you trust me with this knowledge?" he laughed.

Catherine nodded, granting him a small smile. *If only he knew what else I will trust him with.*

They rounded the rocks, stepping gingerly over the seaweed sprawled on the sand, its salty stench assaulting their noses. She peered around the corner. There it was. The gaping hole in the cliff. Over time the entrance had eroded further by the punishing assault of the waves.

She ducked her head to step into the cave and waited for her eyes to adjust to the darkness inside. The air smelled dank, causing her to wrinkle her nose, but was much the same as she remembered it. The sand where she stood never dried, she recalled, but farther inside the cave, where it sloped upwards, the sand was soft and untouched by the tide.

"Catherine?"

She turned as the already dim light darkened even more. The mouth of the cave was blocked by Jonathan's silhouette, his shoulders almost spanning the width of the entrance. The walls reverberated with his potency.

With trembling hands, she pulled on the ties of her gown. She breathed deeply as the bodice loosened and she felt the gown fall away slightly from her skin. As the moments passed, anticipation took to seed, growing palpably around them. Jonathan moved not a muscle, though Catherine could see his body poised and controlled. Keeping her eyes on him, she slid her gown off her shoulders and carefully pushed the sleeves down her arms. For a moment her courage waned and she stopped, feeling woefully inexperienced in the art of seduction.

Jonathan instantly closed the gap between them and tangled his hand in her hair, pulling her face to his.

His kiss was hot, fierce, instantly setting her on fire. He teased her mouth until she parted her lips. His tongue, velvet heat, stroked her own and branded it as his.

She released the grip on her gown and twined her arms about his neck. She could taste in his kiss that he wanted her as desperately as she wanted him. It was a heady feeling, an aphrodisiac that took over. "Touch me," she whispered against his lips.

He pulled back and looked down upon her for a long, agonizing moment. "Catherine…"

Her body ached for his touch. Anywhere and everywhere. "Please."

Slowly, with one hand still fisted in her hair, Jonathan trailed the other down her neck to rest just above the soft swell of her breasts.

She arched and pressed upwards in encouragement. "Please," she begged again.

His fingers tugged at the top of her gown and gently pulled it down, freeing her from the confines of the fabric.

She bit her lip at the sudden desire to be more for him. She wanted him to think she was perfect. She looked down at herself, wondering…was she good enough for him?

"Look at me, Catherine."

She raised her eyes and all doubt vanished.

His fingers followed the crevice and touched her lightly beneath her breasts before cupping her fullness in his hand.

She couldn't have look away if she wanted to. And still he hesitated.

She pressed into his hand, wanting him to take more. "I am not a fragile flower, Jonathan. I am a woman grown."

With a husky moan, he cupped her breast and slowly rubbed his thumb over her nipple, teasing it to a hard peak.

She threw her head back and cried out, reveling in the tiny shivers that raked her body.

He planted steamy kisses on the soft skin beneath her ear, along her jaw, and trailed down her neck, and stopped, resting in the curve of her neck. Pulled hard against his chest, she felt his body quiver against hers, fighting to regain control. Harsh breaths shuddered through his chest as he held very, very still.

"I cannot possibly behave like a gentleman when you bewitch me so, milady."

"Then," she whispered, "be not a gentleman and call me not a lady."

His grasp on her slowly released and Catherine gently pushed him away. They stood apart, yet bound together by undeniable attraction. She dared herself to go on. She slowly raised her hands and hooked her thumbs at the top of her gown, which hung loosely about her waist. She eased it down and pushed it past her hips, letting it crumple to her feet. A shiver ran through her body.

The lack of light concealed the true depths of Jonathan's reaction as she stood before him. She had the disadvantage of not being able to see his face clearly, but the way he stood so still, muscles coiled tight, she knew neither of them would be turning back from what they were about to do. She could feel the heat from his eyes as he soaked up the sight of her and watched her every move. Encouraged, and driven by her own curiosity, she unhurriedly trailed her fingers up along the length of her thighs, over her lush hips, and across her flat, smooth belly. Her body flushed at the touch of her own hands as they brushed underneath her breasts, smoothing over her nipples before trailing back down again sensuously to her hips. She stepped out from the gown gathered at her feet and stood a fingerbreadth away from Jonathan.

He looked down upon her, his lower lip caught between his teeth. She took his hands in her own and turned with him slightly so that the light shining off the water and pouring into the cave would reflect upon his face.

His amber eyes had turned liquid gold, heavily lidded with desire. He cradled her face in his hands before he treated himself to the taste of her lips in a slow, luxurious kiss, his tongue finding hers once again.

But that was not enough. She needed more. She ached to feel his skin under her hands, her flesh against his. She pulled up hard on his tunic to give her access to what lay beneath. Her hands splayed against the ridges of his stomach and slid up over his powerful chest.

A low growl rumbled deep in his chest when he broke their kiss. He held her face apart from his. But she would not hesitate. She would not waste what moments she still had with him. Her hand snaked around his back, as she touched her tongue to her full lips, swollen by his kisses.

He needed no further encouragement. Jonathan released her and stripped himself of his tunic and untied his breeches, dropping them to the ground.

Catherine's eyes grew wide at his bronzed skin pulled tight over his wide shoulders, smooth expansive chest, bundled muscles of his arms, rippled stomach, and narrow hips...and his rising desire.

"Catherine..."

"Shh..." she managed to say. "No words. Come." She pulled him deeper into the cave and turned to him, pressing her body against his, reveling in the searing heat at every point their flesh touched. She felt his hardness against her belly and moved wantonly against the swell.

Pushing away her hair to expose the curve of her neck, he dipped his face and planted feather-light kisses along her jaw and down her throat, his hand stroking the small of her back. He lowered her to the soft sand and, in one fluid motion, he stretched the length of his body next to hers and ran his hand along her waist and hips, drawing her leg up over his.

Her skin flamed anew where he squeezed her buttock, pulling her closer to him. The intimacy with which they lay, with his shaft pressed hard between the moistness of her thighs, fired such an exquisite longing within her. She could not stop herself from touching him wherever she could. Her hands ran over the corded muscles of his shoulders and back, the smooth skin over his tight buttocks. She wanted to know everything about him. She wanted to etch into her memory, right down to her soul, what he felt like.

She never knew her body was so capable of tightening with such pleasure. Her fingers threaded through his thick hair and pulled him into a soul-searing kiss, searching for a release.

But he would grant her no such boon. Sliding his hand slowly up her side and finding its way to her breast, his kiss softened and slowed. He pulled on her lower lip, flicking his tongue at the corner of her mouth. Her sigh of satisfaction melted into a moan when he gently massaged her soft mound, nipping the tight bud between his fingers.

The fever that ran through her when she first kissed him paled compared to the inferno that melted her now. She thought she would scream in agonizing pleasure when he took her in his mouth to suckle her. She arched her back in response with her breath coming in short bursts.

She shuddered. "Love me now, Jonathan. Please."

He raised his head and shifted his body over hers, putting his weight on his elbows. Their hearts beat furiously against one another, their flesh hot and slick between them.

His teeth grazed her jaw before nipping the lobes of her ears. Then his words brushed across her even more gently than his touch. "There is no reason to rush. We have much time, my love."

"No. No time." She was hungry for him. She wanted him to fill her now, until she no longer felt separate from him. "Now." She shifted under him until her thighs cradled and tightened around his hips.

He laughed softly. "You are much too impatient." But he conceded, and slowly slid into her hot, wet tightness.

She gripped his shoulders as she gently filled her, and reveled in the explosive union of body and soul. "More," she breathed.

When he met resistance against her thin barrier, he stopped.

"Catherine?" Jonathan searched her face for words she might not say. All was quiet but for the noise of the distant ocean as the waves pulsated against the rocks outside.

"Please do not stop," she pleaded.

"You must be certain."

"I have never been more certain of anything in my entire life. *Please*. I *want* this."

He nodded as he considered her words. Then he pressed deeper, his hips moving against hers, slowly at first, then stronger as her heat wrapped around him. He thrust hard, penetrating the barrier between them.

Catherine arched against the pain that shot through her and Jonathan's mouth captured the sounds that would have escaped her lips. He stilled, letting her accustom herself to the size of him inside her.

"You are so beautiful, Catherine." He rested his forehead against hers. "You cannot possibly know what you do to me."

The knowledge that she had the power to excite him made her bold. She smiled wantonly. "Show me."

He studied her, as if weighing her commitment. "As you wish, milady." He claimed her mouth and began the dizzying torture of seduction, probing her mouth with his tongue. With a long draw on her lower lip, he broke the kiss, and as she wished, he began slow, deep strokes, watching her face as he moved inside her.

The friction against her very core brought her to a precipice where, wave upon wave, the air trapped in her lungs swelled and burst forth, filling her heart, spilling over into her loins, and exploding beyond her very soul. His name stuck in her throat as she gasped for air. She road the crest, clutching his hard buttocks, bringing him closer, and then, when she thought she could go no higher, she shattered into a thousand fiery stars.

His rhythm pounded faster, his thrusts deeper as she tightened her legs around his waist, demanding more of him. He rose above her, filling her, driving harder, before calling out her name with his own release, then collapsing against her.

She unlocked her ankles, sliding her heels up and down the length of his strong thighs. A satisfied smile danced on her lips. She marveled at the way their bodies fit, at the way her skin was still afire where he touched and kissed her, where he lay within her. His back tightened in response to the lazy lines she trailed with her fingers. Planting small kisses upon his shoulder, she strove to remember the taste of him upon her lips.

Jonathan rolled to his side and propped himself upon his elbow, watching her, his hand resting protectively across her hip.

She smoothed back the wild tangle of his hair and smiled. "Thank you."

His brows rose in question.

"For showing me. For giving me something to remember."

She closed her eyes to his tender caress upon her face, across her shoulders, and down to the hollow space between her breasts.

"Nay, 'tis you who have given me something to dream about, Catherine. It will be sweet torture until I return." He leaned close and brushed his lips against hers. "I want more of you. More than this." He gestured about the cave. "Not just when I find myself in port, but every moment of every day. I want you forever."

Her heart lurched. Their moments together were stolen at best and the moments were fast running out. Jonathan would leave. Galen and her father would return. What then? What if she failed to convince her father of Jonathan's worthiness? What if Galen refused to let her go?

Jonathan lifted her chin to search her eyes. "What say you? Am I alone in these feelings? Tell me you want me to return."

She knew not what tomorrow would bring. But she was certain of one thing. "Aye," she whispered. "I would like that very, very much."

Chapter 31

Bryce stared at his clenched hand, a piece of paper choked in its grip. Proof. But what, he thought, if this was just a sick, twisted joke? Brandi certainly wouldn't be above stooping this low to hurt Eryn. She obviously had a personal vendetta against her. Blinded by his own jealously, he had stepped right in the middle of it. And now Brandi had him by the balls. But if he played along, he thought, he had a good chance of getting out of this with his marriage intact and with Brandi out of their lives for good.

Slowly he eased his fingers open, exposing the crushed page from Eryn's journal. He ignored the slight trembling of his hands as he pulled the crumpled paper apart and smoothed it out on his desk.

I missed you last night. I realize how dark it is without you by my side. You are my light by which I navigate my day. But lately the days and nights are becoming one as the line between hopes and dreams and reality is erased.

The page once again became a ball in his fist.

"Now do you believe me?" Brandi had been watching from the doorway, her shoulder resting on the frame. She sauntered across the room to stand behind him.

With calculated intent, her nails scratched a rhythmic, soothing motion along his back. "Let her go, Bryce. You need someone who appreciates you, someone who loves the same things you do. Someone who is loyal."

"And you're that *loyal* one?" he hissed. "You, who was so anxious to fuck your best friend's husband?"

Her hands froze and her voice turned icy. "I didn't hear you complaining when you were slamming into me." She shrugged. "Whatever. Like I've been trying to tell you, we're perfect for each other. We *need* each other."

His fisted hands ground into the desk. "Why are you doing this to us?" The words were low in his chest, the growl of a caged animal.

"You'll thank me for it later, Bryce." Her hand slid down to grab his ass before she turned and left. "She never deserved you."

~ ~ ~

"...the eyes are windows to the soul...an inner feeling beyond dispute that they know each other and have known each other across space and time, and so they come together, tossing aside social rules and propriety, all manners of custom, just to rejoin..."

"When twin flames are apart in this physical plane, there is a feeling of loneliness, incompleteness. Your twin flame makes you feel whole again, like coming home."

"Let's leave."

Eryn looked up from the book she found at a second hand store, *Twin Souls – Life Beyond Life*. She stared at Bryce, wondering if she heard him right.

"Now. Tonight," he said.

"Where? And why?"

"Do we need a reason to get away together?" He raked his fingers hard through his hair.

Eryn cocked her head to one side, sensing the desperation in his usually calm voice. "But what about the Cohen deal? I thought you were up against a deadline?"

He shrugged. "He can wait. And if not, he can find somebody else."

She knew how much that would hurt his ego - to have someone else put together the plans for the much-anticipated performing arts center. The financial gains aside, this had been a project he had been itching to get his hands on for a long time.

"Where would we go?" Eryn wondered at his sudden need to be alone with her. Would it really make a difference?

Bryce walked over and knelt in front of her. "You name it. We'll go there."

Here he was, practically begging to go away with her, just the two of them. She had never seen him so serious, so desperate. If there really was a chance for them, she was willing to try.

"Well, I guess I need a couple of days to get ready. Besides, I don't want to just leave Brandi here alone." The moment the words left her lips, she was sorry.

Other than his jaw tightening, his face went still.

"Name the place, Eryn." He said.

"Okay, okay. Let's see," she said quickly. She narrowed her eyes trying to remember the most exotic place she had seen in a travel magazine. Someplace secluded. Someplace where maybe, just maybe, they could find some common ground again.

"How about Fiji? There's an island where we can have our own hut with our own private staff." The image grew in her mind as her pulse quickened. "I read that if you want lobster for dinner they'll go out and catch it for you. And the water is crystal clear."

Bryce's face softened as a smile pulled at the corners of his mouth. He leaned in and kissed her hard, pressing her back in her chair.

"We'll leave in a couple of days," he promised.

Eryn bit her lip, watching him stride out of the room. Something still wasn't right. For him to give up the Cohen account, to be in such a hurry to leave, was really odd. Too spontaneous for Bryce. She tapped a finger to her pursed lips. More than likely, Brandi was pushing his patience over the edge. That woman had a way of doing that to people.

"Shit." She needed to get Brandi out of the house before they left.

Eryn grabbed another book, and, flipping though the pages, she found what she had noticed earlier. *We choose to be a part of soul groups to learn lessons, but not all relationships in the group are beneficial. If the negative feelings are not dealt with in this life, it will carry over until it is. The negative karma attracts interpersonal problems time after time.*

"They must have had Brandi in mind when they wrote that one," Eryn murmured, shaking her head. Whatever lesson was in this, she had to face it. Tonight.

Chapter 32

Galen's steps were brisk upon the stone floors leading to Catherine's chambers. It had been so long since they had really talked, as they once had. His prolonged stay at Rynonshire had allowed too much time and space to grow between them. Fortunately, Lord Roberts had sent Galen, along with some of his men and Sara, back to Elderidge while he tied up some unruly ends at Rynonshire. Galen would soon return to take over the steward's role.

Most importantly, Lord Roberts had promised that when he returned to Elderidge, he would tell Catherine of his intent to bind her and Galen in union.

He knocked lightly on the door. "Catherine?" He pushed the door open as he announced himself. "Catherine, it is I, Galen." Receiving no answer, he peered into her chambers. The sunlight streamed through the window onto the papers strewed upon her writing desk. The bedcovers were spread neatly upon the bed. He looked around. There was no sign that she had been here this afternoon.

Galen ran his fingers through his hair in frustration. A gust of wind funneled through the window, lifting the edges of the papers, and sending them scattering. He lunged for them, but was unable to catch them before they fluttered to the floor.

"At the very least, milady, I can keep your chambers tidy for you," he said softly. As he set the papers upon the table, one letter caught his eye.

My Dearest Jonathan,

A chill gripped his body. He instinctively looked behind him. Looking back at the letter, he quickly read, placing his hand on the table for support.

I do not know where to begin. Everyday I wait. How many times will the sun set before I see your beautiful face again? How many of my dreams will be empty and dark without your light to take me to the dawn? I search for you like a blind woman, looking through sightless eyes, and like her, I see nothing. By day I must remain Lady Catherine, strong, commanding, and responsible. Oh, to see you would surely be my undoing, for I would become a servant to you! My love for you would insist I be at your side, to care for nothing but you...

Galen became intensely aware of the way his blood pounded in his ears and how his chest constricted, making even the shallowest of breaths near impossible to draw forth. There had to be some mistake. This letter was unsigned. It could have been written by someone else's hand, could it not? He stood at the desk, the letter in his hand, shaking ever so slightly.

"No! No!" he hissed. "This is not hers!" His aguish ran deep, and his heart knew the truth. Slamming the letter back onto the desk, he ran from the room in search of Catherine.

"Galen! What is the meaning of this?" Catherine gasped.

He had run around the corner directly into her with such force, she had been sent teetering on her heels.

"Catherine!" He grasped her shoulders to steady her. "My apologies! I was in a hurry." His words spilled out. "Are you harmed?"

She smiled at his flustered state. "No, no, Galen. I am fine. Please do not fuss."

She paused when she saw fear and uncertainty glimmering in his eyes. Holding his face with her hands, her voice was gentle, "Whatever is the matter?"

Without hesitation, Galen's lips covered hers, desperately searching for a response. Catherine, startled at first, acquiesced, letting Galen fulfill her need of intimacy she missed since Jonathan left.

But it was Galen who pulled away. "I am sorry, Catherine. I merely wanted to tell you..."

She looked at him patiently, one brow lifted in a delicate arch.

With an effort, he pushed the thought of the letter away. He didn't need to know. She was here and the merchant was gone. Catherine would be his wife.

"I merely wanted to tell you I love you, Catherine. 'Tis good to be home."

~ ~ ~

At nightfall, Catherine stood on the edge of the cliff, looking out across the vast ocean. The wind was cold and menacing, lifting the crests of the waves high into the air until they could stretch no longer, and then letting the water crash down with a deafening roar onto the jagged rocks below. The coal-gray skies were a stark contrast from that morning's glorious blue. Drawing her cloak tighter around her body did little to ward off the cold.

Where was Jonathan now? How would his ship fare the brewing storm? He had sent word he would arrive within a fortnight, but this storm twisted her stomach in a queasy knot. A violent shudder ran through her as she turned and walked back towards her horse. The hooded cloak sheltered her from the elements, but could not hold at bay the deep fear that shook her.

Back at the castle, she crept up the winding stairs towards her bedchamber, her feet light on the stones. She slipped down the corridor to her room and silently pushed open the door to step inside. Candles illuminated the room, casting a soft glow against the walls.

A startled gasp escaped her lips as Catherine took in the figure standing in front of the fireplace, his hands braced against the mantle. Galen said nothing as he stared into the dancing flames.

"Ah, there she is. I told you she would return." The voice dripped with mockery.

Catherine looked sharply in its direction and found her sister sitting in her bed, propped up with pillows.

"What goes on here?" Catherine looked from one to the other, a frown creasing her brow.

Sara slid off the bed and breezed past Catherine towards Galen, who continued to remain silently fixated on the fire.

"Galen was looking for you. I offered him company while he awaited your return." Sara stood by him, gently placing her hand on his shoulder for a moment before he shook it off.

"Get out, Sara." Catherine commanded.

Undeterred by her sister's icy voice, Sara spoke to Galen. "What would *you* have me do?"

Catherine's fingers curled into fists at her side as she bit back hard on her anger. Only when Galen nodded his head in the direction of the door did Sara move from his side.

Galen waited until Sara closed the door before speaking.

"Where have you been?"

Catherine cringed at the accusation in his voice. She fought back the tears that welled, her heart aching. Gone was the innocence of their youth and the trust they once had.

"I simply could not sleep and needed some fresh air." It was not a lie, she reminded herself. Her sleepless nights were indeed a part of her now, spurred by the longing and worry for a man she could not have.

Galen pushed himself from the mantle and turned to face her. Silhouetted against the glow of the blaze, he looked defeated, his broad shoulders drooping. When he walked towards her, his steps were hesitant, and when he stood before her, his face was weary and sad.

"What keeps you awake at night, Catherine?" He reached up to touch her face, his thumb tracing the circles beneath her eyes.

She tasted another lie. They came too easy for her now. But she could not tell the truth. "I do not know," was all that she could say, but his eyes told her he knew otherwise.

His jaw clenched, and his eyes grew colder.

She stood motionless as he abruptly walked past her to the door. She pressed her lips together, bracing herself against the gnawing guilt. She spun around at the sound of the bolt sliding into place, but Galen was still in the room.

"I will have you, Catherine. Now." He glared at her with the determination of a trained warrior. Galen stood his full height, his chest expanded to its full breadth. "I will not have that merchant take what is rightfully mine."

Catherine raised an eyebrow to his declaration. "Rightfully yours? I am not a horse to be sold or bargained for, Galen."

"So you say, dear lady, but I question your judgment. It seems to be clouded of late."

He dropped his belt and pulled his tunic over his head, tossing it aside. His golden hair fell around his broad shoulders, the muscles tensed with anger.

She swallowed hard. She had never thought of him as a lover, but now, his sculpted chest, his rippling stomach, and his powerful thighs, gave her a moment's pause. But only a moment, for with one stride he was in front of Catherine, staring hard into her eyes.

She defiantly lifted her chin and stared back.

Reaching out to stroke her cheek with the back of his fingers, his face softened and the harshness of his eyes was suddenly gone.

"I have always adored your fire, Catherine. You have so much passion in your soul." He dipped his face close and brushed his lips against hers. "I love you to the depths of my own soul, Catherine."

Though they were the tender words any other woman would yearn to hear from such a man, Catherine could not accept them.

"No, Galen. I cannot." She tried to push him away, but his hand reached around her back and pulled her against his hard body. Their eyes locked and Catherine shivered at the coldness that once again turned his steel eyes to ice.

In one swift move he picked her up and carried her to the bed.

"Galen! No!" she cried, beating against his chest with her small hands.

"Do not care deny me, milady," he growled. "I have been patient with your folly too long. I have been your faithful servant for long years, but now I will be your lord."

Throwing her roughly on the bed, he pulled up her arms and pinned them over her head. He then sprawled his full length over her body, letting her feel his desire.

"Let me see the same blaze of fire that lights up your eyes when you see that merchant."

His crushing kiss halted her denial. His lips were harsh, bruising her mouth.

She pressed her lips together against his tongue's assault.

He pulled away, smiling coldly. "Very well then, my lady, just a warm glow will do." He kissed a line along her jaw to her ear and whispered, "If you would only give me but a morsel of the passion you feel for him, I would die happy."

He moved over her, pushing her knees apart with his own, his free hand cupping her breast, squeezing her nipple between his fingers. His breath was hot against her skin wherever he pressed his urgent kisses.

A scream worked its way up Catherine's chest and throat, a scream of anger and panic. She knew he loved her, but she had asked him to wait. And to reward him for his patience, she fell in love with another man. Though she knew she had pushed him beyond endurance, he still had no right to take her like this! She squeezed her eyes tight, willing herself to stay calm. She would despise him for this, but he would hate her even more when he discovered she was no longer a maiden. She lay there, unmoving, as his hand worked its way under her dress, to her buttocks, pulling her closer.

Then he went still.

She waited for his anger to explode, waited for the sounds of ripping fabric, waited for the invasion of her body, but instead his grip slowly relaxed on her wrists.

He held his face inches from hers. "You may stop praying, Catherine."

She opened her eyes and saw that the anger in his eyes had been replaced with sadness.

"I want you to come to me freely. I want your desire to match my own. If you cannot give yourself to me, I will not take you against your will."

Pushing himself to sit at the side of the bed, he shoved his fingers through his hair. His breath was deep and labored with defeat. He looked to the ceiling, his eyes distant.

"I have fought many an enemy, but never one such as this. Even if I were to pierce his heart with a sword, I cannot kill what you so obviously feel for him."

She opened her mouth to protest.

He shook his head. "I found your letter."

She was too late to stifle her quick intake of air.

Galen closed his eyes and took another deep breath, his forehead creased in a frown. "Perhaps someday, Catherine, you will see my love is forever. I have no desire to be anywhere but with you."

Hot tears stung her eyes and regret rose like bile in her throat and churned like acid in her stomach. How could a chance meeting with a merchant have turned her life so completely around? Had she not met Jonathan, had she not fallen in love… Aye, things would have been far simpler, but she would have lived her days behind a veil of gray, not seeing the vibrant colors of her own passion.

She kneeled beside Galen and put her forehead against his shoulder.

"I am so sorry," she whispered.

His muscles tensed under her fingertips as she followed the outline of his arm.

"No. Please." His voice was strained. He shrugged her off and abruptly got up to sit in the chair beside the bed. He leaned forward with his elbows on his knees, his head in his hands.

"It hurts so much, Catherine. It hurts because I love you with all of my heart." He whispered as though he were afraid to admit his weakness. "I am hopelessly yours. I have no choice. I can love no one else."

Catherine slid off the bed and again kneeled before him. She could not bear to see him, a man so strong, so fierce a warrior, reduced to this. She hated what she was doing to him.

Galen searched her face for some comfort, for some shred of hope for him. "Can there ever be love between us?"

She could not answer that, for she did not know.

His thumb smoothed the quivering of her lips and wiped away the tears that escaped her eyes. He fisted her hair at her neck and pulled her close to him, drawing her lips to his. Their tears mingled as the kiss deepened. A groan rumbled in his chest and he pulled away, breathless. He got up quickly, pushing her away.

"I cannot do this." He retrieved his tunic from the floor and quickly slid it over his head. "I will not leave your side, Catherine, until you tell me I am no longer welcome. But you cannot have us both and I will not be second to *him*."

He picked up his belt from the floor and wrapped it around his waist, yanking hard to secure it. Running his hands through his hair, he opened the door and left, not looking back.

Suddenly cold, Catherine wrapped her arms around herself to fight off the chill running up her spine.

What had Jonathan told her? *If it makes you happy, it cannot be wrong. Just find what it is that makes you happy and live it.*

She was no longer sure what it was that would truly make her happy.

Chapter 33

There. She'd done it. She had told Brandi to leave.

It's been a long time coming. Too long, Eryn thought. Finally she could see their relationship for what it was. Since the day they met, they'd used each other to feed some compulsion inside of them; her need to give, and Brandi's need to take, with a little bit of vengeance mixed in.

Eryn wasn't sure how much Brandi had drunk tonight, but she had already decided she couldn't wait until her friend sobered up.

Now Brandi's knuckles were turning white as she gripped the bar, and though Eryn couldn't see her face, she figured it was twisted with fury. Brandi's back was rigid, her shoulders and back rising and falling steeply with each breath.

Then Brandi seemed to relax. She picked up her glass and took a sip before turning around to face Eryn.

"So that's it, huh? Just like that? Throwing out the garbage?"

Eryn bit her lower lip to keep from saying anything, afraid she would back down and be the coward she had been all these years.

With each word, Brandi's voice went a step higher. "Do you think it is easy being where I am? Having to look at you day after day? You have it all, Eryn! A big house, too much money. Isn't it enough?"

"You're jealous of me?"

"I forgave you for taking away my boyfriend and now you try to take away the one place I can stay! I have nowhere to go!"

"I tried to help you..."

"I don't want your pity," Brandi spat out. She finished off her drink in one gulp and turned to pour another. "God, Eryn. You take everything for granted. You can't even see what a good friend I've been."

Eryn's jaw dropped in disbelief.

Brandi turned sharply, her drink spilling over the edge of the glass. "And what about Bryce? Look at the way you treat him."

"You don't understand, Brandi. Bryce and I..."

Brandi laughed. "Oh yes I do. I understand that you don't give a shit about him. Do you have any idea what he feels? While you're off taking pictures of those pathetic homeless people, he's home alone. Not to mention," she said, poking Eryn in the chest, "that you're running around with *another* guy. God, how many men do you have to have?"

"I told you before! I am not running around with anyone!"

"Whatever."

"Bryce and I are just fine. We just need to work on some things."

"And you think getting rid of me is going to save your marriage? Ha! You're already doomed. He needs a woman who will take care of him." Brandi was quiet for a moment, eyes narrowed, and then her voice lowered. "Or should I say he *needed* a woman to take care of him."

"What the hell is that supposed to mean?" Eryn's stomach lurched. She and Bryce would be going away in a couple of days. Was he trying to make their marriage better or was he covering up guilt?

Brandi brought her glass up to her lips, looking at Eryn over the top of the glass. The glint in her friend's eyes was sharp and almost, Eryn thought with a shiver, evil.

Brandi's lips curled in perverse satisfaction at the pain she was inflicting on Eryn, seemingly in no hurry to end the suspense.

Eryn's mind reeled with the implications, but she needed to know the truth directly from Brandi's lips. She closed the space between them with two quick steps before slapping the glass out of Brandi's hand, sending it crashing against the wall.

"Answer me, Brandi! What the hell did you mean by that?" Eryn's breaths were coming in quick bursts now, her patience completely tapped out.

Brandi didn't flinch as she studied Eryn's face coolly. "You don't like it when you don't have all the answers, do you?"

Eryn straightened her shoulders as hate surged through her body. She spent too many years of being a doormat for Brandi, making sure she was okay, and now here the woman stood, vile words dripping from her mouth.

Brandi's attention flickered over Eryn's shoulder for a second, then she looked back in her eyes. "I finally took something that was yours." Her smile grew wider. "And he was absolutely incredible." She leaned forward, inches from Eryn's face. "An animal," she whispered.

"God damn it, Brandi!" From the doorway, Bryce's voice shook the room.

"I guess you're really going to kick me out now, huh?" Brandi shrugged as she stared at Eryn.

Eryn felt the blood drain out of her face and pool somewhere in her feet. She couldn't focus and a sharp pain ripped through her chest as she tried to take a breath.

Bryce and Brandi? But he hates her, doesn't he? Why won't he say something? God, Bryce, why are you taking so long to deny it?

"Bryce?" Eryn's voice sounded pitifully woeful to her own ears. A pregnant silence was her only answer. She bit back the nausea that was coming in waves, and then her anger exploded, shattering her confusion into pieces. She looked up at her long-time friend.

Brandi, whose face was cocky with victory, didn't look so much like her friend any more.

Eryn lost what little control she had left and locked onto Brandi's gaze like a vice.

"You!" Eryn shoved Brandi in the chest as hard as she could. "Bitch!"

Before Bryce could reach her, Eryn had slammed her fist into Brandi's jaw, sending her crashing over the bar stools. Eryn lunged for her, but Bryce was there, grabbing Eryn by the waist and pulling her back.

"Don't touch me!" Eryn shook him free and backed herself against the wall, cradling her throbbing hand against her body. The touch of his hands sickened her. She glared at Brandi who sat tangled up in the bar stool legs with a look of surprise on her face.

Brandi kicked the stools from her feet and got up, dabbing the corner of her mouth.

"Huh." She studied the blood that stained her hand. "I think you just lost your crown, Miss Congeniality."

"Get out." Eryn ordered.

"I'll just get my stuff."

"Leave it. I'll send it to the nearest homeless shelter."

"Yeah, right." Brandi's voice was slick with defiance. She turned to the bedrooms. "I'll just be a minute."

"Take one more step in the wrong direction and I'll have you arrested for trespassing." Eryn reached for her cell phone and flipped open the top.

Brandi turned to look first at Eryn and then at Bryce.

"You're right Bryce," she said. "She wouldn't understand." She grabbed her purse from the counter and walked out of the house, slamming the door behind her.

Eryn didn't realize she was holding her breath until she heard the sound of the car's engine finally fade away.

Emptiness filled up her lungs and quickly spread to her arms and legs. It was almost as if she expected this betrayal, for the hurt was eerily familiar. Her body shook, racking hard with tears, with anger, and with pain. The world as she'd known it had just dropped out from under her feet and she was falling hard and fast.

Oh, God. Tell me this isn't happening. Tell me this was just a big misunderstanding. Please, please, please, oh, please.

She waited, her eyes scrunched too tight, but there was no sound, no answer to her prayers. No one

275

was going to fix this for her. She drew a ragged breath through the big, empty hole in her soul.

Finally opening her eyes and straightening her shoulders, she released the grip she'd had on her cell phone and snapped it shut.

"Eryn. Eryn. I'm sorry." Bryce made no attempt to come closer.

Finding her voice, Eryn was surprised at her calmness. She made herself look at him. "I should have seen this coming."

"I had sex with her because I was pissed off! I was angry because you are having an affair! I know it didn't make it right, Eryn, but still..."

"What? You think I'm having an affair?"

He pulled out the crumpled paper that he had shoved in his pocket and held it up to her.

Her face went white. She recognized the pink tinted page from her journal. Brandi had made damn sure the knife was going to go deep.

"Do you deny it?" The look on his face told Eryn he thought he had her. That little piece of paper gave him a valid reason for what he did.

Eryn shook her head at irony. The words she wrote to heal herself were the words that ultimately caused her pain.

"Why didn't you just ask me about it?" When he didn't answer, she just sighed and shook her head. "Those are just words on a piece of paper, Bryce. Call it what you want, but I wasn't having an affair."

Without waiting for a response, she put her phone down and turned to go upstairs.

It wasn't until much later, deep into the night, that Eryn felt Bryce get into bed. Her back was to him, shielding herself. He laid on his back, not touching

276

her, his breath smelling of alcohol. A lot of it. There was no sleep for either of them.

Her anger was gone now and she was ready to tally her options. She knew she was going to leave. Bryce had given her no choice.

Chapter 34

Galen stopped mid-stride and paused, listening. Silence drifted through the corridor. Perhaps it was nothing after all, he thought. Then he heard it again. It was muffled, but it was the unmistakable sound of crying - painful, full of despair, soul-breaking tears.

He followed the sound to Sara's chamber and knocked lightly on the door. "Sara, 'tis Galen."

"Leave me be."

Her voice was anguished, and though he avoided Catherine's sister as much as possible, he could hardly ignore such suffering in any woman. He knocked harder. "Please, Sara, open the door."

A few moments passed before Galen heard the bar slip free and the door slowly open, revealing Sara's tear-stained face. She turned very slowly and walked to the window. Leaning against the sill, Sara seemed lost and deflated, her shoulders bowing under an unseen weight. Outside, the sky was gray, with darker clouds beginning to billow.

Galen closed the door behind him. "What troubles you, Sara?" he asked.

She stood, her silhouette etched against the darkening sky.

Grasping her shoulders, he gently turned her towards him. In the fading light she looked at him with red-rimmed, swollen eyes.

"What is it?" he asked again.

"I know not what to do." Her tears flowed freely again and Galen took her in his arms and held her close, rocking her back and forth, murmuring soothing words.

"It is all her doing, you know. She tries to take everything away from me!"

Galen cringed at the anger and jealousy in Sara's words.

"She has done this to me! This time, I will have my revenge!" Sara pushed herself away from Galen, wiping away the tears from her cheeks. Hatred and vengeance washed over her face. "Do you know, Galen, that she writes him letters? That she goes to him when his ship arrives in port?" Her hands clenched at her sides. "You, Lord Oakley, everyone grovels at her feet. She plays you all for fools." She paced the room, fueled by her own anger. "She chooses and tosses men aside at her whim." She stood straighter, her mood suddenly calm. "But she has not won. No." She looked down lovingly at her hands, lightly touching her belly. Her voice was soft. "I shall be a lady in my own right for I carry the child of Lord Oakley."

Galen stared, his jaw slack. Had he heard her clearly? Aye, from the way she stroked her stomach so protectively, he knew what he heard was the truth. The muscles in his jaw tightened as he fought to control his growing rage.

"He has gone too far this time. I shall rip him apart limb from limb," he said through clenched teeth.

"Nay, you will do no such thing!" Sara stomped her foot.

His steel blue eyes turned icy as he regarded her. "Did he force himself upon you?"

Sara tossed her head, standing tall, chin tilted upwards. "I went to him freely. He said he wanted me. He said I was beautiful."

Galen closed his eyes against his rage. "Do you believe you are the sole female he has ever told that to?"

She glared at him.

"Does he know of this babe you carry?"

"He knows. I told him when we stopped for the night on our way to Rynonshire." She frowned a little. "He was surprised, but he will become accustomed to the notion of being a father once he and I have wed."

Galen grabbed her arms, wanting to shake sense into her. "You believe he will wed you?"

Sara winced under the pressure of his grasp. "You are hurting me!" she cried.

He quickly released his grip and backed away.

She rubbed her arms. "I confided in you because we fight the same foe - Catherine. She takes our love, but does not return it. She did not want Lord Oakley, so I offered myself in her stead and he accepted me, willingly."

"He has you fooled," he gritted. "He will not marry you. He only beds women for his pleasure."

Sara's eyes flashed dangerously. "Am I so undesirable that no man would wish to wed me?"

"Do not twist my words, Sara," Galen snapped. "What will you do if he will not acknowledge that you bear his child?"

She cried, panic in her voice. "He will! He must! I have been with no other, I swear!" She flung her arms around Galen's waist and buried her face in his chest.

Pressed against him now was not the woman she wanted to be, but a scared child. His anger rested heavily on Lord Oakley.

"Hush now Sara." He comforted her as well as he could, but he knew he was ill equipped to deal with such matters. "Go to Catherine. She will know what to do."

"She will hate me."

Galen lifted Sara's chin so she would see him. "She will not. She is not our foe. She loves you and only wants what is best for you."

"I wish that were the truth," Sara muttered. She took a step back and squared her shoulders. "You will leave Lord Oakley alone and you will not speak of this to anyone. I will make Lord Oakley see how blessed we are and prove to him that I shall make him a good wife." With her chin set in determination, she pushed past Galen and hastened to the door, ducking into the corridor before her tears started anew.

~ ~ ~

"You are what?" hissed Catherine.

"I am with child," said Sara, her lower lip quivering and tears pooling in her eyes.

Catherine was unable to speak, her shock so great. Her little sister, so young, so innocent, was telling her she was carrying a babe. Gone was the manipulating, selfish girl that had continually defied her at every turn. Sara's eyes were searching hers, pleading for some understanding and compassion.

"Please Catherine. Please do not look at me like so! I did not know!"

"Did you not stop to think of the consequences?" Catherine, finding her voice, allowed her anger to saturate her words. "Who was it that bedded you?"

Sara shook her head, tears steaming down her cheeks. Her words tripped over choked sobs. "I tried to tell him, but he would not accept it. He called me a whore. He told me if I ever told anyone it was his child he would never admit to it!" She covered her face with her hands, tears spilling out between her fingers.

"Whoever took advantage of your innocence will surely pay." Catherine lowered her voice in an effort to control herself. "You must answer me, Sara. Who was the vile creature that seduced you?"

Sara looked up, eyes red and puffy, but chin set in defiance. "I am not an innocent child, dear sister; not a little girl that no man would notice. While the most handsome nobles and even lowly merchants court you, everyone thinks me too young, too plain to have suitors." Her face became hard with hatred. "But I am not too young to be a seductress! It was your beloved Jonathan I seduced, Catherine! It is *his* child I carry!"

She turned and ran from the room.

Catherine froze where she stood. Sara's parting words echoed in her ears, so loud she thought her head would split. Her heart was aching in a way she did not know possible. Had Jonathan indeed play her for a fool? Had he given his kisses and touches – and his seed – to her sister? Had he merely told Catherine all the things she wanted to hear, meaning none of them?

She thought of the softness of Jonathan's kiss, the warmth of his touch upon her skin, and the words he whispered as he claimed her as his own. Her knees could no longer hold her and she sank heavily to the floor. She buried her face in her hands as if the darkness behind her lowered lids would shield her from more pain.

But no such relief would be gifted upon her. She was forced to look up when Jarrid ran in breathless.

"Milady!" His chest heaved with effort. "Something is not aright with Lady Sara! She has taken her horse and ridden out of the gates like the devil himself was on her heels!"

Catherine barely heard his words.

Sara...horse...gates.

"Milady!" Jarrid crouched before her. "She looked to be a madwoman! She is headed to the cliffs!"

The cliffs. Shame struck her heart. Sara had come to her seeking help, and Catherine had chastised her, shouting instead of soothing, accusing instead of understanding. Though Sara's revelation cut her to the bone, she was nevertheless Catherine's sister. Sara, in her blind rage, was headed for danger and Catherine would not fail her now.

Surging with resolution, Catherine was instantly on her feet. "Find Galen and tell him I am following Sara to the cliffs!" she commanded.

The courtyard was empty, the servants having taken shelter from the pelting rain. The clouds were black and ominous, the thunder moving closer and closer.

Catherine was quick to saddle her horse and even quicker to mount the mare. "Run hard, Sable," she urged. "We must find her!"

The storm that threatened to unleash itself held out no longer. Its rage challenged Catherine's fear, but it did not deter her urgency as she raced to the cliffs. The horse bolted across the space between the castle gate and the cliffs, heedless to the thunder above or the slick dirt below. Catherine held tight, squinting against the taunting rain.

As she drew near, Catherine saw her sister's small body silhouetted against the darkening sky. To Catherine's horror, Sara was standing dangerously close to the edge with her head low against the growling wind.

Catherine reined her horse in sharply and slowly dismounted. Not daring to frighten Sara, she inched forward, her hand outstretched. "Please, please come away from the edge. We can talk over here where it is safer," Catherine said, trying to keep fear from her voice.

Sara did not move. "I have always loved you, Catherine. You are everything I wished I could be. And I also hated you for being everything I knew I could not." The wind whipped her hair wildly about her head as she turned to face Catherine. "I've always felt so alone. But now I have this babe." Sara stroked her belly. "It will be just the two of us."

The wind began to rise with more intensity, pushing rain down upon them.

Catherine could hardly hear her own voice above the storm. "I am sorry if I have wronged you. Please come away from the edge and let us talk!"

Sara's clothes were now soaked through, her hair plastered heavily to her head and shoulders. Her expression remained calm.

"You fear for me?" her voice raised against the wind. "Why? Is it because I have something you want? Have no worries, Catherine. I have no intention of plunging to my death."

Catherine dare not turn at the sound of an approaching horse.

Galen reigned in his stallion and slowly dismounted. He quietly approached Catherine. "What does she mean to do?"

"I do not know!" Catherine cried. "'Tis my fault, Galen. She blames me."

Out of the drenched air arose a tune, a quiet hum that sang of peace.

Catherine and Galen stared at Sara, who stood with both hands on her belly, face raised to the sky, her expression almost angelic.

Long minutes passed and the slow smile that began to form on Sara's face sent chills down Catherine's spine.

"Sara, please. Come to me." Catherine took a step forward, slowly reaching out with a shaky hand.

The humming stopped and Sara looked at her sister. No knife could have impaled Catherine deeper than the soundless words Sara's eyes said to her, for in them were malice, revenge, and triumph.

Catherine drew her hand back to stifle a scream. She saw in Sara's eyes what she now meant to do.

One backward step. One small step that would separate them forever.

Catherine and Galen lunged to catch her, reaching out for her hands, but missing completely. They stared in horrified shock as Sara toppled backwards, dropping with the falling rain, and crashing onto the rocks below.

"Sara!" Catherine's scream was lost in the storm, becoming part of the slashing rain and the roaring wind that surrounding them. Galen grabbed her around her waist, pulling her back from the edge.

They huddled in shocked silence as they looked down at Sara's lifeless body, draped across the rocks below in a grossly unnatural position. The black waters pushed against her arms and legs as if urging her to rise.

Disbelief robbed Catherine of her breath until panic welled up inside, stretching, until a scream finally broke free. Her hands covered her mouth, but she could not stop the noise. She covered her ears to shut out her shrieks, but doing so only made it louder.

Stop! She willed herself. *Think! Think! Sara needs me!* Clamping her mouth against the scream, she looked around wildly, frantically searching for a way down the cliff.

Galen grabbed her by the shoulders, but she cried, "Let me go!" She let loose a barrage of fists upon his chest. "I have to fix her!"

Thrust against Galen's chest, she continued to her fight to escape.

"Catherine! It is too late!"

She twisted from his grip, but he caught her and forced her to look at him.

Wild, crazed eyes met his, fists slamming into his chest.

"No! It is not! It is *not* too late!"

"Catherine…" Galen's voice cracked with grief.

And suddenly, she knew he spoke the truth. He had never lied to her, nor would he do so now. She began to shake uncontrollably, chilled with pain and grief.

Without a word, Galen pulled her against him, wrapping his arms protectively around her.

Burying her head in his chest, Catherine closed her eyes tight, trying to shut out the look in her sister's eyes and the ache of her heart as it broke apart, piece by miserable piece.

Chapter 35

"Brandi!"

Eryn bolted violently upright and drew her arm across her lips to rake away the sweat that had beaded above them. She looked frantically around her bedroom, her heart pounding against her chest. The sheets next to her were cold and undisturbed, the ceiling above white and unblinking, and the walls seemingly gave her wide berth as she tried to catch her breath.

Her mind frantically backpedaled from the nightmare that stared her down.

She and two others, one of them a painfully thin girl, the other a tall man, stood on a cliff high above jagged rocks engulfed by black water that was being thrashed about by the storm. With the thin girl teetering precariously on the edge, they were oblivious to the gale that whipped around them. Eryn was terrified that the girl would be toppled by the force of the wind or perhaps the rain-soaked ground beneath the girl's slippered feet would give way. Eryn looked to the man to implore his help...only to find Bryce staring at the girl with his usual cool and unreadable expression.

Eryn followed his gaze back to the edge of the cliff where, instead of the thin girl, Brandi now stood. Through the wind, she heard Brandi humming a tune, so eerily peaceful and disturbingly calm, but it gave Eryn hope. Eryn thought if only she could coax Brandi away from the edge, they could talk. Eryn just knew she could help her.

She hadn't known how wrong she was until it was too late, until the moment when Brandi ceased her humming and told Eryn with a look so unmistakably filled with hate and jealousy and with a smile that curled with perverse satisfaction, that her death would be on Eryn's hands.

Eryn's muscles ached from the strain of reaching for her as Brandi took a step into nothingness. Eryn would have tumbled over the edge herself had Bryce not grabbed her around the waist and held her against him. Guilt road hard on Eryn, knowing Brandi's death was her fault and that her suicide had been deliberately done to punish Eryn.

Eryn blinked hard, trying to bring her room into focus. She brought very tremulous hands up to her face, wiping away both sweat and tears.

This nightmare had been much like her own life now, she realized. There was a certain darkness that permeated the three of them, tying them together in some kind of karmic cesspool. Eryn hugged a pillow to her chest like a lifeline.

If we don't master lessons in this life, they will carry over to the next lifetime.

Eryn was finally beginning to see the pattern in her life; a pattern of emotional torment and guilt, and possession masked as love.

Taking a few deep breaths, she ran her fingers through her hair and kicked the covers from her legs, suddenly determined. Though Bryce was no longer sharing her bed, he was still sharing her life. He was downstairs. Waiting. Hoping she would change her mind. But their relationship was over. Whatever karma she was carrying over, had to be dealt with.

~ ~ ~

290

"Hey." Eryn said.

She stood in the doorway watching Bryce leaning over his drafting table, his practiced hand sketching and measuring the lines that would make up the newest performing arts center. He was throwing himself into the Cohen project with a vengeance. It kept him busy in the hours when he came home, giving him reason to avoid Eryn.

Bryce had abandoned his attempts to salvage what was left between them. Eryn hadn't encouraged him, too torn by her own feelings. His betrayal had forced her to open her eyes to reality. There were so many things she'd chosen to ignore, and now she realized that obligation alone couldn't possibly hold two people together.

Bryce paused at the sound of her voice, his hand poised, his body still.

"Can we talk?" Her voice held no anger, only weariness. Talking was something they hadn't done for days except for simple courtesies over coffee cups, and now she was breaking the silence with those three little words.

She saw the slight dip of his head, the expansion of his chest as he sucked in a big breath, and the momentary hesitation before he turned to face her.

She cringed. She was prepared for indifference. She was prepared for the absolute control he had over his emotions. She wasn't prepared for the sadness, the regret, and concession. Usually so unreadable, his eyes now hid nothing.

She gestured to the couch tucked in the corner. "Can we sit?" She walked past him, feeling the weight of his stare as he followed her.

He sat next to her, his elbows on his knees and fingers locked together. His eyes were pleading with her, saying what his lips would not.

Unable to return his gaze, she stared at her hands. Her eyes began to sting and her vision blurred. She swallowed hard. "You know I have to leave."

His voice was thick when he finally spoke. "I wish I could take it back, Eryn. You can't even imagine how I regret what I did." He shook his head and took a deep, quivering breath. "It was your journal. There was someone else," he whispered more to himself than to her.

She dropped her face into her hands, fingers pressing along her eyes, moving to massage her temples.

"I'd been having dreams, Bryce. It was all that talk about reincarnation. I just needed to write things down, things that I felt, stuff that I saw. It was the only way I could try to make sense of them. I had no one to talk to about it." She looked at the ceiling and blinked, trying to rid herself of the tears. "Did you know she resented me for everything that I had?" Her voice began to crack and her sniffle betrayed her hurt. "I really don't think she even liked me."

Eryn shook her head as she went on. "All these years I had no idea. She was going to find a way to hurt me, and she used you to do it."

"But *I* just wanted to hurt you."

Eryn twisted her wedding band that still wrapped around her finger. Could there be a shadow from their past that has been covering their relationship all this time?

"Well, maybe that's just it," she said. Like finding that last puzzle piece, it started to make sense.

"Maybe there was something else going on inside you, and Brandi just lit the fuse that set you off. She gave you the excuse you needed."

"What?" His gaze turned sharply at her.

"Even before this happened, I've always felt you've been angry, like you wanted to punish me for something."

"How can you say that?" He reached over and took her hand in his, lacing his fingers with hers. His eyes, gray mist, held hers. "I need you Eryn. Ever since I saw you in high school, I couldn't stand the thought of anyone else being with you."

Eryn finally met his gaze. Big, beautiful, confident Bryce, the man who could have any woman he wanted, was finally opening up.

His voiced was low. "I've never felt you really wanted me, but I wasn't going to let you go."

She knew that admission of need was hard for him. Usually so strong, so controlled, he was now admitting his vulnerability.

"I know I can't ask you to forgive me for what I did," he said. His expression darkened before looking away. "Hell, I know that if you had sex with another man, I'd probably hold a grudge against you forever." He sighed deeply. "There has to be a way to fix this."

She slowly shook her head. The reason she was with Bryce, though she hated to admit it, had more to do with obligation than with love. She cared for him so much, but the passion just wasn't there.

Bryce buried his face in his hands. "Shit. I can't believe how badly I screwed this up."

She slid off the couch and kneeled in front of him. "Bryce, I want you to see that it is not just what you did with Brandi. Things have *never* been right for us, and no matter how hard we try, it's not ever going to work." She crouched lower, peering into his face. "Maybe Brandi had to happen, to get us to move on with our lives." She tucked his hair behind his ears. "Come on, Bryce. I haven't been happy for a long time and you've got to admit you haven't been too happy either."

He let his hands slide from his face, ready to protest, but she stopped him.

"Something here," she said, tapping her chest, "has been calling to me, and I've ignored it for too long."

He pressed his lips together hard, but couldn't stop them from quivering. Dark brows crowded together over his glistening eyes. "This is it then. You're really leaving me."

"Oh Bryce," she said, snaking her arms around his waist. She pressed her cheek to his. "Please know that I love you, but not in the way you need me to."

He held her tight against him, his body trembling. Defeated tears mingled between them. His short intakes of air rumbled in his chest and quivered with each breath he took.

This was harder than she thought it would be, watching and feeling him hurt like this, but she was gaining strength knowing this was the only way. He leaned into her touch as she wiped his cheeks with the backs of her fingers.

"Don't you see, Bryce? When you don't follow your heart, a part of you dies. When you live for others, when you stop living for yourself, that's suicide. I can't do that anymore."

He nodded, once again dropping his face into his hands.

She stood to leave, stroking his hair back one more time. She wondered what it was going to be like, now that she was breaking this destructive cycle. The bundle of oppressiveness, guilt, worry, frustration, and the endless questions she carried for so many years was already slipping from her open palms.

She knew there was something out there for her, waiting until she was ready.

She stood up, determination straightening her back. She was definitely ready.

Chapter 36

"He is asking for you, milady." Emelie whispered her words to Lady Catherine. "Master Jonathan desires an audience."

How quickly things change, Catherine mused. Only a fortnight ago she would have succumbed to the bliss upon hearing those words. *He is asking for you.* Now, those words made her sick at heart.

Her world, once so solid, had abruptly crumbled to pieces beneath her feet. Nothing was the same anymore. Catherine wondered at the chain of occurrences that has led her to this day. Was there something she could have done to prevent her sister's death? Perhaps if she were to have been more caring and patient with Sara, her jealousy may never have taken root. If only she had not made Galen wait so long, had she only agreed to marry him sooner...

Catherine focused on the embroidery she held. Since Sara's death, she had tried to escape into each stitch, meticulously driving her heartache down with each push of the needle. Her fingertips grazed over the needlework she had been laboring over.

"When did his ship arrive?" She asked solemnly.

Emelie stepped from behind Catherine and knelt before her.

"Three days ago."

Catherine nodded. "You have seen Cedric?"

"Yes, milady."

A faint light flickered deep in Catherine's eyes now as she looked up from her needlework. Her voice dipped into a whisper. "And is he well?"

Emelie and Catherine looked at each other, their gazes clinging through the long painful moments that stretched between them. Tears blurred their vision, releasing sorrow in each tear that rolled down their cheeks.

"Yes, milady," Emelie said quietly. "They are both well."

Emelie wrapped her arms around herself to still her trembling, her lips pressed tightly together. Moments passed for a time before Emelie spoke again.

"Master Jonathan wishes to give you his condolences himself, milady." Tears shimmered in her eyes. "I saw sadness in his eyes when I told him of Lady Sara's death. He could not understand what would drive her to such madness. He is concerned for your well being."

They both turned sharply when the door opened. Lord Roberts stepped into the bedchamber, his movements slow and heavy.

"Might I have a word with you, Catherine?"

Emelie dipped a curtsey to Lord Roberts and Catherine before slipping out of the room, closing the door behind her.

Her father's slumped shoulders and his slow and heavy movements made him seem so much older. Gone was the confident warrior accustomed to triumphing over the enemy. Now he was a man who was bested for the second time by death. Though he remained stoic before his people, every night he would withdraw to his chambers to give into his grief, his sobs echoing through the corridor.

Catherine quickly put aside her needlework and went to her father, grasping his hands in hers. The sparkle in his eyes had dimmed, but she could still see the love that fiercely burned within.

With gentle force he pulled her close and wrapped his powerful arms around her, holding fast to his one remaining daughter. She breathed in the closeness, his warmth, and his love, letting them flow through her, willing them to ease her own pain.

He pulled away just enough to look at Catherine's face, keeping her encircled within his arms.

"My sweet Catherine," he murmured, reaching up to stroke her cheek. "So much like your mother. So steadfast and kind."

Catherine closed her eyes and leaned into his touch. He did not know the right of it. If she were indeed so steadfast and kind, Sara would still be alive.

He lifted her chin. "You cannot be to blame for Sara's death, Catherine," he said, as if knowing her thoughts. "Sara was headstrong and irrational at times. You could no more tame such a spirit as to capture a bolt of lightning on the stormiest of nights." He cradled her against his chest, resting his chin gently upon her head. "I pray the heavens have patience with her soul."

"Aye," Catherine agreed.

"I must ask something of you, Catherine," her father said, pulling away once again and holding her hands. For a long moment he looked at her, seemingly struggling with his next words. "I had made this decision some time ago, before I left for Rynonshire, but it is just now that I have realized the importance of that decision." His eyes shimmered. "Now, even more than before, I need to know you are protected."

Catherine searched his eyes, her brows drawn together. "Protected from what?"

His placed his finger gently across her lips to silence her. "Please understand my reasons when I ask you to marry Galen and accompany him to Rynonshire. He is strong and capable. He will be a good husband to you and most importantly, he will keep you safe." He managed to raise the corners of his mouth in a smile. "Perhaps I may even hope to see grandchildren someday." He grazed the underside of her chin with his finger.

With her father looking at her as such, so sad, yet so hopeful of a brighter future, she had no will to deny him. Jonathan's betrayal and Sara's death had left a vast, empty space inside of her that she feared she would soon lose herself within. Perhaps Galen could help fill that void.

"You and Galen have known each other for many summers, Catherine, and unless I have misread your feelings for him, I believe you care for him."

Catherine moved her head in a barely perceptible nod.

"That will be enough for now. The passion and love will come, just as it did for me and your mother."

She wrapped her arms around his waist, wishing suddenly to be a child once again, free of the burdens she now faced.

He squeezed her tightly, placing a kiss atop her hair. "Soon we will have a quiet ceremony."

When he left her chamber, his footsteps not as heavy as they once were. She was grateful to have made her father happy. She knew she would make Galen happy. Only time will tell if she would be happy as well.

A glint of the ocean drew her attention to the window. She would miss waking up to see the water stretching endlessly beyond her imagination. It would be difficult to leave Elderidge, for she had come to love the tranquility the ocean offered. She would forever remember the way the waters moved, the color of its moods, and the strength beneath the surface.

So vastly different than the lands of Rynonshire, where the castle sits high atop a mountain, skirted by rolling hills, with the only water being a healthy river that wound its way down from the mountain and bordered the village below. At Rynonshire she would start anew. There she would try to forget.

~ ~ ~

A heady fragrance saturated the air, daring anyone who breathed its perfume not to feel the joy in simple pleasures of life. Color was everywhere, red, pink, purple, and blue.

Catherine grudgingly admitted that being outside did indeed lift her spirits a bit. She occupied herself with gathering bouquets of flowers for tonight, when a small banquet would be held to celebrate her marriage to Galen. The preparations kept her for thinking about Jonathan, who was still anchored at the port, waiting.

She had rejected Jonathan's repeated requests to meet with her, knowing the futility of such an encounter. What could he possibly say that would change her mind about him and what had happened?

Catherine turned to the sound of pounding feet along the path.

"Milady!" Emelie's ran to her, her voice urgent. "Master Jonathan and his men are gathered at the gates!"

Catherine's heart skipped a beat at the mention of his name and the basket of flowers she held slipped from her hand, scattering the flowers upon the ground.

She did not want to see Jonathan again. She did not want to open the wound that had hardly had a chance to heal, but it appeared she had no choice. She had to see him before Galen did.

Catherine ran past Emelie. She would not have any more blood on her hands.

~ ~ ~

"I believe I made it clear that you are not welcome here," Galen growled at the cluster of men who stood beyond the gates.

It was a sight to see. Dozens of men gathered on either side of the gate, throwing weighted stares at each other like daggers. Lord Oakley, present to attend the marriage ceremony, stood with a cocky stance behind Galen, a twisted grin distorting his already sordid face. So much anger and distrust was spread thickly in the air.

Catherine took a deep breath before speaking. "Galen, allow me to speak to him." Catherine's voice sounded calmer than she felt.

"Nay, Catherine," said Galen his eyes not leaving Jonathan.

"Please, give me only but a moment, so that we may put this to rest."

Galen turned to face Catherine, judging what he could of her intentions. "To what end, Catherine?"

When Galen stepped back, her senses were assaulted by Jonathan's presence. Dressed in black, Jonathan's mood was as somber as his clothes. His eyes were stricken with confusion and grief, and were full of questions. His face was a mask of seriousness she did not know he possessed.

She held Jonathan's gaze as she spoke to Galen. "I will not have you or your men fighting with them. There are things that need to be said. Things he must understand."

Galen looked from Catherine to Jonathan, and then gave the signal for the gate to be opened.

"Catherine -- ," Jonathan started.

She interrupted him. "Sara died with your child growing inside of her." She heard Galen's sharp intake of breath and turned to him. "Tis true, Galen. Sara told me he bedded her."

The sound of swords being unsheathed cut through the air. All of her father's men were poised, ready to defend Sara's honor.

A muscle worked in Galen's jaw, his eyes wide with surprise. His lips parted, but after a sweeping glace at Catherine and Jonathan, he thought better of it and clenched his jaw shut.

"Well, well," Lord Oakley chuckled quietly to him. "It looks like your little problem is solved."

Galen turned sharply toward him, his eyes slivers of ice. "Do not deceive yourself that you are free from blame. I will see you rot in hell for what you did to Sara," he hissed.

Lord Oakley raised his brows. "So why do you not strike me down? Why do you not give the truth to Catherine?"

Galen held a scathing look at Lord Oakley before allowing a glance at Catherine and Jonathan.

"I thought as much," Lord Oakley smirked.

Galen whipped back around and ground out his warning. "If you value your life with your cock intact, you will say nothing."

Lord Oakley, stepped back, and with lids lowered in submissiveness, inclined his head in acknowledgement.

Catherine eyed them both warily. It unnerved her to see their heads so close together, hissing words between them.

Galen turned back to Catherine. "What will you have me do?" He swept his hand, indicating his men.

She looked around her. Both sides had knives and swords drawn, ready to fight. "Pull your men back and let me speak to him alone."

Galen gave the order and he and his men stepped back.

Catherine turned back to Jonathan, waiting for him to signal for his men to retreat with their weapons as well.

They stared at each other for what seemed to her and eternity before he stepped closer. His desperation was palpable.

"Catherine," Jonathan's eyes were pleading. "You must believe me. If she carried a child, it was not mine."

Catherine spoke as if she did not hear him. "My sister was easy prey for any man."

"I did not touch her! You must believe me."

"Did you whisper the same words in her ears as you did in mine?"

He closed the gap between them and grabbed her by the arms. "Hear what I say."

She jerked free. "I have heard too much already," she hissed. She could no longer hold at bay the hurt the memories brought forth. "You made me feel things I never thought possible, not only with my body, but in my heart and my soul. I believed in you! I believed I had a choice in life! I believed a man and woman ..." She drew her fist to her mouth to stifle a cry of anguish.

She closed her eyes tight as she fought for control. "I gave you everything I had. How could you betray me?"

Both hands shot up and his fingers raked through his hair in frustration. "Someone plays us for fools, Catherine! There is no truth to this!" He shot a scathing look at Galen.

"You call my sister a liar?" Her voice turned cool. Catherine did not want to believe her sister would purposefully cause her such immense pain. "Did you know her well enough to believe that she was capable of such lies, or did you just exchange pleasantries before you bedded her?"

Jonathan stood straighter, stung by the accusation. "No, Catherine, I did not know your sister, but *you* know *me*." A heavy breath seemed to deflate him, leaving him without weapons to fight. Hands out to his sides, palms up, he bade her to look at him fully. "Stop and think with your heart, Catherine. Am I capable of what you say? Think upon it. You know the truth of it."

"Aye," she said. "I know but one truth." Her eyes shimmered with unshed tears. "The truth is I gave my soul to you. Now tell me...how do I live without it?" She clenched her hands against the choking sobs that threatened to spill forth.

His mouth suddenly softened and love shone radiantly in his eyes. "Can you not see?" Jonathan said. "I, too, have pledged my heart and soul to you." He lowered his voice so only she could hear. "What we did, what we shared, was more than making love. We became one. When I travel across the seas, I feel you here," he said, splaying a hand atop his heart. "You are a part of me now. You complete me. There can be no other."

She fought to close her heart against his words, but she had felt it too, the blending of their souls. She quickly strengthened her resolve.

"You either loved us both or you loved neither of us." Her voice quivered. "I will not tolerate either."

He moved closer. His eyes held her with such intensity, she gasped.

"Your head denies what your heart knows," he said softly, but with conviction.

She tried to step back, but his voice was a silky balm over her battered heart.

He spoke again, bridging the distance between them by gently grasping her hand. "A love like ours knows no time or distance. You will remember my words, Catherine. You will remember the night we bound our souls together for eternity, and when you do, you need only to whisper my name and I will come. I will be your sun, your moon, and every star in the heavens."

Jonathan looked past her shoulder as Galen stepped forward, a look of impatience on his stern face.

"Even if I were to believe you," Catherine said, staying Galen with an upraised hand, "there is no choice now. I am to marry Galen. Today, before nightfall."

A shadow darkened Jonathan's beautiful face. His back stiffened as he regarded her. "But you always have a choice, Catherine." Jonathan tapped his chest. "Listen to your heart. Do not leave it to others to decide which path you take."

She shook her head. Her heart begged her to listen, but Catherine quickly pushed it down to a place where it would no longer have a voice. She must stay strong for Galen, for her father, and for Sara. Her eyes stung with despair.

Jonathan's chin fell to his chest and stayed there for long moments before he raised his face once again.

He reached up to wipe the tears that trickled down her cheeks. "Do what you must, Catherine. I want only to be cause for your joy, not your sorrow. You may turn me away, but know this. It matters not how much time or space separates us. You will always have my heart." His hand dropped to his side as he drew a deep breath.

Jonathan signaled to the others to follow him and with one last look at Galen, his eyes narrowed in warning. "Have a care with her. Make her happy."

Catherine turned and ran away, unable to see Jonathan walk out of her life. She ran up the steps to the great hall, past her father, past a silently weeping Emelie, and fled straight to her chambers.

~ ~ ~

One last time Catherine watched the sails silhouetted against the setting sun. The ocean was ablaze with the colors of hot, fiery passion, reminding her of the passionate heat she no longer felt. Perhaps with time, though, she could feel it with Galen.

Only an hour earlier, a brief ceremony had bound them together for the rest of their lives. Before God, family, and friends, she had vowed to be a good wife to Galen.

She raised a goblet of wine to her lips and drank deeply. Galen would be here soon, but first Emelie would see to it that she was readied for her wedding night. From this night forward she and Galen would share a bed. She would be naked to him in body, if not in soul.

Catherine finished the wine. She had no illusions about tonight. Galen would never wholly forgive her for giving herself to Jonathan. How much more would she put Galen through? How much more will he tolerate? She hung her head. It would take a lifetime for her to make amends to him.

The door swung open and Emelie hurried in, pulling Elizabeth behind her.

"Milady! Elizabeth overhead something that I think you should know." Emelie's cheeks were flushed with excitement.

Catherine was in no mood for surprises. "What is it, Elizabeth? Speak quickly."

Emelie elbowed Elizabeth's ribs.

Grimacing, Elizabeth spoke. "The babe that Lady Sara carried was Lord Oakley's, not Master Jonathan's."

Catherine paled and struggled to breathe as the words hit her like a blow. She looked to Emelie. "Does she speak the truth?"

Emelie quickly nodded.

Catherine grabbed Elizabeth by her shoulders. "How do you know of this?"

Elizabeth scrunched her face. "I was at Lord Oakley's castle, milady. I heard him and Lady Sara arguing in the garden. He threatened her life if she told anyone of it. He called her a whore!"

"Milady!" Emelie said excitedly. "'Twas but a lie that Lady Sara spoke! Master Jonathan never betrayed you!"

Catherine released Elizabeth's shoulders and dropped her hands to her side. *Dear God. What have I done?* She stepped back, seeking a chair to lean upon. Jonathan, her Jonathan, told her what her heart did, indeed, know to be true. If she thought she could feel no worse, she found she was wrong. She had denied his truth and turned a deaf ear on his pleas. She gave him no reason to fight for her. She let out a small whimper of agony.

"Catherine."

Her hand covered her quick intake of air as she turned to the door. She had not heard Galen come in. *How much had he heard?*

The girls picked up their skirts and bobbed a curtsey before slipping out the door.

Catherine turned quickly to the window, swiping at the tears that fell.

"Galen, I fear I am not yet ready." She said with a shaky laugh. The ache welled up again. If the lie was hard to bear, the truth now crushed her. Catherine had sent Jonathan away. She was wed to Galen. And now, there was no going back.

Galen quickly crossed the room and gathered her in his arms, pulling her back against his chest.

Straining for a glimpse of the horizon, she said a silent prayer and sent her love on wings to Jonathan. She gathered the memories of what they shared, his touch, his laughter, the intense and passionate glint in his eyes, and held them in her heart for a moment before lovingly bundling them together and placing them in the dark place within her broken heart. There they would stay, safe for the rest of her life. There they would stay until she needed to draw upon them for strength, for light, and for love.

As if reading her thoughts, Galen pressed his cheek against hers. "All I have ever wanted was the chance to love you," he said quietly. "I vow to make you happy. I vow to make you forget him, and I will do whatever is in my power to make your heart mine."

Catherine closed her eyes. *Though that will never be enough, it will have to do.*

Chapter 37

"You're going to love living here, Eryn." Melissa pushed open the freshly-painted pale-yellow door and led the way into the two-bedroom beach cottage.

Eryn stopped just inside the doorway, soaking it in. The scent of lemon cleanser lingered in the air, mingling with the fragrance of port-wine magnolias and Sterling Silver roses stuffed into wide-mouthed vases. A soft light bathed the entranceway, drifting down from the skylight above them.

"You called at exactly the right time. The former tenant just moved out. He decided he needed the Arizona heat." She beamed at Eryn. "It's like it was meant to be."

As Eryn gazed around the room, she realized that this was the first time she had ever lived on her own. Right out of high school, she'd stepped from her parents' home into the house she shared with Bryce. She had molded herself to him and his life. But now, this was hers. Her space, her life, her choices. This was her space that she would soon fill with her own music, her own thoughts, and her own dreams. Most importantly, her photography will adorn the walls.

Melissa took the camera pack Eryn held and placed it on the polished hardwood floor. Straightening up, Melissa let out a soft breath, concern etched in her brow. Her knuckles grazed Eryn's arm.

"Are you sure you're going to be okay?"

Catching her friend's hand, Eryn gave it a reassuring squeeze. "Yeah. I'm going to be just fine."

She looked around at the chic furnishings, the varying shades of brown and pastel colors that soaked the walls, the over-sized pillows stacked in the corner, and the built-in bookshelf with its collection of shells. The cheery mango-yellow of the kitchen peeked out from around the corner, brightened by the sun blazing through the bay window above the sink.

Eryn walked in further, her satisfaction growing with each step she took. She released a contented sigh as she stared through the picture window in the living room. It offered a view of a long stretch of beach, the pier off to the right, and the waves straight ahead falling eagerly over themselves onto the sand. Boogie-boarders and surfers slid down the waves and children played at the edge of the water. Eryn tasted freedom.

"This is so perfect," she said, emphasizing each word.

Melissa looked relieved. "Good. I'll give you a few days to get settled and then I'll be by with a bottle of wine to give you a proper housewarming, okay?" She placed the keys in Eryn's hand and closed her fingers around them.

Eryn hugged her friend hard. "I'd like that."

When the door shut behind Melissa, the silence settled in. Eryn smiled and let the coolness inside the cottage drape over her skin.

Now, she thought, her decisions no longer had to be measured by what kind of impact they would have on someone else. They would not have to be filtered through others' feelings or beliefs. Every corner had been swept clean. No baggage was left behind. No cobwebs from the past crowded the corners of the rooms. She looked around at a totally clean slate.

With a satisfied clap of her hands, she took a deep breath. The boxes stuffed into the back of her car could wait, she thought. She had taken so little with her; some clothes, dishes, and her photographs. The rest she would buy. Start fresh. For now, though, it was time to start documenting her new life.

She grabbed her camera out of the case, kicked off her sandals, and headed out into the afternoon. The warm on-shore breeze met her at the door and teased her hair out from under the sunglasses perched on her head. For so many years she lived at this beach, running miles and miles of it back and forth. She thought she knew every nuance, every smell, every color of the water, and the texture of the sand. But today it all felt different. The sand seemed to sift more slowly through her toes and seemed, somehow, sandier. The seaweed lying twisted here and there filled her nostrils with its pungency.

She pulled down her sunglasses against the glare of the sun and walked towards the water's edge, then across towards the pier, toeing at broken sand dollars and shells along the way.

A lone figure stood higher up on the dry sand, arms folded across his chest, watching other surfers jockey for waves. Against the backdrop of the pier, the surfer's muscular body wrapped in a wetsuit and long brown hair blown off his face by the salty breeze, was a picture just too good to pass up.

Framing in his profile, Eryn captured a few images before checking the results. After making a couple adjustments to the settings, she lifted the camera back up to her eye and zoomed in. The shutter clicked again just as he looked directly into the camera. Her finger froze as a smile spread across his face, crinkling the corners of his eyes.

She peeked from behind her camera. There was no mistaking that smile and those eyes. Her heartbeat kicked up a notch. It was the one from the gallery. The same one she practically ran over months before in the beach parking lot.

His eyes never left hers.

She looked down, fiddling with the settings on her camera in an effort to appear busy. She tried to look nonchalant, though she was well aware that he was still looking at her. She lifted the camera again, this time out towards the water where a half dozen or so surfers sat straddling their boards, rising and falling with the rolling water.

So here we are again, she thought. This is becoming quite the habit, running into him. Taking a deep breath, she lowered the camera, pressing her hand to her stomach to quell the beginnings of a butterfly infestation. She let her hair fall over her face and peeked through the strands at him. *I really should go over to thank him for buying my photos. Most people only buy one. Buying three definitely deserves a personal thank you.*

She looked back out at the surfers. *So what are you doing still standing here?* She laughed at herself. *Just stop stalling and get your ass over there!*

"Here goes nothing," she said under her breath. She made her way over to him, her toes sinking deeply into the warm sand. The distance between them shrank quickly. Before she reached him, the feather-light butterflies doing a tap dance in her stomach had found a way to her chest and began to tickle her throat.

He was sinfully beautiful and he had more charisma rolling off him than was healthy for a woman to be around. His thick mane of hair fell easily around his shoulders, framing his high cheekbones and strong jaw. Tanned skin showed telltale signs of good humor; laugh lines cupping his full, sensual lips, with crinkles fanning out from his vivacious eyes. The black rubber of the wetsuit molded to his wide, athletic shoulders, corded biceps, and stretched itself across the wide expanse of his chest. Like a second skin it lay snug against his taut stomach and wrapped around his strong thighs.

And still his eyes never left her.

Her mouth went dry. *Come on, Eryn. He's just a customer who likes your work*, her mind prompted her. She slowed to finally stand a step away from him.

Her heart swooned. *Oh, but you know he is so much more than that, don't you? Who does he remind you of?* Eryn shook that thought away.

"Hi," she said, clearing her throat. "I, um, think I saw you at The Image Gallery about a month back."

If it was at all possible, his smile grew wider and his eyes brighter. "Yeah, that was me."

"I never got a chance to thank you for being there," she said apologetically.

"That's okay. You were busy."

"Still…" She bit her lower lip. "Thank you. I really appreciate it. I'm Eryn, by the way." She extended her hand.

"I saw a picture of you and your husband in the newspaper," he said as he took her hand and held it tight. "I think it was for the music hall opening some years back. It's nice to finally meet you. I'm Shawn."

She glanced down at the difference in their hands. Hers felt so small wrapped in his. Small...and protected. She shook her head as she looked back up. "Bryce, my husband...I mean...We're not together anymore."

His brows drew together. "I'm sorry to hear that."

"Oh, don't be. It's really okay. I mean, I'm doing all right now." She flushed hot, realizing she hadn't yet let go of his hand. "Um, sorry." She pulled back, shifting her camera. She indicated the row of cottages that overlooked the beach. His gaze followed to where she pointed.

"I'm renting that cute cottage down the way. Green house, yellow door."

"Old man Henry's house."

"Did you know him?" Eryn asked.

Shawn nodded. "He used to sit out there and make lures all day. Nice guy. My friends and I would hang out with him every once in awhile."

He turned to face her fully now. "You know, your work is really good. You've got a great eye."

She felt her cheeks start to flush again. "Thanks. I'm glad you like it."

Silence drifted between them, but to Eryn, the ferocious way her heart was beating was deafening.

"So, what is it that you do?" She finally broke the silence.

"I have a small business. I shape boards."

She looked down at his board lying in the sand at his feet. Despite the wax that had been rubbed down onto the top, she could still make out the deep orange and red that bled out from a vibrant yellow spot, spreading like a sunset, before reaching the unmistakable logo of a *triskele*.

Now she remembered. "Epic Breakers?" she asked.

He nodded.

Her jaw went lax. "Small business? But...but it's international, isn't it?"

He shrugged. "Yeah, well, I like to travel. I guess it just seemed natural for my business to follow." He looked down and toed his board a little, looking almost apologetic.

Wow. Eryn mouthed. Her camera was suddenly very interesting as she blew off lint and sand that weren't there. She had heard sometime ago that some of the larger banks were vying for Epic Breakers' accounts because it had some big holdings. How ironic, she thought. Some of those very same bankers who had sat in her living room puffing their Cuban cigars, were chomping at the bit to get a hold of Shawn's money. She stole a glance at him. She never would have guessed.

She draped her camera strap over her shoulder. "So, is your business based overseas?"

He dragged a hand through his hair to smooth it back off his face. "No, I grew up here. I didn't see any reason to base it anywhere else. When I started it up and began taking some orders, I taught a bunch of my friends how to make the boards, and we've been doing it that way ever since."

Somehow she had known he would be that way. Loyal and giving to the core. At ease with the elements and one with the sea.

Something about his eyes reached somewhere deep down inside her. Just like...yeah, like the

Jonathan of her memories. Her insides flipped. Wow. Even it she were to entertain *that* thought, that wasn't something she was willing to say out loud.

"You know," Eryn said thoughtfully, "we've met before. About ten years ago at Solstice Beach."

His eyes crinkled at the corners as he flashed her a grin.

"You were playing volleyball and I..." she started.

"You came over to watch. Sure. I remember that."

His smile took them from strangers to friends in the space of less than her runaway heartbeat.

She smiled and shook her head. "I knew it was you. I realized it the day I almost hit you with my car in the parking lot." She wrinkled her nose. "By the way, sorry about that."

He laughed. "No worries. Besides, it was Kenny you almost hit." He nodded in the direction of the water. "I was behind him."

Eryn shielded her face from the sun with her hand, searching for Kenny. She would have to figure out which one that was so she could apologize to him.

"I almost asked you out that day."

His admission caught her off guard. With Kenny totally forgotten, she turned to him. "Really?"

Shawn gave her a boyish, lopsided grin. "Yeah, really. It looked like you had a boyfriend, though."

All these years I've been kicking myself that I didn't ask him out and here he had the same idea!

"Would you have said yes?" he asked.

Her brows furrowed as she sought for an answer. If she knew then what she knew now, then definitely, she would have said yes. But at the time she believed it was Bryce she needed to be with.

"I would have *wanted* to," she admitted. "I mean, I definitely would have considered it, but things were kind of complicated with him."

He nodded in understanding. "That's what I figured."

Already she was securing packing tape over her box of memories from years past. She rubbed her finger where her wedding band used to be, to remind herself she was on her own now. No more guilt. She was single. Free to follow her heart. A heart, she thought, which was beating unreasonably fast.

"What about you? Wife? Girlfriend?"

His attention drifted back to the waves, watching his friends. "I've had a few relationships. Nothing very serious, though."

Eryn had no idea her heart and stomach could do simultaneous flips, but the fact that he was unattached sent everything in her body spinning.

He started toeing the sand again. For a few minutes the gentle breeze swirled around them with its tantalizing breath.

"So what about now?" He was first to break the silence.

She raised her brows to his question. *What about now?*

"Would you say yes now?" He locked his eyes with hers and held her there.

She found she couldn't look away. She swallowed the thudding of her heart, but it just slammed even harder against her chest.

"Are you asking me out?" She teased, trying not to sound as giddy as she felt.

He laughed. "Only if you are going to say yes. Otherwise it would be idle curiosity." He put his hand over his heart. "I do have my male pride to protect, you know."

That was the moment she knew. Without a doubt this was where she was meant to be. This felt right. *He* felt right.

"Then yes. Definitely yes." She felt flushed, hot, tingly, lightheaded, girlish, womanly, sexy, scared, all at the same time.

"Cool." His white teeth flashed under his entirely too-enticing lips. Relief seemed to wash over his face. "Would tonight be too soon?"

She was amazed. It never occurred to her that maybe he was just as nervous as she was.

"Not at all. It'd really like that."

He nodded and grinned. He bent down to grab his board and said, "I'm going to get a few sets in, okay?"

"Oh, sure. Please, don't let me keep you."

He reached out and gently wrapped his hand around hers, grazing her knuckles with soft strokes of his thumb.

Everything but Shawn seemed muted as he touched her, his eyes locking with hers.

He lifted her hand and brushed his lips across the top of her fingers. "I'll pick you up at 6 o'clock then."

All she could do was nod. He did things to her heart she couldn't explain, filled her head with notions she couldn't ignore. She watched in silence as he tucked his board under his arm and jogged down to the water and into the oncoming waves.

Eryn slowly turned and walked back down the beach, a smile lingering on her lips. Looking around for something to photograph, she watched as a crab scuttled towards the safety of the water. Down at the water's edge a baby in droopy, soggy diapers crouched down with a fistful of sand, and a black Labrador paddled in the foamy surf. So many choices lay before her. Her choices. She closed her eyes and listened to the drumming of her heart.

With another glance at Shawn, she smiled. There would be plenty of time to talk and discover everything about him. But for now, this was it, she realized.

She was home.

AUTHOR'S NOTE

Thank you so much for spending your time reading *Again.*

I invite you to sign up for my newsletter to receive news about sales, new releases, and other fun news. Don't worry, though. I won't flood your email box with unnecessary stuff.

As a writer, I encourage any comments you might have. I would very much appreciate it if you would take a few minutes to leave a review on the site that you purchased this novel and let me know your thoughts. If you do, please email me at dianamurdockauthor@gmail.com with a link to your review so I can thank you personally.

I'd love to hear from you! Please feel free to connect with me at any of the following sites:

Website: http://www.dianamurdock.com/
Twitter: @Diana_Murdock
Facebook: www.facebook.com/diana.murdock
Pinterest: pinterest.com/dianadmurdock/
Email: dianamurdockauthor@gmail.com